# LOOKING UP AT CASTLE PERILOUS . . .

"Gene, look at the ceiling," said Snowclaw.

Gene stopped and looked up. The ceiling was in steps. "Odd."

Odder still was the sight of a man in a long gown walking up them. Gene was hit by a sudden dizzy spell.

The man tilted his head up—down—and did a double take.

"My!" the man said. "You gentlemen seem to have gotten yourselves turned about, haven't you?"

Gene regarded the man on the ceiling. "What about you?"

The man laughed. "Well, a matter of where one is, I suppose. Good day to you." He went off, chuckling.

Gene and Snowclaw looked up.

There was a group of people seated at a long table magically affixed to the ceiling.

They were enjoying a very elaborate meal.

---

"John DeChancie has written a wild and original fantasy novel. *Castle Perilous* is just plain nifty!"

—Craig Shaw Gardner

"*Castle Perilous*. It's got everything: unremitting action, laughs, and a heart-stopping climax if ever I read one."

—Esther Friesner, author of *New York by Knight*

*Ace Books by John DeChancie*

CASTLE PERILOUS
CASTLE FOR RENT
CASTLE KIDNAPPED
(*Coming in November*)

*The Skyway Trilogy*

STARRIGGER
RED LIMIT FREEWAY
PARADOX ALLEY

# CASTLE PERILOUS

John DeChancie

ACE BOOKS, NEW YORK

This book is an Ace original edition,
and has never been previously published.

CASTLE PERILOUS

An Ace Book/published by arrangement with
the author

PRINTING HISTORY
Ace edition/March 1988



ISBN: 0-441-09418-X

Ace Books are published by The Berkley Publishing Group,
200 Madison Avenue, New York, New York 10016.
The name "ACE" and the "A" logo are trademarks
belonging to Charter Communications, Inc.

PRINTED IN THE UNITED STATES OF AMERICA

10 9 8 7 6 5 4 3

To my son Gene

# Keep—East Wing—Northwest Tower

Something was following Kwip up the dark spiral stairwell. He was sure of that now. It was something that walked on taloned feet with thickly padded soles. Some inhuman . . . *thing,* little doubt. His heart frosting over, Kwip wondered what variety of shrieking nightmare it would be this time.

That it was intelligent, there could be even less doubt. With calculated stealth it matched him footstep for footstep, masking the click of its nails against stone with the sound of Kwip's movement up the stairs. When Kwip stopped, it stopped. When he picked up the pace, it followed suit instantaneously. He was sure it wasn't his imagination.

As he saw it, panic was one of only two choices, should he find a locked door at the head of the stairwell or should the thing choose to begin sprinting up the stairs in pursuit. The alternative was to draw this sword he had stolen, turn and meet it. A clear choice, but his heart was voting *panic!* as it banged against his breastbone. His head was somewhat in agreement, but reason still held the deciding ballot. Kwip did not want to start running and give the thing ideas. He was tired. He'd been climbing for hours, it seemed. Running would drain the last of his strength. Doubtless he would need every scintilla if he wished to continue his career in a onepiece body. Lose composure now, and these dark stone walls would be smeared with his innards. Such decor was not to his taste.

He thought an experiment was in order. Trying to maintain the same interval, he mounted two steps in one stride, then continued normally, listening. The barely audible clicking behind him did not change rhythm. He allowed himself a tiny sigh. He had gained a step on the thing. Try again. He jumped another step with his right foot and did the same with his left, then resumed mounting one per stride. He listened again. Three steps gained . . .

The thought occurred to him that he should give serious consideration to changing professions. A thief's life had much to recommend it, but the dangers were considerable. Case in point, the present moment. Now, if he found the castle's treasure room, it would all be worthwhile. But for the moment there was the problem of getting through this charming episode.

With a suddenness that turned Kwip's bowels to water, the thing behind him began scrabbling up the stairs. Kwip lunged forward, taking six steps at a leap, dashing madly up the twisting passageway. But the thing was heart-freezingly quick, clicking and scuffling in pursuit. It was gaining. The stairwell wound upwards in an unending gyre. For an eternity Kwip ran and was chased.

Almost before he saw it, the top of the stairwell was upon him. The stairs dead-ended into a blank stone wall.

With raw fear pumping a last desperate strength into him, Kwip drew his sword, whirled, and charged down the stairs, his demented battle yell rending the silence of the tower.

He met only emptiness. By the time he was three or four turns down the well, he began to realize that he should have met his pursuer by now. He halted, stumbled, slid down a dozen more steps before he managed to stop himself. He froze and listened. Nothing. Where was it? Had it retreated? Or . . . gods of a pig's arse! Had he actually imagined it after all?

No. Inexplicably, the thing was above, descending the stairs at a leisurely pace. He lurched to his feet. Invisible! The buggering thing was invisible! But was it also incorporeal? He must have charged past it. But, no. There wasn't room enough.

Whatever it was, it was coming around the upper turn. Kwip made a motion to flee, but halted. When he saw what it was, his eyes bulged.

It wasn't an *it,* after all. It was a *them.*

Feet. They were feet. Two disembodied, taloned, reptilian feet, almost comically monstrous, hollow costume feet looking for all the world to be made of papier-mâché. They came tripping down the stairs. Kwip flattened himself against the wall as they passed. Thunderstruck, Kwip watched. When they disappeared behind the curving stone of the lower turn, he heard them begin to run down. Then he heard laughter, a high, thin, chittering, fading with the footsteps. In a short time the silence of the tower returned.

Kwip stood in shock, immobile. Then he collapsed to the stone steps, his breath coming in racking heaves.

When he had composed himself, he rose slowly and sheathed his sword. He felt the front of his breeches. They were wet.

"Gods of a poxed doxy."

He had bepissed himself.

He scowled and turned up his nose. "Damn me for a small-bladdered, craven—" He stamped his booted foot. "*Balls!*"

Presently he began to laugh. At first it was a snicker, turning to crazed giggling. Then he exploded into full-throated laughter, tears coming to his eyes.

Some sixty stories below, Lord Incarnadine, whose castle this was, passed by the entrance to the stairwell and heard faint echoes of mirth. He paused briefly to listen. Smiling, he wondered who it was. Then he walked on.

# KEEP—WEST WING—SOUTH WALL

"THERE YOU ARE, Jacoby."

The corpulent man with fleshy, hanging jowls and a pendulous double chin turned toward the doorway leading out onto the balcony. "Dalton . . . my dear fellow." He smiled, lifted a thin glass of amber liquid to his lips, took a sip, then turned back to take in the sweeping view of the countryside, which, from this high vantage point of the castle, spread for miles to the south and west. There was much of interest.

Dalton, a tall thin man with graying temples, came out onto the balcony holding a long-stemmed wineglass in one hand and a tan-colored cigarette in a holder in the other. He was dressed in green breechclouts, brown leather doublet, and brown suede boots. He wore a hat of soft green cloth that looked something like a Tam o' Shanter. From the room behind him came sounds of laughter and pleasant conversation, overlayed with strains of music from antique instruments.

"How goes the battle?"

"Well, from here it looks as though the outer wall has been breached."

Dalton leaned over the rail of the stone balustrade. "Really?"

Jacoby, who still preferred the conservative Savile Row tweeds he had arrived with, took another sip. "Yes. Hand-to-hand fighting down there." He pointed. "Among those outbuildings. Do you see?"

Dalton peered down. "You're quite right. We should announce this to the other Guests." He straightened up and drew a thoughtful puff on his cigarette. "Brings up an interesting question that's been entirely hypothetical until now. What exactly will our situation be, vis-à-vis the invaders?"

"Are they aware of us?"

Dalton shrugged. "Aside from Our Host, I've never met anyone who could answer that question with any authority."

"I suspect they do. You're right—Incarnadine would know."

"I should think."

"Has anyone ever asked him?"

"I don't think Our Host has made an appearance since the siege began, several months ago. At least, no one I know has seen him."

Jacoby nodded and looked out at the battle again. For miles around, vast armies lay camped on the plains below. From this distance the clumps of brightly colored tents looked like a sprawling, endless carnival or festival. The sprawl stopped at the foot of the rocky promontory upon which Castle Perilous stood. There, hanging against the sheer cliffs, began a massive array of wooden trestles, scaffolds, ramps, and platforms—the means by which the besieging armies had scaled the heights. Even now troops of soldiers were mounting them in an endless stream from the plains, some dragging huge battle engines up the ramps, using complicated systems of ropes, cranes, and pulleys.

"There's a certain inevitability about it all," Dalton observed. "Our intrepid defenders have given a good account of themselves, but I think the outcome is a foregone conclusion. That army is a wave that can't be stopped."

"You may well be right."

"I suppose, then," Dalton went on, "somebody should approach the other side and find out how the Guests figure into things."

"Rumor has it they mean to destroy the castle."

Dalton snorted. "I've heard that. Ridiculous. Do you know how big this place is on the outside alone?—to say nothing of the worlds of room within. Look down."

Jacoby did so.

"Must be eighty stories to this part of the keep. And look at those towers. How high, would you say?"

"I have no idea."

"Have you ever been to the north wall?"

"No."

"It must be a mile distant from us."

"That much." Jacoby didn't seem oversurprised.

Dalton's eyes narrowed. "Yes." He paused, looking at Jacoby. Then his gaze was drawn out over the rail again. "This has to be the biggest edifice ever constructed. Anywhere."

"Must be."

Dalton drank from his glass and exhaled noisily. He smiled. "Exquisite, as usual." He smacked his lips, deliberating. "A bit too fruity, perhaps."

"Do you think there's a chance we'll be permitted to remain here?"

"That depends on our future landlords."

"Yes. That is, if they succeed in overcoming Lord Incarnadine's formidable defenses."

"Formidable indeed. You missed some of the best battles. Those armored war birds . . . and the horrific dragon things, spewing fire. Men burning . . ." Dalton gave an involuntary shudder. "The invaders took heavy losses. But apparently they've made them up. So, it just might be a good idea to contact them, apprise them of our neutral position."

"Or perhaps offer our assistance."

Dalton arched an eyebrow. "And turn against Our

Host, after all the hospitality he's shown us, all of us?"

"I am not ungrateful." Jacoby took a drink, then ran a sausagelike index finger around the lip of the glass. "But if he can no longer guarantee my safety, I have no qualms about protecting my best interests by acting as the situation demands."

"I can sympathize with that." Dalton placed his wineglass on the flat stone of the rail.

"I wonder . . ."

"About what?"

Jacoby gestured with his glass. "About them, the invaders. Who they are. The hosts of some rival lord?"

"A fair guess. Maybe an alliance of rivals."

"Yes. And what are they after? The legendary jewel, perhaps. What's it called again?"

"The Brain of Ramthonodox."

"Strange."

"Appropriate to the place."

"Very."

Both were silent for a moment. Inside, the ensemble struck up a waltz. Then Dalton said, "This idea of yours—helping the invaders. What could we possibly offer them?"

"Information?"

"Concerning what?"

Jacoby turned a chubby palm upward. "The whereabouts of Our Host, for instance. Doubtless they'll want him as a prisoner."

"But no one knows where he is. He's probably hiding, and he may have left altogether."

"Perhaps we could locate him. Mount an expedition . . . a search party."

"Few of the Guests would participate. And it's a safe bet the invaders will be looking for him themselves."

"No doubt," Jacoby conceded. "Still, we should make some attempt to find him before the castle falls."

"You could hide for years in here," Dalton said, speaking through teeth clenched on the stem of the cigarette holder. "Forever, maybe."

"You're entirely right, of course. As you said, the

immensity of this place is almost beyond imagining." Jacoby drank the last of the liqueur and placed the glass on the flat stone of the rail. "Escape will be easy, but it will be a pity to lose the castle." He exhaled and shook his head. "A tragedy."

Dalton blew out a stream of smoke. "Yeah. As pleasant as some of the nicer aspects are, I don't relish the prospect of having to pick one of them to live in permanently. And who's to say the invaders won't follow us through the portals and hunt us all down?"

"I doubt they'd bother with us," Jacoby said.

"Well, frankly, I agree. I'm not exactly worried about it. But not being able to come back to the castle would be damned inconvenient. I'd hate to go back to working for a living again." Dalton sighed. "Still, if it has to be, it has to be. There are a number of very pleasant worlds on the other side of the portals."

Jacoby shook his head. "I like it here."

"Yes, this place does have its delights—as well as its dangers. But this castle belongs to someone else. You would be forever a Guest, never an owner."

"I feel . . . alive here," Jacoby said with sudden animation. "This magnificent construct . . ." He turned and lifted his head to look up the high wall of the keep. "This colossal monument to power—it excites me. You say never an owner? I can't bear the thought of it. Anything is possible here. Anything."

Dalton did not look up. He was eyeing Jacoby circumspectly.

"I want to—" Jacoby felt Dalton's gaze, turned back toward the rail and gave a slightly self-conscious smile. "You'll forgive me, but my experiences here so far have given me an overwhelming sense of freedom, of promise. I can't quite . . . well, it's exhilarating, to say the least. And the newfound powers, these abilities I've acquired—"

"Don't let it go to your head. We've all acquired them, to varying degrees."

Jacoby's smile faded into something akin to indignation. "I'd be willing to wager that mine are more than usually developed, for such a recent arrival."

"I have no reason to doubt you."

Jacoby's smile crept back. "Do forgive me."

"It's nothing."

"Since we're on the subject, do you mind giving me a small demonstration of your own abilities? I hear they're quite advanced."

"Well . . ."

"Please. I'd be very interested—if you don't mind." Jacoby's smile was warm.

Dalton nodded, stubbed out his cigarette on the rail, and slipped the holder into a leather pouch attached to a wide belt around his waist. He picked up the wine glass, drank the last of its contents, and replaced it on the rail. He then extended a stiffened right hand perpendicular to the ground, aiming it in the direction of the glass. His hand began to vibrate slightly. At the same time he commenced an unintelligible, monotonous chanting.

Presently the glass rose tentatively from the stone to a height of perhaps a few inches. It stopped and hung there, rotating slowly about its longer axis and precessing lazily. This went on for a few moments; then, abruptly, the glass fell to the rail, toppled over without breaking, and rolled. Dalton quickly reached out and saved it from falling over the far edge.

"Damn. Lost it there. I can usually hold it for about a minute before my concentration breaks." He set the glass upright and turned to Jacoby.

"Still, very impressive," Jacoby said. "You use a mnemonic phrase?"

"Yes. It seems to help focus the forces . . . whatever."

"I see. Very good. Very good indeed. And now me."

Dalton's body suddenly went rigid, his expression turning first to one of puzzlement, then to alarm. "What . . . ? What is it?"

"Me," Jacoby said.

"I—" His next words were choked off. With jerky, marionettelike movements, he started edging toward the rail. His face drained and his eyes grew round with fear. His right leg spasmed, rose, lowered, then rose again until his foot was even with the rail of the balustrade. He slid forward until he straddled the rail, knocking his empty wineglass over the side in the process.

Jacoby, meanwhile, was standing ramrod straight, the pupils of his eyes shining like tiny polished black stones. His jaw muscles clenched and relaxed spasmodically, making his jowls shake. The loose, bloated sac of his chin quivered.

Resisting fiercely every inch of the way, Dalton lowered himself over the rail. The process was agonizingly slow.

"You see," Jacoby said when Dalton was hanging by both hands. "My powers are to be reckoned with even at this early stage."

"Yes . . . you—"

"There is total freedom here. One only needs the will to do what one desires, without fear of retribution."

"Let me up."

"I could let you drop."

Dalton started to raise himself.

"I could, you know. I doubt if any of the other Guests would bat an eye."

Dalton's body shook and grew rigid again. "Pl-please!" he managed to say in a strangled gasp. His left hand withdrew from the rail.

"There you dangle, eighty stories up," Jacoby said. "Subject to my will."

Dalton emitted a muffled scream.

"I could let you drop." Jacoby's body relaxed, his jowls going loose once again. "But not today."

Dalton's left arm shot up to hook over the rail. With some effort he hauled himself upward until he was able to throw one leg over. Struggling, he inched upward until he was straddling the rail again, then slid off and fell to the flagstone floor of the balcony. After a long moment he got up on all fours, then lurched to his feet. His face was bloodless, tinted with ghastly shades of green.

Jacoby looked at his glass. "I need a drink," he said, and walked inside.

It was some time before Dalton followed.

# Elsewhere

"Mr. Ferraro?"

"Here."

A tall, curly-headed, dark-haired man, about thirty, rose from among the Waiting Dead. Apex Employment Agency was busy that day. At least three dozen people occupied chairs in the reception area. Most had been sitting, slumped and hopeless, for hours. Gene Ferraro was lucky, having had only a forty-minute wait.

"Hi. Jerry Lesko."

Gene took the kid's hand—Lesko was no more than twenty-five, probably a good deal younger. "A pleasure."

"Come on back."

"Sure."

Gene picked up his attaché case and followed Lesko through a maze of desks and partitioned offices until they came to a cluttered cubicle, which they entered. Lesko took a seat behind a gray steel desk and motioned for Gene to sit in the small hard-backed chair next to it.

"First we gotta get you to sign this," Lesko said, placing in front of Gene a large yellow filing card densely inked with small lettering. "Read it and sign if you want to."

Glancing over it, Gene recognized it as the usual

agreement to fork over a certain percentage—in this case a healthy fifteen percent—of the signee's yearly salary, payable immediately and in full should the signee accept any job offer resulting from the agency's referral. Fine. You pay to work. Dandy.

Gene signed it, slid it across the desk to Lesko.

"Good. Now fill this out."

"What is it?"

"Credit check."

"Why?"

"Company policy. You may have to borrow to pay the fee. Fifteen percent of your salary, you know. Just put down your bank account, and list any major credit cards."

"I don't have a bank account, at least not a checking account. No credit cards either."

"Oh. Did you ever have a student loan? Says here you have a degree . . . couple degrees, in fact."

"Never did. Scholarships, fellowships, teaching assistantships, that sort of thing. My parents covered whatever shortfalls there were."

"You're lucky. Must be pretty smart. Well . . . have a savings account?"

"Yes."

"Put that down."

"I'm afraid I don't have the passbook with me, and I don't remember the account number."

"Well, just put down the name of the bank."

"Sure." Gene did so and handed the form back to Lesko.

"You live with your parents? Hard to get along without—"

"Yeah, temporarily, until I find work."

"Good idea. Can't hurt."

"Yeah."

Lesko passed his eyes over Gene's resumé. Gene got the impression it was the first time he'd seen it.

"You have a master's degree. What in?"

"Says right there. Philosophy."

Lesko found it. "Oh, yeah. Really? I have a cousin who majored in psychology. She had a hard time finding—"

"Philosophy."

"Huh?"

"Philosophy, not psychology."

"Oh. It's different?"

"Very."

"Uh-huh. Gee, you've had a lot of schooling."

"Unfortunately, when you put it all together, it comes up short of a marketable skill."

"That's too bad. Economy's in real bad shape too. It's going to be hard to place you."

"I know. In fact, I more or less just said that . . . unless I'm badly mistaken."

Lesko frowned and averted his eyes. "What . . . uh, what were you studying for? To be a . . . philosopher?"

Sighing, Gene answered, "I wanted to teach. Teach in a university—do you understand? I was after an assistant professorship, tenure-track, and I was just at the point of writing my dissertation when it dawned on me that the job market had completely dried up. Even with the Ph.D., getting a job was unlikely. I quit and went to law school."

"Yeah, I see. You quit that too."

"Right. The lawyer's path is rocky with ethical dilemmas every foot of the way. Most lawyers simply step over them. I stumbled on the first few, and decided it wasn't for me."

"Yeah?" Lesko said emptily.

"Also, competition in that field is stiff too. Every field. Post-war baby boom, the demographic bulge." Gene shrugged. "You know?"

"Uh-huh, uh-huh. Well . . . what did you do after that?"

"Worked in a car wash, then bartending, then . . . for years, a series of odd jobs. In my spare time, I wrote."

"What did you write?"

"Poetry, fiction. None of it publishable, I'm afraid."

"Oh, you're a writer? Well, we may have something in that line." He went through the card file again. "Ever do any technical writing?"

"No."

"Oh. We always get listings for technical writers."

"I had two semesters of mechanical engineering."

Lesko's eyes lit up. "Hey, right. We may have something for you."

"I changed to liberal arts when—" Gene blinked. "You do?"

"Yeah. Says here, 'In-House Technical Writer.' Now, what a technical writer does is—well, he sort of . . . um . . ."

"Right."

"Takes technical stuff and . . . you know."

"I have a fair idea of what the job entails."

"Oh, good. Tell you what, why don't you go back to reception and have a seat. Let me contact the employer and see if I can sell them on you."

"Fine with me."

"Can't promise anything. I mean, your employment history . . ."

"I drifted a lot."

"Yeah. It's kind of hard. Look, go out and have a cigarette or something and we'll see what we can do. Can't hurt. Right?"

"Fine."

Gene was surprised to see Lesko again in only ten minutes.

"Mr. Ferrari? Look, I—"

"Ferraro."

"Right. I talked to the personnel manager over at USX—that's the employer—and he says they have over two hundred applicants for that job already. But he has a cancellation today, and I talked him into seeing you. Can't hurt. Right?"

"Can't hurt," Gene said.

"Just give him this card. Okay?"

"Can't hurt."

"Huh?"

When he emerged from the lobby of the office building into the wilting August sun, Gene saw that his blue VW bug was in process of being ticketed and towed away. He sprinted across the street, talked the cop out of following through with the tow, and settled for the twenty-five-dollar ticket. Then he got in, fired up the Bug and drove away. Thinking that he might as well spring for the two bucks or whatever it was for the underground facility at the USX building—couldn't afford the risk of another whopping fine—he turned up Forbes Avenue, then hung a right on Grant Street, there to bump along the cobblestones, threading his way through the almost-rush-hour traffic. The USX building hove into view as he approached the intersection of Bigelow Boulevard. It was an immense, peculiar-looking edifice of reticulated surfaces and myriad small windows. It was the exact color of rust, this so because of the special steel of its exposed frame (expressive of its organic structure, don't you know), a remarkable alloy designed specifically to accrete a protective layer of oxidation on its surface, but no deeper.

Gene saw USX PARKING and turned in, traversed a narrow roadway that skirted the edge of an expansive plaza, and plunged into the mouth of a tunnel that spiraled down into the bowels of the underground lot.

The first level was full, as was the second and the third. So was the forth. There, he chanced across an attendant removing barriers blocking a ramp descending to still lower depths. He leaned out of the window.

"Hey! How far down does it go?"

"Got me, I just started today. Go ahead down. Plenty of room."

"Can't hurt."

"What?"

Reaching the fifth level, he felt a wild hair at his fundamental aperture and decided, what the hell, let's see how far down it does go.

Two more sub-sub-basements down, Gene was amazed. The place was vast, tomblike in its silence. Gene picked an arbitrary slot marked by parallel yellow lines and pulled in. With the motor off, the stillness fell like the lid of a sarcophagus.

Now I know, Gene thought, where to run when the

balloon goes up, as the boys at the Pentagon are wont to say.

He locked the car and struck out into the dimness of the reinforced concrete cavern, looking for a way up, his footsteps echoing hollowly. He couldn't find a sign. Coming to the mouth of the ramp, he looked up, saw it was a long way to walk—dangerous too—and decided there must be a stairwell, or better yet, an elevator around somewhere.

He searched in vain. He did find a featureless corridor which met another at a T. To his right the way was dark, so he turned left, turned again at an L, and found himself back in the concrete-walled silence of the garage again. Sighing, he retraced his steps, passed the intersection of the first corridor and continued on into the darkness. Feeling his way, he went about thirty paces until he bumped into a wall. The passageway turned to the right, still unlighted, and continued interminably.

"Absolutely ridiculous."

Another turn, and there was light up ahead. Gene could see a stairwell.

"Now we are getting somewhere."

Once into the light, coming from a strange fixture mounted on the wall at about eye level, he noticed that walls of the corridor were now of masonry, meticulously executed, with dark stones set in intricate patterns. The stone itself was dark gray in color, spangled with tiny glowing flecks of red, blue, and green. Then he noticed the light fixture. It looked more or less like a torch, a long wooden handle mounted into a bracket affixed to the stone, but at the top of the handle there was a glowing bulb shaped like a faceted jewel. The light it emitted was bright and of a faintly bluish cast.

"USX's medieval period, I guess."

He mounted the stairwell, which turned to the left, then to the right, and came out into another passageway identical to the one below, complete with the odd light fixture and another stairwell set into the opposite wall.

Four stories up he began to wonder what the hell was going on. This could not be . . . no, categorically impossible . . . could not be the USX building. Where the hell was he?

As he thought it over, sounds came from his right. He listened. A low rumbling, then . . . a scream? He walked on down the passageway toward the noise, coming to the pool of light cast by the next jewel-torch. Farther down, another corridor intersected. The sounds came from the branch to the right. He approached the corner.

What he heard next made him drop his attaché case. It was the full-throated yowl of some hell-spawned behemoth, the thunder of its rage shivering the stones around him. He backed away. He heard another scream. From the adjoining corridor came the sound of running feet, advancing toward him.

Bursting around the corner came a man in full flight. He came right at Gene, saw him, yelped, danced around him and ran on into the shadows.

"Hey!" Gene yelled after him. "Hey, buddy!"

He was gone. Gene picked up his briefcase and trotted after him for a few steps, then stopped. He scratched his head. The man had been dressed strangely.

The horrific noise sounded again, much nearer. Gene took a few more paces in pursuit but stopped again, unsure of what to do. He looked back toward the intersecting passageway.

What came running around the corner this time froze him solid to the floor.

It was large, maybe seven, eight feet, walked on two legs, and was covered head to foot with silky white fur. Oh, and the head. The head was smallish, but the mouth was not, agleam with razor-edged teeth and curved three-inch fangs. Bone-white claws tipped its fingers. Its shoulders were almost as broad as the beast was tall, and from them hung long sinewy arms. But with all that bulk, it was fast. And it was coming toward him.

Somewhere within Gene's mind, a part that had not as yet turned the consistency of Cream of Wheat, he was thinking, *Movie, they're filming a movie. Oh, yes, that's what it is.*

As the beast neared, the glow from the jewel-torch fired

its eyes, luminescent yellow agates. An alien intelligence burned within them, fierce, cruel, and unhuman.

The sound of the hell-beast shook the passageway.

But the white-furred thing ran right past him—and as it went by, it spoke.

It said, "Run, you fool!"

# INNER PALISADE—SOUTH-SOUTHEAST TOWER

THE VOICE SPOKE to him as he lay in meditation in the Hall of Contemplative Aspects, a grouping of adjacent rooms at various intervals along the curving wall of the tower. In each room there was a wide unglazed window reaching almost from floor to ceiling.

He reclined on a couch set back a short distance from the window, head propped on an arm. About him, the room was a seraglio of painted screens, velvet cushions, wicker baskets, luxurious carpets, low settees. Here and about were inlaid tables upon which lay assortments of finely crafted objects—brass oil lamps, rosewood boxes, carved tusks, scented candles, incense burners, and other curios. Tapestries and decorative rugs draped the walls. Scents of exotic perfumes hung discreetly in the air.

Outside the window, two moons—one larger and of a pale blue color, the other bronze tending toward gold —were becalmed above a quiet sea, its waters a-dance with fingers of moonlight. Sparkling combers washed a narrow beach, above which lay a town of white stone buildings topped with domes, minarets, and campaniles. Above, the night was starry. Glowing filaments of nebulous gas stretched across the firmament. Faint sounds of exotic music arose from the town, and here and there among the buildings, festival lights could be seen. Tall broad-leafed trees stirred in the salt breeze.

But when he heard the voice, the mood was broken.

*The time of my freedom is imminent.*

"No doubt," he answered aloud.

*Unfettered, corporeal once again, I shall soar . . . I shall destroy. . . .*

"As one of my Guests is fond of saying, 'Whatever turns you on.'"

*I crave the fastnesses of the air above the earth . . . the cold sky . . . the icy winds . . . I have been too long in bondage. . . .*

"We all have our sundry problems."

Sighing, he arose and walked out of the room. Passing through an archway, he entered another of the chambers, this one sparsely furnished: a single table with an ensconced candle on it, and a low wooden bench. The window opened onto a vast level plain populated with huge monoliths in various geometric shapes. He seated himself on the bench and endeavored to recapture a meditative state of mind.

To no avail.

*Already the Spell Stone sings to those who seek it, drawing them near. . . .*

He let a few moments of silence go by before he said, "Indeed."

He got up and approached the window, stepping out through it, and stood in the sand. A mild wind blew in from his right, carrying fine grains of sand to tickle his cheek. He felt the desire to walk out among the monuments, touch them, sit within their shadows. He stepped farther out.

*Where are you going?*

The voice diminished as he withdrew from the suspended rectangle of the window.

*You will return.*

The sound of the wind through the monoliths was drear, but somehow comforting. The sky was violet. A triangle of three bright stars shone just above the horizon to his left. All was simplicity, clarity, peace.

*I remember . . .*

He was farther from the window now. The voice was partly lost in the moving air.

"What did you say? You remember? What?"

*Your father's father . . . or was it your father's father's father . . . he who spoke my name . . . he who enchained me.*

"What of him?"

*How long ago? That I do not remember.*

"Do you remember what you are?"

*No, not completely. I do not entirely know my nature. Much has been lost.*

He halted. The voice was a whisper now.

"Why do you speak now? You have not done so in a hundred years."

*That long? I did not know. Was it you to whom I spoke?*

"Does it matter?"

*No. It is sometimes difficult for me to ascertain individuality . . . and I do not care in any event.*

"You spoke to me. I ask again—why have you broken your silence?"

*I speak now because I sense an impending liberation.*

A spark of light above caught his eye, and he looked to the zenith. A falling star scratched a trail across the heavens. It glowed with a phosphorescent green light.

"Ah."

*What is it?*

When the star had descended, he looked down, his face troubled.

"Nothing." Presently, he said, "A moment ago you spoke of soaring, of destroying. Is that your nature?"

*I feel it must be.*

"You also spoke of the Spell Stone. What is it?"

*That which both holds me in bondage and denies me knowledge of my nature.*

"But what is it? Where is it?"

*I do not know.*

"I see." The song of the wind rose up again, and he turned toward it. He felt drawn to the open spaces before him. But the shackles of obligation held him back. He chafed at them.

He shook his head, turning to the window. On the other side of the sky a blue-white sun was setting. Here, the freedom of nothingness was comforting. But he knew he could not stay. He had many tasks before him.

"Tell me this," he said. "Do you remember your name?"

*No.*

"That is good."

After taking one last look at what lay about him, he strode toward the window and stepped inside it.

# Southern Barbican—Near The Keepgate House

Two lords and a lady sat inside a tent at a table made of rude planking. A draft from the breach in the outer wall, very near, ruffled the cloth walls of the tent.

At one end of the table stood an imposing mountain of a man, wearing battle dress executed in the style of the Eastern Empire, and the finery of it spoke of the highest rank. He wore a burnished helmet of bronze, set with blue stones and decorated with bars of white enamel. His long-sleeved tunic was of vermilion wool, bordered at hem and cuffs with gold embroidery. The massive breastplate shone like a golden sun, and a blue cape flowed over his shoulders and down his back like a cataract.

The other men were dressed for battle as well, though in more utilitarian style: suits of mail under long sleeveless tunics, on which were emblazoned their respective coats-of-arms. The lady occupied one side of the table by herself. She wore a long cloak dyed a bright orange. Behind her stood a man in a long hooded gown.

From outside came the gruff voices of soldiers, the rattle of wagons, the whickering of destriers.

"You say we have begun undermining the inner palisade?"

Prince Vorn turned to Lord Althair, who sat nearest him.

"Last night, though work progresses slowly, by hand. We must use the bore sparingly, since its noise could give us away. Moreover, the spell that runs the engine does not work well below the earth. Bores are meant for walls above ground."

"Even in its proper element," Lord Dax, seated to Althair's right, remarked, "your bore did not excel. Three months to breach the outer wall."

Vorn turned a withering dark eye on him. "Three months to bite through stone that is more like metal than metal itself."

Dax lifted a silver flagon of wine to his lips, pausing to mutter, "True," before drinking.

Lord Althair, a thin-faced man with light brown eyes, scratched his long nose with a finger. "We started last night? I suspect they have already begun to countermine. Incarnadine has anticipated our every move. We have taken inordinate casualties."

"Most of which have been from among my best regiments," Vorn said.

"Your regiments make up the bulk of our combined forces, so it's hardly surprising. That is why we three have formed an alliance with you. Without aid, we could never have begun to take Castle Perilous."

"Then why complain?"

"I do not complain. I state facts."

"You would do well not to state the obvious."

Althair's lips drew up into a pout.

"To business, then," Vorn said, drawing up a chair and sitting down. "The Spell Stone. I should like to hear again what its function is and how we may go about locating it."

Lady Melydia of the House of Gan, a woman of delicate features and bold blue eyes that glowed with a curiously discordant intensity, inclined her head toward the man standing to her left. "Osmirik will tell you."

Osmirik reached up and drew back his hood. His hair

was long and black, matching his beard. "If it please His Royal Highness . . ."

"It would please me if you were brief this time."

"I shall endeavor to obey His Royal Highness."

Vorn snorted and leaned back.

"The Spell Stone may be likened to the keystone of an arch," Osmirik said, "without which the arch would collapse. It is the core of the castle's strength. Find the Stone, abrogate its spell, and the castle shall undergo detransmogrification."

"Bandy no scholar's jargon with me. Are you speaking of magical transformation here?"

"Yes, sire, though of a higher order than usual. Once the spell is broken, the castle will revert to whatever it was before it was transformed."

"What would that be?"

"I do not know, sire."

There was a moment of silence. Vorn glanced around the table, then looked at Osmirik. "Is that all?"

"His Royal Highness requested brevity," Althair said with a snicker.

Vorn ignored him. To Osmirik, he said, "Continue."

"Sire?"

"You have no idea what the castle would revert to?"

"Most likely the Stone itself and a pile of rubble. Or it may be that Castle Perilous is a transmogrified conventional castle. There is no historical evidence to support this supposition, but it may be true nonetheless."

"We know," Dax said, "that the castle has existed for the last three thousand years. The written record goes back no farther."

"However, there are legends, my lord," Osmirik said.

"Legends?" Vorn brought a meaty hand up to scratch his trimmed black beard. "What do they say?"

"Legend has it," Osmirik said, "that the ancient home of the Haplodites, of whose line Incarnadine is, was far to the south, in another part of the Western Pale. Indeed, there are ruins in that region such that, if one undertakes a comparative analysis of architectural styles—"

"Which I hope we will not do this moment . . ."

"No, sire."

"The upshot, scribe. The upshot."

"The upshot, sire, is that it may very well be that Castle Perilous is the only edifice ever to have existed on this site."

"In which case, once the spell is broken, the place becomes a pile of rocks. Is that it?"

"Perhaps, sire. Perhaps not."

Vorn scowled. "Is it possible to get an answer from you that does not twist three ways at once?"

"Of course, sire. However, when—"

"Enough!" Vorn took a long drink from his gold chalice, wiped his mouth with the back of his hand. "Why must there be a Spell Stone at all? Suppose the castle is real, in and of itself?"

"Impossible," Dax said. "Its sheer bulk alone . . ."

Vorn looked at Osmirik. "You agree?"

"Yes, sire. It has long been taken for granted that Castle Perilous must be a magical construct. Human instrumentality alone could not account for its existence. The technique of construction by magic has long been known, but has been rarely practiced. Spells are tenuous things —most are, that is. People are loath to live in dwellings held up by a magician's skill alone. As a result, the art has been lost over the years. Castle Perilous is doubtless a product of the craft at its highest level of advancement."

"I see." Vorn turned his head to Lady Melydia. "My lady. Forgive me if I bring up an indelicate matter . . ."

Melydia smiled mirthlessly. "You are forgiven, Your Highness. Since I was once betrothed to Incarnadine, you wish to know if I can confirm the Spell Stone's existence. I cannot. Incarnadine never mentioned it. And though I stayed at Castle Perilous on many occasions as a Guest, I do not know where it is located."

"I, too, have been a Guest," Althair said. "I even asked him about it once. He took great pains to avoid answering."

"It must be found," Dax said.

"Now," Vorn said, "let me ask this. Why can we not

simply find Incarnadine and induce him to tell us where it is?"

"You could spend a lifetime trudging through that monstrosity," Althair said dyspeptically.

"Sire, the castle is also known as the House of 144,000 Aspects. It contains gateways to other worlds, other planes of existence. Incarnadine could slip through any one of them to elude us."

"May he not already have slipped away?" Vorn asked.

"Yes, sire, that is very possible. However, it was my impression that the object of this campaign was not Lord Incarnadine's capture—"

"We are not interested in your impressions, scribe," Melydia said.

"No, my lady."

"Why not forget the Spell Stone," Vorn went on, "and simply look for the treasure room?"

"That, too, would be difficult to locate," Osmirik answered. "But if His Royal Highness would permit me an opinion, I would agree that this would be the best—"

"That is enough," Melydia said.

Vorn looked at Melydia, eyes a trifle suspicious. "Is there something . . . ?"

"A scholar's daydreams, sire. He'll propose a dozen different theories, then take the negative and argue each one into absurdity. It is naught but casuistry."

"I merely meant to add, my lady, that—"

*"You will be silent!"*

Vorn, on unsure ground, stroked his beard thoughtfully. "I would be interested, Lady Melydia, in what he has to say."

Melydia sighed. She inserted an index finger between her cheek and the white cloth of her wimple, letting air in. "Forgive me," she said, her hands going up to her pie-shaped orange hat to adjust it. "This man is a member of my household. I must put up with his convoluted gibberish and insubordination on a daily basis." She fanned her face with her hand. "Yes, yes, by all means . . . go on."

Osmirik stiffened. "Thank you, my lady. There are other legends concerning Castle Perilous. One of them has to do with the jewel known as the Brain of Ramthonodox."

"Ah, yes, the jewel," Vorn said, smiling. "It would likely be in the treasure room, would it not?"

"I do not know, sire. I do know that the name Ramthonodox appears in certain ancient writings—"

"Musty books he has his nose stuck in all day," Melydia said.

"Yes, my lady. In one particular volume, the *Archegonion*, or *The Book of the Most Ancient of Days*—a compendium of classical texts in fragmentary form—one reads of a day long past, when the earth and the men who dwelt in it were subject to the depredations of great demons. It was a time of fear and desolation, when men scratched out a miserable existence in a world of waste and ruin."

"Yes, yes," Vorn said impatiently. "We have similar legends in the East. Go on."

"The name Ramthonodox appears at various points in the texts. Unfortunately, the references are not clear, due to difficulties in translation. The original Tryphosite codices have been lost. All we have is an early Zamathian translation. However, in marginalia added to copies of the Zamathian codex done about fifteen hundred years ago, we find—"

Vorn struck the table with a mailed fist. "Get to the point!"

"Yes, sire. There are also references to—"

From inside the barbican there came a terrific sound like a clap of thunder. There were shouts and general commotion. Then, men screaming in agony.

Silence at the table.

"They have found our mine," Dax said.

Vorn nodded grimly. The three men rose and walked solemnly out of the tent.

Melydia stood up slowly, turned and faced Osmirik, drawing up to him until the tip of her nose fairly met his.

"You think the art of colossal transmogrification lost?"

Her breath was hot on his face. "Not quite, my lady."

"True, it is not. I have it, and I will transmogrify you into a mountain of *pig shit* if you vomit forth any more of your bookish nonsense!"

"My—"

*"Silence!"*

Osmirik's body went slack. He took a deep breath.

"I have warned you before, and I do so now again." Melydia stepped back. "Take heed, scribe."

She turned and left.

Osmirik's face grew pensive. He paced the length of the tent for a while, then halted.

"Library," he said in a whisper. "The library . . ."

## KEEP—EAST WING—FAMILY RESIDENCE

THE ROOM WAS lovely in the daylight. The walls were paneled in dark wood, the furniture beautifully carved in a style she did not recognize. There were even curtains. She had had no trouble sleeping here. She had never slept in a canopied bed.

She threw off the covers, sat up and dangled her feet over the side of the bed, feeling for her wooden-soled sandals. She had slept in her clothes—faded jeans, and a T-shirt with faded iron-on lettering that read IT'S HARD TO FLY LIKE AN EAGLE WHEN YOU WORK WITH TURKEYS, accompanied by a cartoon rendering of the sentiment. She needed to use the bathroom, and she wanted a shower. If they had bathrooms in this place. She rather doubted it. She got up and stretched. It occurred to her to look under the bed. Yup, there it was: the chamber pot. Yuck. Well, she could put it off for a little while longer. Not like yesterday, when she had to . . . No use dwelling on that.

She went to the window. Here, unlike in other parts of the castle she had seen, the windows were glazed, lovely old leaded glass. Turning the wrought-iron handle, she swung one casement pane outward. She leaned out. She couldn't tell exactly how far up the room was, but it was high. Below and beyond the outer walls a carpet of dense green forest spread out and upward, mounting to the foothills of snow-tipped peaks far in the distance. Not a sound. The air was cool and sweet-smelling.

Someone opened the door to her room, and she jumped. Almost everything in this place made her jump. But this time it was only a middle-aged woman carrying bedding. She was dressed in a long gray undergown with sleeves full to the elbow. The sleeveless overgarment was white. She wore a white cloth cap tied around twists of gray hair to either side of the head. The woman's face was pleasant, if a bit plain. Her complexion was ruddy, and she had few teeth. She looked friendly.

"Good morning, mum," the maid said, smiling.

"Good morning."

"May I . . . ?"

"Um . . . yes. Yes, of course."

The woman came into the room and began stripping the bed.

She stood watching for a moment before she said, "Uhh . . . I'm Linda Barclay."

The maid smiled again. "Pleased to meet you, mum. Rawenna's my name. Sleep well, I trust?"

"Yes. Yes! Marvelous. I—"

The maid looked up from her work. "You were saying, mum?"

Linda shook her head. She crossed to the footboard of the bed and ran her hand over the carvings. "You know . . ."

"Yes, mum?"

"I found this room by accident. I really don't know . . . I mean, I hope I wasn't—"

"Oh, don't trouble yourself, mum. Any room where you'll be comfortable."

"But I'm not really sure I'm supposed to be here!"

"Oh?"

"I don't even know where I am. This place . . ."

"You're in the keep, mum. Forty-sixth floor, east wing."

"Yes, but where? This is a castle, I know, but *where* is it?"

"Well, where are you from?"

"I live in Santa Monica, California."

Rawenna stopped plumping the pillows long enough to think it over. She shook her head. "Sorry, mum, never heard of the place. I'm sure it's nice, though."

Linda nodded, then sighed and took a seat on a low stool beside the armoire. She propped her head up on one hand, elbow on knee. "I'm probably going crazy."

"Such talk, and from a pretty young girl like you."

"This is probably a hospital, and you're probably a nurse, and I'm hallucinating the rest."

"A nurse, mum? Me? Oh, I'm much too old." She put a hand to her ample bosom. "Dried up long ago, I did. I've nursed a few whelps in my time, though. I certainly did."

"That's not—" Linda giggled. "God, this is so nutty." She watched the maid fit the bed with fresh sheets.

When Rawenna was done, she tucked the sheets in, drew up the beautifully quilted bedspread and smoothed out the creases.

"I don't even know how I got here. Or why I'm here."

Rawenna stooped and slid out the chamber pot.

"I didn't use that."

She pushed it back under the bed.

"I don't know if I can. I guess I'll have to."

"If you prefer to use the bath, mum, it's just down the corridor."

Linda brightened. "You have a bathroom? With a toilet?"

"A water closet, you mean? Yes, we do. Some of the Guests prefer it. Others . . . well, like me, they're used to what they're used to."

"Guests?"

"Why, yes. The other Guests."

"But I'm not a guest. I can't be. No one invited me here."

Rawenna looked at her. "How did you come to be here,

mum? If you don't mind my asking."

Linda rubbed her forehead with a palm. "You'll think I'm crazy."

"Not at all."

"I was in the closet, in my bedroom. At home, where I live . . ." She threw up her hands. "Oh, I can't even say it, it sounds so insane."

Rawenna considered it. "Sounds to me as though you got yourself lost, and found yourself in the castle. Am I right?"

Linda spread her arms wide. "Sounds good to me."

"Then you're a Guest, all right." Rawenna finished with the bed and gathered up the sheets she had draped over the footboard.

"But who am I a guest *of*?"

"Why, of His Lordship."

"His Lordship? Well, it fits." Linda stood up. "Does he have a name?"

"Incarnadine is his name, mum."

"Incarnadine. That's his full name?"

With both hands Rawenna whumped the sheets into a manageable pile. "No. He's called Incarnadine of the House of Haplodite, King of the Western Pale, Liege Lord, Protector of the— Oh, it goes on and on."

"I see." More to herself, she said, "A genuine castle, and a genuine feudal lord-type person."

"Beg pardon, mum?"

"Oh, nothing."

"Would you be wanting breakfast in your room, mum? Or would you care to join some of the other Guests?"

"I suppose I should meet them. Maybe they know something about all this."

"Two floors down in the small dining hall, mum. I'll take you there if you wish."

"Thank you—after I take a shower, or a bath? It's been two days. The other night I slept in a dusty old storage room full of crates."

Rawenna shook her head and clucked. "Pity, a young lady of good breeding having to do that. We send out the men every night to gather up any new Guests, but . . . sometimes I think this drafty old place is just *too* big."

Linda laughed. "*That* is an understatement."

"I'll fetch some fresh towels for you."

# Keep—Somewhere Else

"Snowclaw."

"What?"

"Is it my imagination, or is the ceiling lower than it was a minute ago?"

The great albino arctic beast came over to where Gene was standing. He looked up, then brought his gaze down to peer at the juncture of floor and wall. "It's your imagination," he said. "What's really happening is that the floor is rising." He absently scratched his furry stomach with one clawed finger. "Either way, let's get out of here." He yawned, recovered with the snap of his toothy jaws slamming shut. "Great White Stuff! I'm tired. Hungry too."

"Over here."

"We just came through there."

"Couldn't've. This doorway wasn't here a second ago. I watched it appear."

"Damn. I'm getting confused."

Snowclaw followed Gene into a small foyerlike area with three more arched doorways leading to other rooms. The place was bare, as were most of the chambers they had been passing through for the last hour or so.

"Which way?" Gene asked.

"The floor's still rising in here too."

"This way?"

"Fine with me."

They chose the left exit, moved through another small room, this one with a single exit leading into a narrow corridor. Following it, they went straight for a good distance, then to the left at an L. The corridor then went into a series of lefts and rights, finally debouching into a room that looked identical to the one in which they had first noticed the rising floor—stone walled, bereft of furnishings, and somewhat trapezoidal.

"Right back where we started."

"Maybe," Snowclaw ruminated.

"Well, we'll just go back to that foyer and take another . . . oh, hell."

"What foyer?"

"Great."

Snowclaw pointed to the doorway straight ahead. "Did you see that one appear . . . just now?"

"No, I was looking—"

"Look at it!"

The doorway was moving slowing to the right, drifting over the stone like a reflection over the surface of a pond, yet carrying the room beyond with it. It began to pick up speed, sliding toward the far wall.

"Run for it!" Snowclaw said.

They did. As if to elude capture, the doorway put on a burst of speed and disappeared enigmatically into the corner. Now the room was exitless.

"Wonderful," Gene said.

"Here comes another one."

They walked along the wall to meet it. This doorway was moving at a more leisurely pace. It opened onto a stairwell going up.

"Should we?" Snowclaw asked.

"Not my bus. Wait for the next one."

After the stairwell vanished, the wall remained blank. There came a rumbling sound. The floor quivered a little.

"Uh-oh."

"We should have taken it," Snowclaw said.

"We have to get to the ground floor of this place, get the hell *out* of here."

"Agreed, but . . ." Snowclaw reached up and tapped the ceiling. "Look."

They waited. When Snowclaw was able to place the flat of his palm against the ceiling, the far corner generated another doorway, this one gliding across the wall at a brisk pace.

"Get ready."

Suddenly, a sliding wall dropped from the ceiling, slamming down to cut the room in half. The moving doorway didn't make it past the new corner.

"Well, freeze my icicle," Snowclaw said.

"Hey, look."

Behind them a new door had materialized. They sprinted for it. As they did, the rumbling sound grew to a tremendous roar, rocking the flagstone floors, shivering the walls and deafening their ears. The next few minutes were a Keystone comedy of sliding walls, dropping partitions, narrow escapes, rushing from crazy room to crazier room.

"Over here!"

"No, this way!"

"God."

Floors began to tilt, walls to list inward, outward, generating migraine-provoking angles and nauseating perceptual tricks. Walls bulged and ceilings drooped. Bottomless wells appeared in the floor.

"Yahh!"

"Watch yourself, Gene."

"Jesus Christ."

They came to a sheer drop at the end of a corridor, and this time it was Snowclaw who almost went sailing over the edge. Gene grabbed a handful of white fur and yanked back, though he really wouldn't have been of much good had Snowclaw actually been falling. The white beast must have weighed over three hundred pounds. Snowclaw grabbed the carved stone of the pilaster below the archway and swung himself back.

"Thanks," he said.

They looked down. The doorway hung in the curving wall of a great circular shaft plunging endlessly into the heart of the castle. It seemed to go up just as far, lighted in both directions by arrays of jewel-torches every twenty or thirty feet.

"I think I'm getting ill, Gene. I can't tolerate heights."

"What, a big fellow like you?"

"Drift crawlers too."

"What're those?"

"Little nasty things that . . . ahh, let's get away from here."

They moved back down the corridor, which by this time had transformed itself from straight to serpentine, now twisting and coiling back on itself, leading nowhere. The floor still heaved, and sounds like huge bowling balls rolling came from within the walls. At long last the corridor ended, and they came out into a rotundalike room with a white polished dome ceiling. Here was the hub from which the spokes of at least a dozen other corridors radiated outward. Of course, the room had not been here when they had entered the corridor.

"Eeny meeny miney moe. That one."

"What, exactly, is 'eeny meeny miney moe'?"

Gene didn't answer. This corridor looked straight and stayed that way for a long while. There were no exits. However, after what seemed like a quarter of a mile it terminated in a stairwell leading down.

And down. And down still. And when it finally ended in a small featureless stone chamber, the only way out—save for doubling back—was another doorway initiating a second stairwell, which led . . . up. And up.

And up. They climbed for ten minutes.

Gene said, "I'm bushed." He sat down heavily; in the process he let go of his attaché case. It went sliding down the steps, caught a corner, flipped, and went tumbling. Gene watched it until it was out of sight, though the sounds of its crashing continued to be audible until long after.

"Why did you hang on to that thing, that carrying box, whatever it was?"

"Little piece of reality. I had it when I blundered into this place."

"I see. Me, I wasn't carrying anything. I was at the bottom of a crevasse, having been stupid enough to push my sled across the ice bridge over it without testing the damned thing first. The sled went over, I clawed the wall all the way down until a ledge stopped me—crawled along that a ways until I came to the mouth of an ice cave. Carved by water, I guessed, and I was hoping to follow it back to the bed of an underground stream, but a little ways back it turned from ice to stone block . . . and I wound up here." Snowclaw sat down next to Gene. "Good thing too. Never would have made it out of that crevasse."

"I was thinking . . ."

"Eh?"

"You say you didn't understand 'eeny meeny miney moe'?"

"Well, I got the drift."

"The words were unfamiliar. Right?"

"Right."

"But you heard the words."

"I guess. Yeah."

"Which means that the magical running translation that goes on around here breaks down when you start using essentially untranslatable words and phrases."

"Makes sense. Does that phrase you used mean anything?"

Gene thought about it. "Not really."

"Well, there you are."

Gene frowned. "Still don't get it. I mean, to me you speak perfect English—better than that, completely natural colloquial American. But I damn well *know* you're not speaking it."

"And you seem to have an unnatural command of Back-Ice Chawaharsee."

"You see? Chaw . . . Chawa . . ."

"Chawaharsee."

"That's mostly a growl to me. Okay, but . . . now, take that guy I first met when I came in. The one who almost knocked me over. He had a bit of an accent. Why? Why didn't he speak colloquial American?"

"I don't know, Gene." Snowclaw turned it over in his mind. "Maybe it has something to do with the fact that we became such good buddies so quickly."

"You think?"

"Yeah. For some reason—though for the life of me I can't think of what it could be—there's a rapport between us."

"I agree. Maybe that's it. If true, then I'd expect the guy who owns this place to speak in Elizabethan couplets."

"What? That came out as something like 'snow queen poetry.'"

"Close." Gene scratched his head, then brushed dust off his rumpled gray three-piece suit. "You're right. I didn't like that little guy. Screaming all the time."

"Neither did I, though we shouldn't speak ill of the dead."

"We don't know that he's dead."

"If that leaping purple thing had grabbed me, I'd be dead, and I don't die easily."

They sat in silence for a moment.

Presently Gene said, "Hear that?"

Snowclaw cocked a pointy ear. "What?"

"Nothing. Things have settled down a bit."

"Good. Got your second wind?"

"Fifth. Let's get moving."

"Don't you want to go retrieve your carrying box?"

"Who needs reality?"

They resumed mounting the stairs. Some distance up they came to a landing flanked by descending stairwells.

"We should have a coin to flip for these occasions," Gene said.

"You mean cast bones, something like that?"

"You don't have coins where you hail from? Money?"

"Some. Pretty scarce."

"Oh. Left?"

"Right."

For some reason the stairwell, which descended in ninety-degree turns, was unlighted. They groped, tripped, and cursed in the darkness; came to landings, went up, came back down; traversed corridors that dead-ended, swore mightily; found another stairwell, continued down, went up yet again, and finally wound up clumping downward again, doing it all in pitch blackness.

Lighting fixtures appeared again, and they found themselves descending a spiral stairwell.

"Gene, look at the ceiling."

Gene stopped and looked up. The ceiling was in steps as well. "Odd."

Odder still, farther down, was the sight of a man in a long gown walking up them. Gene was hit by a sudden dizzy spell.

The man tilted his head up, down, and did a double take.

"My!" the man said. "You gentlemen seem to have gotten yourselves turned about, haven't you?"

Gene regarded the man standing on the ceiling. "What about you?"

The man laughed. "Well, a matter of where one is, I suppose. Good day to you." He went off, chuckling.

"What do you make of that?" Snowclaw asked.

"'As I was going up the stair, I met a man who wasn't there . . .'"

At long last . . .

They debouched into a large room—a strange one. After crossing a columned portico that bordered the main area, they stood on the edge of what looked like an empty swimming pool with chandeliers rising like crystal trees from the bottom. A swimming pool . . . but if you twisted your head, it looked a great deal like a ceiling. Gene and Snowclaw slowly looked up.

There was a group of people seated at a long table magically affixed to the ceiling.

They were enjoying a very elaborate meal.

# Keep—East Wing—Queen's Dining Hall

"I SAY, YOU two up there! Had your breakfast?"

Linda twisted her head around in an effort to see whom in the world Thaxton could be talking to. When she caught sight of the gray-suited man and the furry white monster standing on the ceiling, she dropped her coffee cup to the stone floor.

"My God! How . . . ?" She stared in amazement. After a moment she regained enough composure to look down at the mess on the floor.

Jacoby was already handing her a fresh cup. "Here you are, my dear. Don't worry about it."

"Th-thank you." She took the cup.

"Are you all right?"

Linda gulped some coffee. "Yes, thank you. It's just that I'll never get used to this place. Surprises at every turn."

"Oh, you'll get used to it rather quickly. In time you'll come to the realization that this is rather a wonderful place to stay. Our Host could make a fortune if he charged the going rates."

"If he could guarantee a way home," DuQuesne said.

"But think of the throngs of people who would pay

anything to go on holiday here," Jacoby said enthusiastically. "Surely with an organized effort, the major portals could be located and maintained. Why, then you'd—"

"But that would be a task of major proportions, I'm afraid. Impossible, perhaps."

"Well, perhaps . . ." Jacoby said, suddenly deflated.

"Hello, up there!" Thaxton was calling. "Coming down?"

After much discussion it was agreed that the ceiling-hanging pair should make their descent by walking down a nearby column. This they did, with success. Applause. Then the gray-suited man tried to walk back up, and fell on his buttocks.

Gene picked himself up. "I can't figure it."

"Where do you think we got turned around?" Snowclaw said.

"Who knows."

"Where did you fellows come from?" Thaxton wanted to know when the two arrived at the table. "Coffee, tea?"

"Coffee, please," Gene said, pulling up an ornate chair. "We took a tour through an Escher painting, I think."

"Oh, yes. The one who does the trick perspective things, isn't he?"

"That's the one. Hello," Gene said, nodding to various people around the table. "Hello, hello."

Snowclaw prowled around the long table examining the sumptuous assortment of fare. He grabbed a whole roast squab, bit off half of it, bones and all, and chewed. "Not bad," he said, then reconsidered it. "Not good, though. *Ptoohey!*" A spray of semimasticated bird flew forth. "Y'got anything to eat around here?"

"Won't you try the paté?" Thaxton offered, brushing fragments of bone and meat from the shoulder of his morning coat.

"What's that?" Snowclaw said, tearing off a leg of turkey.

"Going back to your resort idea," DuQuesne said sotto voce, leaning toward Jacoby, "you'd have to restrict the clientele."

"Of course." Jacoby smiled.

"This would be a nice hotel," Linda said. "The area around here, I mean."

"Most of the Guests stay in the family residences," Jacoby said.

"The rooms are so nice," Linda continued. "And the staff is helpful. They speak English too—which I can't figure out. In fact, everybody around here—"

"But, my dear, they *don't* speak English," DuQuesne told her. "As a matter of fact, neither do I."

Linda stopped chewing her mouthful of omelette. "Huh?"

"Don't listen to the sense of what I'm saying for a moment, listen to the sound. The sound of my voice. Am I speaking English?"

"I don't quite know what you mean," Linda said, swallowing.

"Listen carefully. Are you sure that the language I'm speaking is English? Listen."

Linda's eyes narrowed, and she cocked her head to one side.

*"Ecoutez bien. Donc. Quelle langue est-ce que je parle maintenant? J'ai parlant français, n'est-ce pas?"*

Linda's jaw dropped. "You *are* speaking French! But I can understand you, and I don't speak a word of French!"

DuQuesne grinned at her. "Remarkable, isn't it?"

"Oh, well, this is just too much. How could I not have noticed?"

"Part of the spell," Thaxton said, having overheard. "Part of the magic."

"Magic . . . yes." Linda sat back.

"You got any raw meat, something still kicking?" Snowclaw asked, tossing the half-chewed turkey leg into the tureen of escarole soup.

A blue, shimmering cloud with a vague suggestion of a human form within it approached the table, having ghosted in through the main entrance. It glided to an empty chair and seated itself.

"Good morning," came a voice emanating from within the phenomenon. The voice was feminine, and sounded as though the speaker were underwater.

"Merikona, how nice to see you," Thaxton said. "Where have you been keeping yourself?"

Gene, Linda, and Snowclaw were watching, mouths agape. The other Guests smiled and went back to eating.

"I found an aspect opening onto a world somewhat in phase with mine. I spent some time there. It was pleasant to have spatiotemporal intercongruence with one's environment again. But I missed my friends here, and . . . as you can see—"

"How nice," Thaxton said. "Tea and scones, as usual? Some over there, I think."

"What's on the agenda today?" DuQuesne asked brightly.

Linda had recovered from the shock of Merikona's entrance enough to ask, "How did . . . how did Merikona get back from the world she went into? I thought someone said the doorways or whatever you call them shifted around."

"I'm for tennis. Up for a few sets, DuQuesne?" Thaxton called.

"I'd rather golf today, if you don't mind," DuQuesne answered, and immediately went on speaking to Linda: "Marikona traversed an aspect, of which the castle has 144,000, or so rumor has it."

"Ah," Jacoby said. "A number pregnant with mystic significance."

"Quite so."

"Best of three sets, then," Thaxton proposed.

"Not today, Arnold, thank you. As I was saying, my dear, many of the castle's aspects are stable. One may pass to and from those worlds without trouble. Unfortunately, most are very unstable. They appear and disappear with disconcerting irregularity. Lord help you if you wander through one. It could close up and leave you stranded on the other side. That could be most unpleasant."

Thaxton wouldn't give up. "How about you, Dalton, old boy?"

In the middle of lighting a cigarette, Dalton said, "And drop dead after the first set? No thanks. Golf's my game too."

"Bother. Well, golf it is, then."

Linda asked, "Don't these unstable aspects ever open up again?"

"Possibly. No telling," DuQuesne said. "And there's no telling *where* in the castle they'll appear if they do open up."

"It's catch as catch can, I'm afraid," Jacoby said.

Linda sat back and smiled wanly. "I suppose the aspect leading back to our world is one of the unstable ones."

"I'm afraid it is," DuQuesne said.

"Isn't there any way of finding it? Can't we search for it?"

"No one we know has found a way back," Jacoby said.

"But that doesn't mean that a way back to our world won't eventually be found, by somebody," DuQuesne protested. "Or that somebody, some Guest, at some time, may not have found one and gone back to the world we know. This castle is thousands of years old."

"Then . . ." Linda's right hand went to her face. "We're stranded here."

"Temporarily," DuQuesne said gently. "That's the way it's best to think of it."

Gene had finished his plate of ham, sausage, scrambled eggs, smoked whitefish, buckwheat cakes, lox, and herring in sour cream. He looked around the table and noticed there were serving plates of food more commonly appropriate for lunch or dinner. He helped himself to chicken cordon bleu, stuffed cabbage, rigatoni in meat sauce, and sauteed mushrooms, with an artichoke salad and a plate of coleslaw on the side.

Snowclaw was munching the last of the candles, which he had been dipping in Thousand Island dressing first. Addressing Thaxton, he said, "What's tennis? Sounds interesting. I'd like to take a try at that."

Linda gave a surprised squeal, and everyone looked.

"Oh, this is it," she said, shaking her head in wonder. "This takes the cake." She was looking at something cupped in the palm of her hand.

"What is it, Linda?" DuQuesne said.

"A Valium. See?" She held it up between thumb and index finger.

"Yes, Linda. What's wrong?"

"Just a minute ago I was thinking that I really needed a trank—a tranquilizer. I used to take them . . . a lot of them. Kicked the habit, but when you told me about us being stuck here, I was thinking to myself, God, what have I got to lose, I wish I had one right now, right in my hand. And I had my right hand clenched . . . and just now I opened it and looked . . . and, well, here it is."

Significant looks were exchanged around the table among the seasoned Guests.

"Materialization," DuQuesne murmured. "Interesting."

"How long have you been in the castle, did you say?" Jacoby asked pointedly.

"Huh? Oh . . . uh, two nights. Yes. Two nights and a day."

"I see," Jacoby said, and sipped his demitasse thoughtfully.

# Keep—King's Redoubt

Incarnadine strode around a railed arcade overlooking a high, expansive chamber, the entirety of which was occupied by an immense and astonishingly detailed simulacrum of Castle Perilous itself, showing the tumult of activity that now stormed about its southern perimeter. In scaled miniature the simulacrum displayed the new belfries that the besiegers had constructed, mammoth wooden towers whose tops rose above the thirty-story-high battlements of the inner curtain wall. From their perch atop the belfries Vorn's archers now commanded the inner ward. With most of the parapets cleared of defenders, Vorn had brought up his siege engines to work at close range. A hail of boulders now pummeled the inner ward, flung from gargantuan versions of trebuchet, mangonel, and arbalest.

Incarnadine made the circuit of the arcade, gaining every possible angle. He could see no alternative but to counterattack immediately. If the belfries were not destroyed forthwith, the inner gatehouse would fall to enemy hands and the castle's reduction become an inevitability. The keep was possessed of its own fortifications—ring walls, turrets, bulwarks, and other structures—but Vorn would hardly let these daunt him now. Once the portcullis of the gatehouse was raised, Vorn's soldiers would come pouring through to the grassy expanses of the ward, there to prepare for the final assault on the keep. Although the keep's immensity would prevent it from ever being completely taken—even Vorn could not muster enough invaders to penetrate its every recess and sanctum—its penetration would complete the fall of Castle Perilous. This, then, was the final battle.

Lines of soldiers protected by wheeled wooden barricades were hauling the last of the giant belfries into position. They were under light fire from the defenders, who had withdrawn to the flanking turrets of the inner wall. From there they could barely annoy the enemy, subjected as they were to a withering barrage of arrows from the belfry-mounted archers.

Incarnadine stopped pacing and watched. The simulacrum filled the three-story-high chamber, the parapets of the keep almost touching the domed ceiling. Even at this scale individual figures were minute. He raised his right arm and with one finger traced a simple pattern in the air. The murky area at the edges of the simulacrum quickly grew to overshroud the whole scene, then parted, revealing a much closer perspective. In silence, the battle raged on. Incarnadine flicked his wrist once, and the scene focused on a single belfry. It was a gigantic construction, barely able to hold up its own weight without substantial buttressing in the form of an elaborate trelliswork of timber fanning out and down like a pyramidal skirt from the tower's midpoint. It had taken months to put together out of thousands of precut and partially assembled pieces. Vorn must have expected the tactic of undermining to fail, and had come prepared to take the castle by escalade if necessary. In fact, the battles in the mines, though they had cost Vorn dearly, might only have been a delaying tactic.

A figure approached, walking along the gallery. Incarnadine turned to look.

"My lord . . ."

"Captain Tyrene."

The captain of the Guard saluted, bringing his right palm to his chest. "My lord, I have come to report that the south inner ward will soon be in enemy hands unless we attack with special forces now." Tyrene turned to regard the simulacrum. "If my lord will forgive me. You likely knew this before I did, but I felt I had to report it to you in person." Turning his dirt-streaked face to Incarnadine he added, "The situation is grave, my lord."

Incarnadine nodded and leaned forward, gripping the iron rail with both hands. Light from the simulacrum sculpted his bearded face. In his dark red cloak and saffron-yellow undertunic, he stood a head taller than the Guardsman. His face was extraordinarily handsome and perennially young. The dark eyes were intelligent, thick-browed and serene. His hair was dark brown, coming down to a bit below the ear in slight waves. Around his neck he wore a simple gold medallion on a gold chain; he wore no other jewelry. The medallion bore the image of a strange winged animal with the head of a demon.

"Soon, my friend," Incarnadine said. "When the belfries are completely manned and ready to be drawn up to the walls."

"Then I will return to my men." Tyrene made a motion to leave.

"No, stay awhile. I shall have orders to give you."

"Very well, my lord." Tyrene took off his metal-studded black leather helmet, brushed dust off his chain mail doublet, and leaned against the rail. He took a deep breath and sighed.

"Weary, are you?"

"Yes, my lord."

"You have fought bravely and well against overwhelming odds."

"Thank you, my lord. Though I fear . . ." Tyrene's gaze fell to his feet and he sighed again. He shook his head, his expression pained and vexed. "It makes no sense."

"What doesn't?"

"Vorn going to all this trouble. What are his motives?" Tyrene's eyes rose to the simulacrum as Incarnadine changed the perspective again, this time to a wider view of the outer ward. "It's insanity. What's more, it's bad war making. Vorn could have chosen to besiege a lesser fortress, thereby establishing his presence in the Western lands. He could have collected his quitrents and gone his way to finish the campaign in the South. He must know we have no offensive might to bring to bear against him. Instead, he allies himself with weaklings, the very ones he could have squashed, and pours his life's blood into sands of our impoverished Pale trying to take Castle Perilous." Tyrene pounded the rail with a mailed fist. "It makes no sense!"

"He may succeed."

Tyrene's face fell. "Yes, my lord. And I accept full responsibility."

"No."

"At risk of contradicting you, my lord, I—"

"No," Incarnadine said again, softly but firmly. "You will not berate yourself. You have done your very best and have inflicted grievous losses on the enemy. You have made him pay in blood."

Tyrene protested with a quick shake of the head. "Were it not for special forces—"

"Tyrene." Incarnadine's smile was benevolently admonishing.

The captain's shoulders slumped. "Yes, my lord. I will say no more." He shuffled his feet and muttered, "Still, it makes no sense."

"Don't you think the castle a worthy prize for a conqueror?"

"Why . . . I suppose. But what good can it do Vorn? Surely the last thing he needs is another fortress."

"Perhaps he means to steal our magic."

Tyrene knitted his brow, nodding. "Yes, maybe that's what drives him. But even he should know that only a Haplodite can tap the castle's deepest source of power."

"It may be he does not know. Or has been deliberately misled."

"Aye, it could be. If so, it's *her* doing."

Incarnadine did not answer. He shifted his weight and

placed his left foot on the lower crossbar of the rail. "Then, of course, there is always the attraction of booty."

Tyrene laughed. "I have lived all my life in and about Castle Perilous and have yet to catch even a whiff of where the treasure room might be."

"Again, he may not be aware of the peculiarities of this place." Incarnadine mused for a moment, then said, "I think I would have trouble finding it myself. Haven't been there in years. As I remember, it lies within one of the more stable areas, but its position may have drifted somewhat over time."

With a sweep of his hand, Incarnadine changed the scene below to full perspective.

The line of gigantic belfries was moving slowly toward the curtain wall. The infantry marched in files behind, ready to mount the stairs inside the towers. When the belfries drew close enough to the wall, the invaders would pour out through the top, crossing to the wall walk by means of drawbridges let down from the tops of the towers.

"Then again," Incarnadine said, "it may be Vorn has taken a fancy to our Pale and wants a summer residence."

Tyrene regarded him gravely for a moment, then broke into sudden laughter. "A fine jest, my lord." His mirth was disproportionate, being, as it was, an overdue release from the tensions of battle.

Incarnadine waited until Tyrene had wiped the tears from his eyes, then took his foot from the rail and straightened.

The infantry were marching in double-time, and had begun mounting the stairways inside the belfries.

"The time has come," Incarnadine said.

"The sky dragons again, my lord?"

"I think not—this time."

Incarnadine stood back from the rail and raised both arms. He closed his eyes and stood unmoving for a moment. Then, quickly and with great precision, he commenced tracing patterns in the air. Touching the tips of his index fingers together above his head, he parted them and brought them around and down in two semicircles to meet again at the bottom, thereby completing the Great Circle. He stepped back to examine his work, as if the figure were visible. Stepping forward again, he outlined a series of arcs linking points of the circumference, connecting the midpoints of these with lines to form a square within the circle.

He executed more lines, more figures within figures, his brow knitted, tiny beads of sweat springing to it like a sudden dew.

Watching, Tyrene stepped back warily.

Presently, Incarnadine's spell figure, composed of faintly glowing red filaments, began to take form in the air.

# KEEP—ELSEWHERE

"WE'RE LOST AGAIN," Snowclaw said.

"Tell me something new."

Gene scratched his head and looked around. They had followed a spiral stairwell down to this, a spacious airy room with numerous window alcoves. An Oriental rug covered the flagstone at the far end of the room, and on it were positioned various pieces of furniture—a divan, a few straight-back chairs, two low tables. A sideboard set against the wall held several wrought-iron candelabras bearing the stubs of burned tapers. The alcoves were set at even intervals along the right wall; a single flush window was cut into the far wall, and to the left, an arched doorway led through to the descending spiral of another stairwell.

Gene said, "Linda, do you remember Dalton saying to go right at that first landing? Or was it left?"

Linda stepped past him, following Snowclaw toward the windows.

"I'm sure he said right. And we went right. That's all I'm sure of, though."

"Damn. Well, maybe we just keep following the stairs.

But it seems to me we should have come to that grand ballroom by now."

Yawning, Gene walked to the far end of the room and flopped down on the divan. He yawned again and keeled over on his side.

"Tired," he said quietly, closing his eyes.

Snowclaw said, "Hey, Gene. Come look at this."

Gene's eyes popped open. "What?" He cranked himself up and shuffled over to the alcove into which Snowclaw and Linda had squeezed themselves. They were leaning out of the narrow Gothic window and looking up, Linda bending and ducking her head under Snowclaw's outstretched arm. Gene craned his neck, couldn't see a thing, so he stepped back and went into the next alcove. He looked out.

There was nothing above but clear sky. Hundreds of feet below, waves crashed onto black rocks at the foot of a shear cliff. There was nothing below the window. Gene gasped and put his arms out, bracing himself against the stone jambs. The window was suspended in air, floating a few feet above the edge of the cliff. The angle was disorienting; the window was canted vertiginously forward, unnaturally raising the horizon ahead. The whole world out there was cockeyed. Gene stepped back and turned around. The room was level, just as before. He looked out again, trying to adjust to the strange perspective. Nearby, other craggy promontories rose from the water like the heads of sea monsters. He bent and looked out. The dark band of a squall line edged the horizon. Between it and the rocks, about a mile out to sea, a long, high-masted ship tacked through choppy waters, its sails billowing, a voluminous spinnaker blooming off the prow.

"Hey, this is weird."

"You said it," Snowclaw agreed. "Look at that thing."

"What, the ship?"

"I guess you could call it that."

"What would you call it?"

"I dunno. A floating city."

"Huh?" Gene leaned out as far as he dared and glanced around. "Where?"

"Up there. You mean you can't see it?"

Gene looked up. "What're you guys talking about?"

"Great White Stuff! Gene, how could you miss it?"

"Where? I don't see anything but that sailboat out there."

"Sailboat. What sailboat out where?"

"That yacht, or whatever you call it. Out to sea."

After a pause that contained much bafflement, Snowclaw said, "What sea?"

"What . . . ? Now, wait just a minute . . ." Gene left the window.

"Where in the world are you looking?" Linda asked as Gene came into the first alcove.

"Move over, Snowclaw."

"Sorry." Snowclaw edged aside for him.

The three of them looked out.

This window opened onto a different world. A drop of only a few feet ended on the grassy slope of a high hill. Below was a valley through which a tree-lined stream meandered. The day was bright and sunny, a stiff breeze stirring the tall grass.

"That's what we were talking about," Snowclaw said, pointing up.

Gene looked.

It was a city in the clouds, moving slowly and majestically across the sky. The main structure was a lens-shaped silver disk at least a mile in diameter, studded top and bottom with clear bell-shaped bubbles that housed complex structures within them. The silver disk gleamed brilliantly. The city had come out of a bank of puffy clouds, and now its leading edge cut into another. Gene watched as the clouds enveloped it. The city soared through and began to exit into a clear patch of blue-violet sky.

Gene shook his head slowly. "I've never . . ." He shrugged.

"Yeah," Snowclaw said. He looked at Gene. "Now, what was that about a sailboat?"

Still transfixed, still awed, Gene delayed answering for a moment. Then he said, "Huh? Oh." He scratched the stubble on his chin. "You better go look for yourself."

Snowclaw left the alcove. Linda stayed, leaning her hip against the windowsill and absently resting a hand on Gene's shoulder.

"Beautiful," she murmured. "I wonder who they are and how they came to build such a thing."

"And how the hell they did it," Gene said. "Your genuine antigravity-type flying city. My God."

"Or is it magic, I wonder?"

"Great White Stuff!" came Snowclaw's shout from the next alcove. "Linda, you've got to see this."

Gene continued to gaze at the airborne marvel until Linda's squeal drew him away from the window. He walked past his companions and went into the third alcove down.

Here, again, was a totally different vista, this one of a vast desert of yellow sand wind-combed into furrowed dunes. Dark needles of rock poked up here and there, throwing stark shadows across the sand. Huge winged creatures—they were too big and too strange-looking to be birds—wheeled in a sky washed out by a searing, blue-white sun. With great batlike wings they soared on rising thermals, circling, searching. For some reason Gene didn't think the object of the search was something that had died.

The next window looked out on forested mountains, and the drop to the ground was over a hundred feet.

The three of them began running from alcove to alcove —there were fifteen in all—oohing and ahing, yelling for each other to come look at this or that. There was another seascape, this one of an ocean washing a bone-white beach under a sky of bilious yellow. And another forest, though the vegetation was unearthly, funguslike and strangely colored. There were mountain views, wide aspects of parched wasteland, nightmarish landscapes with odd-colored skies, pleasant vistas of scenic countrysides. One window looked out into almost total blackness—nothing out there but a vague suggestion of looming shadows.

When Gene went back to catch one more glimpse of the flying city, it was gone. He noticed that the window was slightly higher over the hilltop now. These aspects, it seemed, were not entirely stable.

He left the alcove and went to join Linda on the divan.

Snowclaw sat with one leg up over the arm of a carved wooden chair, still musing over what he'd seen. "Crazy," he said, shaking his head, massive white brow creased into a frown.

"Yeah," Gene agreed. He sat down heavily.

Linda said, "I was wondering why every time I looked out a window, things looked different. I thought it was just because the castle was so big."

Gene said, "You've run into this before?"

"Yes, but the castle was under me when I looked out. Not like this, floating along up in the air and all. I would have totally lost my mind."

Gene considered it. "That might mean that the castle itself exists in other worlds. But not in all of them. Like the one we come from, for instance."

"No big castle in my world either," Snowclaw said. "Leastwise, none that I know of."

"But it's only under siege in one of them," Gene said. "So far as we know."

"We know nothing," Snowclaw muttered. "We can't even find our way to the pisser."

"What was it we're supposed to be looking for?" Linda asked.

"The armory," Gene said. "Dalton suggested we might need weapons."

"Oh. I'd like some clothes. It gets cold here sometimes, and this thing . . ." She plucked at her T-shirt disdainfully.

"Yeah, I'd like to get out of this monkey suit," Gene said.

Smiling toothily and rubbing his white pelt, Snowclaw said, "I'm rather attached to this coat."

Linda giggled. "It must keep you really warm."

"Yeah, too warm for this climate. I should begin to shed some of it soon, though, if I stay here much longer.

"Unfortunately," Gene said, "it looks as though we're going to be stuck here for a while."

Linda's face fell. "Yes. It is unfortunate, isn't it." She stared moodily into her lap. "I don't know how long I can last before I go completely to pieces."

"Sorry, Linda. I didn't mean it to sound as if we'd never get out. If anyone thinks we're going to stay lost in this funhouse on a permanent basis, they have another think coming. I intend to find a way back home. Somehow." He reached and gave her shoulder a playful shake. "So buck up."

"I'm sorry."

"It's okay. I'm scared shitless myself."

"Want a Valium?"

"Huh? Are you still conjuring those things?"

"I haven't taken it yet," Linda said. "I'm debating."

"If you think you need it, go ahead."

Linda looked at the white pill in the palm of her hand. She closed her fist over it. "I don't think I will . . . just yet."

"Good."

"I could use a drink," Snowclaw said.

"Alcohol, you mean?"

"I don't mean snow melt. I've been looking for a drink ever since I came into this place. Didn't care for that smelly flower water they had upstairs."

"What do you drink usually?"

"It's called *shrackk*. Made from the blubber of a big land mammal."

"Something like a seal?"

"What's a—" Snowclaw regarded the ceiling with a look of mild surprise. "Yeah, I guess I do know what a seal is. Or at least I know what you mean. Right, it's sort of a seal but with big teeth and claws. Pretty dangerous if you let one corner you. They can be outrun pretty easily, though. I hunt 'em. That's my trade."

Gene asked, "Is there civilization where you come from?"

"Oh, sure. I make it into town about two, three times a year. I sell my pelts, get drunk, kick some butts, rip a few heads off, generally have a good time." He snorted sarcastically. "And lose all my money and wind up strapped again." He yawned and snapped his massive jaws shut. "What a life. What a life."

"Sounds like a colorful occupation," Linda commented.

"It's a living."

They rested awhile, then left the room to continue down the winding stairs.

They reached a landing and went out into a hallway. Turning right, they walked for a while before coming to an intersecting corridor. To the left a short way down was a doorway spilling light. They went in.

"I don't believe we found it," Linda said.

Looking like a museum, the room was filled with ancient and odd-looking military apparel. Suits of mail hung upon wooden dummies, suits of armor stood by themselves. The walls were festooned with shields of various shapes and sizes. At the far end of the room was an opening and a counter. Behind the counter stood an elderly man dressed in a red-hooded shoulder cape. He was smiling, leaning on the counter with hands folded.

"Good morning," he said pleasantly.

"I guess this is the armory."

The man nodded. "It is, sir. And I am the armorer."

"Uh-huh." Gene glanced around. "Do we just take what we need?"

"If you wish, sir. However, I am available to serve you should you need assistance. If you desire a weapon, I must fetch it from the storeroom."

"Oh." Gene knocked a knuckle against an iron breastplate. "Thanks." He stepped over to examine a shield emblazoned with a particularly interesting coat-of-arms.

"Do you have any clothes?" Linda asked the man.

"I'm afraid I have nothing but military apparel, which would hardly befit a gracious lady such as yourself."

"Oh. Do you know where I could—"

"I think you'd be wanting to see the seamstress, my lady."

"Oh, good. And where—"

"I'm afraid her shop is a long way from here. It's on the other side of the keep, on the twentieth floor of the Queen's Tower."

"Oh."

Gene came back to the counter. "I want a sword," he said. "And a knife."

"A sword . . . and a knife."

"Uh, yeah."

The man sighed. "Would you have any idea as to the *type* of sword or knife you'd be wanting?"

"Well . . ."

"There are many varieties, you know. All lengths and sizes, all used for various and sundry purposes."

"Well, I sort of want a general . . . you know, *sword.*"

"A sword befitting a general?"

"No, no. Your average all-purpose, general-utility thing."

The man frowned. "Hmmm."

"Something about yea long."

"Ah, a longsword. Two-edged, then?"

"Uhhh . . . yeah. Two-edged."

"Two-handed or one-handed haft?"

Gene shrugged. "Whatever. Two-handed."

"Cross hilt or decorative?"

"Um." Gene crossed his arms and rubbed his chin.

"I might not have the decorative in a two-hand-hafted longsword, come to think of it. One moment, sir, and I will look."

The man went back to a row of free-standing shelves, returned with a huge sword and laid it on the counter. "Will this do, sir?"

"Holy heck." Gene picked the thing up, grasping the haft with both hands. The sword was heavy and unwieldy, almost impossibly so, and about half again as long as it needed to be. He glanced at the elaborately wrought hilt and laid it back on the counter. "You have anything a little easier to handle?"

"Many things. Perhaps a shortsword would better suit you."

"Yeah. What do you have?"

"Many kinds."

"Uh-huh." Gene shrugged. "Like . . . what?"

"Well, there are two-edged shortswords and one-edged

shortswords. There are swords of various curvatures and of various blade widths. There are swords used for hacking, and there are those more suitable for thrusting at one's enemy. And, of course, there are swords suitable for both. There are blades of various tempers and degrees of strength. There are broadswords and sabers, court swords and backswords. We have rapiers and épées, we have falchions and scimitars. There are swords with cup hilts, cross hilts, decorative hilts, basket hilts, and hilts molded to the individual hand."

"Uh—"

"There are ceremonial swords, calvary swords, infantry swords, swords for infighting, and swords to keep a distance. Now, as far as knives—"

"Hold it."

"—there are many different kinds. We have various styles of dirk and dagger, stiletto and poniard—"

"Hold it! Look, all I want is a sword about that long."

"Are you sure a sword is what you want, sir? It may be you'd be better off with an ax or mace."

"No, a sword."

"A morning star? Perhaps a good, heavy club."

"A sword."

The armorer took a deep breath, folded his hands and smiled pleasantly. "And what kind of sword would you be wanting, sir?"

Gene's shoulders slumped. "Morning star?" he said weakly.

"A spiked ball affixed to a short chain which is in turn attached to a handle."

"Oh, yeah. No, I don't think so."

"A lance, then? Or a pike?"

"Umm . . ."

"A halberd, perhaps? Or a broadax?"

"Well—"

"Could you use a spear?"

"Spear?"

"I would, however, have to know if you intend to use it for throwing or for thrusting."

"Not a spear, for crying out loud. I want something that

I can fight with. Something that'll do some damage."

"Do some damage." The armorer thought it over. "Perhaps an ax, then. Would you like to see one?"

"I guess."

"Broadax, poleax, or taper ax?"

"Oh, boy."

"Do you want something that will unseam a man from nave to chaps, or simply wound him mortally?"

"I—"

"This . . ." The armorer turned and walked off, then returned bearing a large ax with a long wooden handle. ". . . is a broadax."

"Look, could you show me a couple of different swords?"

"Certainly, sir. What kinds would you like to see?"

"Oh, for Christ's sake."

Snowclaw, who had been browsing the room, stepped up to the counter. He picked up the broadax, looked it over once, raised it with both hands and crashed it into the countertop directly in front of the armorer, who shrieked and danced back just in the nick of time. The ax cleaved the counter in two, continuing down to split the boards underneath almost to the floor.

Snowclaw wrenched the ax out and examined the blade, running his thumb delicately over it. He looked at the armorer sharply. "This'll do for me. How about taking care of my friends, and we'll be on our way."

Face paling, the armorer nodded. "Yes, sir. Anything you say."

"And get some clothes for the lady, here."

"Immediately, sir. Will there be anything else, sir?"

"Do it."

"I will fetch the seamstress. She will be glad to come."

"Fine. And if you don't come back, I'll come looking."

The armorer swallowed. "I shall return at once, sir."

# Outer Curtain Wall—Southeast Tower

From an embrasured window Melydia looked out at the long line of belfries lumbering toward the inner curtain wall. The assault was going well, but she knew Incarnadine had yet to act. She was prepared for anything he might do. She had been preparing for years.

She watched as siege engines hurled boulders, some as big as a house, over the inner curtain wall, there to crash into the forebuildings and other structures of the ward. A few stones fell short, bounding off the wall or smashing into the crenelated battlements, to the dismay of the few defenders who manned them. The engines were working well. They would not have worked at all were it not for Melydia's magical assistance. Each engine was under a spell that enabled it to violate those natural mechanical laws which ordinarily would have precluded handling such massive projectiles. By rights, a trebuchet's throwing arm should crack like a toothpick under the weight of stones that size. Even if the strain could be borne, mundane engines simply lacked the power to throw these projectiles, or any projectiles, over a thirty-story wall. Only magical ones could do the trick.

The spell was a difficult and subtle one, but it worked.

She heard the clack of hard-leather soles coming up the spiral staircase behind her. She turned to see Vorn mounting the landing.

"There you are, my lady. I had wondered . . ."

She smiled and turned back to the window. Vorn came up beside her and gazed out.

"The lookouts report nothing brewing," Vorn told her. "Of course, that means little. Incarnadine is sure to play his hand now."

She nodded. "He will."

They watched. The moving towers, now very close to the battlements of the high inner wall, were almost completely manned. Archers, occupying the topmost platforms, were still keeping the walls clear of defenders. Incarnadine's castle guards weren't showing their heads. The Guardsmen had chosen not to engage the invaders at close quarters along the wall; they were outnumbered and they knew it. There were fifteen belfries and five thousand men to flow from them and spill over into Castle Perilous proper. No, the mopping up would proceed from tower to tower all the way around the perimeter until the entire inner curtain wall was secured—slow, dirty work, but it must be done. And it would be done.

"Have you slept?" Vorn asked. When Melydia gave her head a shake, he said, "You must be exhausted."

"After taking on six thousand soldiers in one night? Why would I be?"

Vorn was taken somewhat aback. A voluntary grunt of laughter escaped him, though he did not smile.

Melydia did. "You are shocked by my coarse humor," she said.

Vorn's mouth softened. "A bit. Forgive me."

"No, it was inappropriate. I must beg pardon."

"I shouldn't have been shocked. Though you are a lady, you ought not to be judged by the usual proprieties applying to women of quality. You can't be. They are much too limiting. You are an individual of power, and . . ."

She turned slightly, one eye peeking around the edge of her blue headdress. "And?"

"I admire that." He smiled.

"In a woman?"

"In you."

Her hand, wrist hung with folds of her white cloak, came up to caress his beard. He seized it and kissed her palm.

"Melydia," he said.

"In the midst of a battle, Vorn?"

"In the middle of Hell, if the occasion warrants."

She made to withdraw her hand, and he reluctantly let it go.

"Notwithstanding your jest," he said, "you must be weary beyond measure. To have cast six thousand spells in one night—"

"Fourteen hours without stop. I could barely raise my hand."

"Fourteen—" Vorn was awed. "Indeed, I did not know. I grew weary and retired shortly after you started." He considered it. "Even so, it does not seem sufficient time."

"It wasn't. It gave me but seconds to effect each one. An ancillary spell was needed, one to facilitate my working unnaturally fast—and another to prevent me from collapsing. That spell yet sustains me, though it grows weaker by the minute."

He clucked. "Must each soldier have been done individually? Is there not such a thing as a blanket spell?"

"Yes, but a blanket thrown over six thousand covers not many."

"I see." Vorn's eyebrows drew together in a worried frown. "But will it work? Could any spell be sufficient to fend off Incarnadine's evil? It is said he is no mere mortal."

"He may be mortal. That is, he may one day die. But he has lived some three hundred years."

"I have heard that, too, though I scarce believe it."

"You may believe it. All the Haplodites have been long-lived."

Arms akimbo, Vorn turned, paced away from the

window and stopped. He brooded for a moment, then wheeled slowly around, his gaze on the floor. "Against magic so powerful . . ." he began.

"We have fought and have nearly prevailed." She went to him, took his hands and pressed them to her breast. "Have you had cause to doubt me up till now?"

"No."

"Come."

She led him across the semicircular room to the staircase. They mounted it, she leading him by the hand. They went up six turns until they came to a hatchway at the top. Vorn threw the hatch aside and they climbed out onto the turret. Stepping over the dead body of a Guardsman overlooked by the clean-up detail, they went to the battlement.

"Look," she said, her hand sweeping across the scene. "Walls thirty stories high, a keep whose upper floors are sometimes hid in cloud. Walls within walls, towers that touch the sky, black adamantine stone immune to the elements—a fortress of magic and power unimaginable—and you, Vorn, are about to prevail against it. History has never known such a siege. Future generations will scarce credit it. You will be legend." Her voice rose over the din of shouting soldiers, the whoosh of the catapults, the crack of a thousand crossbows and the ping and clatter of bolts striking stone. Come here."

She lead him to the south side of the turret.

"We are a thousand feet above the plain."

Vorn looked out across the dark lands of the Pale. Gray-black mountains hove in the distance, ringing a valley of dirt and dust. Here and there rude farm huts dotted the terrain, and miserable, near-barren fields made haphazard patterns.

So poor a land, Vorn thought. But it was a fleeting thought.

"Was ever a fortress more inaccessible, more invulnerable? You levitated an army a thousand feet straight up."

"There was no other way," Vorn said. "Else they would have picked us off one by one as we marched up the trail."

"You did it by the power of your will."

*The power of my will . . .*

The thought crowded into his mind, nudging doubt aside.

"You did it, Vorn. Not me."

His chest swelled, then fell slowly, a doubting cast returning to his eyes.

"But you . . ."

"I love you."

He looked into her face. Framed in the folds of her headdress, it was partly hidden now as the wind fetched the cloth across her nose and mouth. Her eyes contained a hundred emotions he could not fathom.

"Melydia," was all he could say.

"Do you believe me?"

He looked out again at the dust into which he had poured his army's blood.

*For what?* came a small voice, barely heard. *For what?*

"Do you believe me?"

His gaze was drawn to hers.

"Yes."

They embraced as a stronger wind blew his cloak around them.

Presently they became aware of a hush that had fallen over the battle. They parted and returned to the north side of the turret.

Melydia pointed. "Behold."

Airborne objects approached from the northwest. Their flight was swift, and in formation—like migrating birds.

"What this time?" Vorn said. "What manner of hellish thing?"

"We will know soon."

"Aye, we will. Too soon."

"Are you afraid?"

He cast a dark look at her. "You think that deserving of an answer?"

"No, my love. Forgive me. I know you fear nothing."

He encircled her within his meaty left arm.

The objects soon revealed themselves to be bowl-shaped, with appendages that at a distance could have been taken to be wings, but as the objects neared, took the form of pairs of human hands, disembodied human hands.

"Mother Goddess," Vorn breathed. "What . . . ?"

Each pair of hands bore a gigantic metal caldron that looked much like an ironsmith's crucible.

Melydia stepped away from Vorn and stood against the battlement, hands on either side of a crenellation, leaning out, her face awry with strange, conflicting emotions. There was hope and expectation and fear and dread. There was hatred. And underneath it all, she knew but strove to suppress with every grain of her being, there was love.

She did not know that there was madness there as well.

"Yes," she said as thunder rolled to their ears, dark clouds piling over the castle. "Yes!" she screamed over its roar.

A finger of cloud passed across the sun, plunging the countryside into shadow and revealing an eerie blue glow emanating from the castle itself. Webs of lightning shot from tower to tower and bright blue prominences arose from the keep. A storm wind lashed the citadel, but no rain fell. Dust devils whirled about, sucking up the debris of past battles.

The flying caldrons broke formation and descended, revealing themselves to be of immense size. They swooped, then reformed into a line, each caldron poised above a belfry. The hands that bore them were the hands of malign gods—huge, sinewy, and punishing.

A bolt of lightning hit the tower on which Melydia and Vorn stood.

The prince was thrown down. Struggling against the ever-rising wind, he got up and staggered to Melydia, who seemed unaffected. She was still screaming, unintelligible now over the crack of thunder and the howling wind.

"We must go," he shouted into her ear, then tried to move her toward the hatch.

She was like a pillar of iron. He tried to shake her, but her body recoiled like a spring, her knuckles white against the stone, face uplifted toward the fearful apparition above the castle wall, the line of caldrons that now began to tip. From within the caldrons came a bright red-orange glow.

Vorn looked over the rampart. Men were bolting from the bottoms of the towers, fleeing in panic. He let Melydia go and hopped up on the wall.

"You!" he screamed. "Man your stations!" His voice was lost in the din.

"Back! Get back, I say! Return to your—" He broke off. It was useless. Too much to expect mortal men to face doom at the literal hands of the supernatural. Vorn looked aghast at the slowly tipping caldrons. Too much to expect even the bravest man to face that. For the first time in his life Vorn knew that he, too, was afraid. Yet he stood there.

Liquid fire poured from the crucibles, splashing down on the belfries in flaming cataracts. At once the belfries and the men in them were engulfed. Like animated torches, soldiers streamed from the belfries into the ward, some jumping to their deaths. Those who didn't fell to the ground and rolled, or ran in panicky circles slapping at themselves in a frantic attempt to put out the flames.

Vorn's heart sank. He had never tasted defeat, and now it sat on his tongue like a lump of brass, hard, cold, and bitter.

There was chaos in the ward. Weapons lay strewn about. Soldiers ran and scattered like coals from an overturned brazier. The belfries stood unmoving, mountains of flame, funeral pyres all.

Vorn could look no longer. He stepped down from the wall and walked to the opposite side of the turret. He drew his royal-blue cloak about him and gazed emptily out at lands of the Pale, lands he would curse till he drew his dying breath. He closed his eyes, his chin dropping to his chest.

Presently he felt a hand at his shoulder. He turned.

"You must see," Melydia said.

He stared at her, his face ashen. He had no words to speak to this woman whom he thought he had known.

Now it was as if she were a stranger. Her face was transformed.

"You must come," she said, smiling as if inviting him to inspect the preparations for a grand ball. "Look what we have done."

He stared at her for a while longer, striving to find in that delicately beautiful face some clue, some explanation to her mystery.

He found none.

She took his hand and led him across.

The men had stopped running amuck. They stood about, talking, exclaiming, gesturing at one another.

They were all still in flames.

Vorn shook his head, uncomprehending.

"They burn but they are not consumed," Melydia told him. "Neither are the belfries. Look."

It was true. The belfries' structural members were still the color of fresh-cut timber; they had not blackened. Stranger still, no smoke came from the fires at all. The flames seemed to dance on the surface of the wood, furiously trying to penetrate but unable to.

"Soon the men will overcome their shock. The battle will then proceed. They need you now, Vorn."

She traced a quick pattern in the air and spoke a word under her breath.

"There. They will hear you now. Speak to them."

Color returning to his face, Vorn mounted the battlement and faced his troops.

*"Soldiers of the Emp—"* He stopped, tongue-tied by hearing his voice boom out louder than the thunder. Heads snapped in his direction. Arms raised, pointing.

Vorn spoke. *"Soldiers of the Empire! We have faced the Devil's minions and have fought bravely. Now we have come through hellfire itself unscathed."* He paused. *"Can any man doubt that our cause is just and holy? Can any gainsay our righteousness? Behold the fortress of Evil itself. It looms before us in all its malevolence. Let no man fear it. We have come to vanquish it, and vanquish it we shall, though all its forces be arrayed against us. Return to your stations. Fight on, bravely, as you have up till now.*

*The Goddess is with us, her blessings are upon us, and her victory will be ours."*

He withdrew his sword and raised it high.

*"Fight on, for Goddess and Empire! Fight!"*

A great shout rose up from the troops. They all saluted, then picked up their weapons and ran to the belfries.

Vorn sheathed his sword, looking up at the line of crucibles still hanging above. Now empty, they were beginning to fade.

He jumped from the battlement. Melydia waved her hand to abrogate the voice amplification spell.

"Why?" he asked her. "Why did you not tell what was to happen? Why did you not warn of this, so that we would know what to expect?"

"Because *I* did not know what to expect. The spell I cast over each soldier and each of the belfries was general in nature, a protection against whatever form Incarnadine's magic would take. I could not predict the form, though of late I have dreamt of fire. But I have dreamt of other things too. I cannot see the future. That is not a power of mine. Would that it were. No, the spell was general, which was why it was so difficult to effect. Neither was I sure that it would work. But it did, as you can see."

Vorn watched his men remount the belfries. The flames were weaker now, and had turned dull red.

Melydia had turned her gaze up to the keep.

"He holds back," she said. "Still he does not tap his deepest source of power." Her voice was a murmur. "Perhaps he is afraid. Afraid of me. Of himself. Afraid . . ."

She swayed, put her palm to her forehead.

"The spell of stamina. It is almost gone. . . . Vorn, I—"

He caught her as she fell, and picked her up. She lay across his arms like a limp doll.

The pattern, its arcane geometries defying the eye with their complexity, was fading. At the height of the spell it had glowed blue-white and had emitted great heat, so much that Incarnadine could barely approach it to complete the last lines. Now it had reverted to dull red, its power quickly ebbing. Incarnadine stepped up to it again and traced across it the Stroke of Cancellation.

With a hiss like molten metal quenched in water, the pattern disappeared.

Shed of his cloak, his undertunic untied and open across his chest, dripping with sweat, Incarnadine came to the rail.

He saw, and he understood.

He grew aware that Tyrene still awaited his orders. He turned.

Tyrene began, "My lord—"

"The castle has fallen," Incarnadine told him. "Not yet, but soon. You will withdraw your men to the keep, fighting only those rearguard actions necessary to protect lives."

Tyrene was appalled. "My lord!"

"Hear me. Once in the keep, you will offer only enough resistance to delay its fall for three days. Thereafter, order your men to disperse through whatever aspects they choose. Do not leave the wounded behind. Do not let anyone be taken prisoner. Order your men to abandon their positions before being overrun. Above all, let no more lives be lost. We have lost too many."

Tyrene was almost in tears. "Yes, my lord." Fumblingly he put his helmet back on. "What about the Guests?"

"I will see to them."

"Yes, my lord." He stepped forward. "My lord, I—"

"Go, Tyrene."

Tyrene left.

He waved the simulacrum to a closer view of the outer curtain wall, then focused it even closer . . . closer still.

There was Vorn. And there was Melydia, in his arms. The prince looked lost, helpless. Strange mien for a victor.

He waved the scene still closer. Melydia's face, blurred by the great distance across which the simulacrum fetched its image, took form below, bigger than life. She looked calm.

"You do not sleep, Melydia, my darling," he said, "though your eyes are closed. You do not rest. You will not—until you have destroyed this castle . . . and me."

He regarded her for a moment, remembering.

Then, a wide sweep of his hand, and the simulacrum was gone. The vast stone floor below lay bare.

"So be it," he said, walking away.

# KEEP—EAST WING—ARMORY

"HEY, YOU LOOK great," Gene said as Linda came out of the storeroom.

"Thanks. You really like it?"

"Sure."

Linda twirled once. She had chosen not to go around attired as most women did in this world, in long gowns and coif. Instead she had picked an outfit more befitting a teenage boy. It was composed of a yellow long-sleeved undertunic, a brown overtunic with a hood-collar and pleated sleeves to the elbow, tan hose and brown soft-leather boots to mid-calf. The hem of the overtunic rode high on her thighs.

"It's a little too short," she said. "My rear end sticks out a little."

"Well, that's not necessarily bad."

She laughed. "Maybe not." She touched the scabbard of the dagger hanging on her narrow leather belt. "*This* thing," she said, "is not me at all."

Gene withdrew his sword (one-handed, double-edged, broad-bladed and cross-hilted) halfway from its sheath. "This isn't exactly my métier either."

"Your uniform looks nice."

"Thanks."

Gene had taken a Guard's uniform, minus the chain mail, which he had found inhibitingly heavy. Over his red undertunic he wore a black leather jerkin with winglike leather shoulder flaps. The front of the jerkin was covered with silver studs. The rest of the outfit consisted of black padded breeches, red hose, and high black boots.

"Actually, it's kind of kinky. I feel like a gay medieval Nazi."

Snowclaw came back from relieving himself in a privy down the hall. "Hey, Gene, you look like a gay medieval Nazi."

They laughed.

Gene did a take. "Hey, you said that in English."

"I heard you. You can turn off the running translation if you listen closely. Funny language, Englitch."

"English."

"Whatever. I'm having a little trouble with *Nazi*, but *medieval* comes out to mean 'middle years'."

"Close."

"Yeah. Are Nazis usually happy?"

"Happy? Oh. That's not what I meant . . . Uh, forget it."

"Anything you say." Snowclaw scratched his stomach. "When's lunch?"

"You hungry? I'm not. Kinda stuffed myself at breakfast. Which should have been supper for me." Gene yawned. "I'm tired, myself."

Linda said, "I could use a bite to eat. Do you want to go back to the dining room?"

"That won't do me much good, actually," Snowclaw said. "I didn't care for that stuff much. I wish I could find someplace to hunt."

"Rawenna—that's my maid—said that if you want—"

"Oh, we have a maid, do we?" Gene twitted.

"All us noblewomen do, didn't you know? What I was saying, Snowclaw, was that if you need special food, you just have to tell the cook and he'll whip up a spell or two and give you what you want."

"Yeah? Magic, huh?"

"Pretty much. All that food upstairs was created by hocus-pocus. Leastways, that's what Jacoby told me."

"The guy who looks like Sidney Greenstreet?" Gene asked.

"Is that who he looks like?"

"Only shorter."

"Hm. Well, that's what he said."

"Look, why don't you try whipping up something for you and Snowclaw?"

"Me whip up something. Huh?"

"Yeah. Materialization. Isn't that what you have, what you can do?"

"Whoa, there. Valiums are one thing—"

"Why should Valiums be one thing?"

"You know what I mean."

"No, I don't. Why don't you try it, Linda? An experiment. I mean, this magic stuff is really fascinating."

"Oh, come on."

"Seriously."

Linda threw up her hands. "Where? *Here?*"

"Anywhere. On this thing."

Gene cleared helmets and other accouterments off a small table.

Linda looked at it.

"Well," Gene said.

"'Well' what?"

"Do your thing."

Linda was annoyed. "Really."

"No, come on, Linda. You can do it."

"This is so insane."

"Seriously. Go ahead."

"Oh, shit. All right."

"Think of food."

Linda closed her eyes. "I'm thinking of food. What kind of food am I thinking of?"

"I give up."

"Well, what should I think of? Come on, Svengali."

"What do you want to eat?"

"Uh . . . uh . . . a Big Mac. And french fries . . . and

a real thick strawberry shake."

"Yuck. Okay, think of that."

"I'm thinking, I'm thinking." She opened her eyes. "Whaddya mean, 'yuck'? Who's the magician here?"

"Okay, okay, go ahead." Gene turned, saw Snowclaw, and said suddenly, "Hey, wait a minute. You have to think of something for Snowclaw."

"Oh, gee. How can I do that?"

"Forget about me, Linda. See if you can do it."

"Isn't there something . . . ?"

"Well, I like *kwalkarkk* ribs marinated in *shrackk* and done just right, but forget it."

"Well, I'll think of barbecued ribs. Maybe that will do it." Linda closed her eyes. "Okay, here goes."

She took a deep breath and stood motionless for a moment. Then she opened her eyes, threw out her arms and said, "Abracadabra. Nothing."

"Oh, come on," Gene chided. "You can do better than that."

"Silliest thing I've *ever* done. Okay, one more time."

She tried again, same result.

"This is ridiculous. The pill must have been a fluke—or maybe I had it on me all the time and didn't realize it."

"That's unlikely," Gene said. "Do you remember how you did it?"

"Well, I was just—" Linda broke off and dismissed the whole thing with a disdainful sweep of the hand. "Look, I'm definitely not in a magical mood today. Let's forget it."

Gene sighed. "Okay. Sorry. Actually, I was thinking that a little magic might help us find a way back home."

Linda bit her lip. "You know, you're probably right." She thought about it. "But I'm no magician. I really don't think I am."

"It's okay. Well, we should head back to the dining room, I guess."

"We ought to find a way out of here, is what we should do."

"Yeah. But how is the question. Snowclaw? You have any ideas?"

"I'm not an idea man."

Gene snickered.

Linda asked, "Do you guys think you could find your way back to the part of the castle where you came in?"

Gene shook his head ruefully. "I'm very pessimistic about that, but I think we have to try."

"Snowclaw, when did you stumble into this place?"

"Just a short time before Gene did."

"And you guys met up right away. That might mean that your gateway and Snowclaw's are close together."

"Might," Gene said, "if they still exist at all. What about the one you came through?"

"Forget that. I know it disappeared right after I crossed over. I saw it."

"Hmph. Straight through your bedroom closet, huh?"

"Yeah. Right out of a kid's nightmare."

"Wow. 'Course, coming through by way of a parking garage in an office building isn't exactly rational either."

"Not much about this place is."

"Yeah. Well." Gene placed his left hand on the hilt of his sword. "What do you say we poke around a little, try to get the feel of this place, if that's possible? If we can get our bearings, maybe we can search systematically without getting ourselves lost again. We just might luck onto another gateway back home. Maybe not the one we came through, but a way back nonetheless."

"But the way these aspects pop in and out seems so random," Linda said. "We might come out in the middle of the Gobi Desert, for all we know."

"Or Times Square . . . or Red Square, for that matter. We'll have to take our chances."

"I guess we will."

"Snowclaw, can you hold off eating for a while?"

"Sure. I'll probably faint, but—"

"A big guy like you?"

"How do you think I got to be such a big guy?"

Linda said, "You know, I really could go for a Big Mac. It'd be a little piece of home. And I really am hungry. I just picked at breakfast, and after running around all morning—"

"Linda."

"—I think I really worked up a— Huh?"

"Linda, turn around."

"Turn ar— Oh, my God."

There, on the table, was a cardboard box bearing the familiar symbol of a fast-food restaurant chain, a red cardboard envelope full of french fries, a strawberry milk shake, and two plates: one, of normal size, held a rack of barbecued spare ribs; the other was large and bore what looked like the entire spine and rib cage of a fair-sized animal.

"*Kwalkarkk!*" Snowclaw shouted, throwing down his broadax. He went to the table, tore off two or three ribs and bit into them, crunching both meat and bone between his huge, gleaming teeth. He chewed briefly, swallowed, and said, "Hey, these are great! How did you do it, Linda?"

Gene was awed. "I don't believe you ate the bones."

"Best part."

Linda opened the box and peeked in. "It's a Big Mac," she said quietly.

"Wow." Gene picked up the fries and sniffed. "They're warm."

"So's the burger." She wiped a tear from her eye.

"Yeah, and the ribs . . . What's wrong, Linda?"

Another tear rolled down her cheek. "Scared," she said.

"Gee, I don't know why. This is great." Gene scratched his stubbly chin. "Yeah. I guess I do know why. It's all very . . ." He shrugged. "All very hard to get used to. Are you okay?"

"Yeah," she said, sniffing. "I'm okay."

Gene went to her and put his arm around her shoulders. "Sure you'll be okay?"

"Sure I'm sure. I'm a goddamn magician, aren't I? I'm a witch." She gave a short, semihysterical giggle. "Just call me Samantha."

"Yeah, and I'm Darin. And this is all a TV sitcom."

She laughed, tilting her head to his shoulder. "Now, if I

could only wiggle my nose."

"Try it."

She did it, and they laughed.

Snowclaw had already wolfed down most of the *kwalkarkk*. "Anybody want these little ribs here—what're these from, a bird, or what?"

"Go ahead," Gene said, still laughing.

Snowclaw picked up the plate, flipped the spare ribs into the air and caught them in his mouth. He crunched and chewed clinically. "Not bad," he pronounced. "Kinda tasteless, though. Hey, are you guys gonna eat any of this?"

"Oh, help yourself, Snowclaw," Linda said, recovering from the giggling bout. "If I get hungry, I'll just go poof and conjure up a cheeseburger or something."

"Is that what this is?" Snowclaw asked. He popped the Big Mac into his maw, gave it three perfunctory chews, gulped it down, then tilted his head back and upended the box of fries into his wide-open jaws.

"Let's go, Emily Post," Gene told him, walking arm in arm with Linda out the door.

"Be right with you, Darin!"

"Are we lost again?"

Gene looked around. "Oh, hell, I guess—"

They heard pounding feet. Three castle guards rushed out of a crossing corridor and double-timed it away from them down the hall. One of the Guardsmen looked back, giving Gene's uniform the eye. But he didn't stop.

"Looks like something's up," Gene said. "I wonder what."

Linda said, "Well, there's a war going on outside."

"Yeah, a siege. I wonder what happens if the besiegers win—happens to us, I mean?"

"We can hide."

"Let's hope."

They walked on down the corridor. Along the wall here and there were empty niches and alcoves. Arches swept across the hallway at even intervals, supported by massive columns to either side. One door led through to a spiral staircase. They came to the intersecting corridor and stopped.

"Which way, gang?" Gene asked.

"I think we've been here before," Snowclaw said. "I smell you guys."

"You're no rose petal yourself, kid," Gene retorted.

"I didn't say you stank," Snowclaw said, sounding a little miffed, "now did I? It's just that I've got a good nose, and you hairless types have a distinctive smell."

"Just kidding, Snowclaw. I can't say you have any sort of scent at all. Humans don't have a well-developed olfactory sense."

"Olwhatory?"

"Smell, smell. Anyway, I apologize. I didn't know you were sensitive."

"Oh, it's all right. For some reason I'm edgy." Snowclaw sniffed the air. "Don't know what it is."

Suddenly the floor began to vibrate and a low, growling rumble came from what seemed like the entire structure of the keep.

Linda clutched at Gene's sleeve. Gene took her hand and pulled her back down the hall, ducking into a nearby alcove. "Come on, Snowclaw!"

Snowclaw crowded in with them.

About five seconds later the alcove began quickly to rise.

"Whoa!" Gene yelled, poking his head out the opening. "Hey, we're—"

Snowclaw yanked him back just as the thick stone edge of the ceiling—and the floor above—swept past. "You'd look funny without a head."

"Thanks. Sorry, that was stupid."

Another floor went by, then another. Then the moving alcove slowed. A fourth cross-section of stone slid down across the opening, coming to a stop at a level smoothly flush with the floor of the alcove.

"Is this lingerie, do you think?" Gene asked.

The three jumped out.

Linda marveled, "A stone elevator."

The vibrations grew stronger.

"Hey, look," Snowclaw said, pointing down the hallway, which was identical to the one four stories below except that it ended in an archway leading to the outside, or so it looked. Bright sunlight poured through the opening.

"An aspect, I guess," Gene said.

"Oh, look at the walls," Linda said.

The stone around them glowed faintly, emitting an ethereal blue light. The rumbling sound grew, and the floor became uncomfortable to stand on, transmitting nauseating vibrations up through the body.

"Let's get out of here," Gene said.

They ran for the opening, dashed through, and came out into a jungle clearing.

The ground was motionless. Stopping, they looked around. Tall palms with scaly bark bordered the clearing, and dark green fronds grew within, a wide footpath cutting through them. A tropical sun warmed the heavy, moist air.

*"Shashrackk vo hunnra nok,"* Snowclaw said. *"Ba nan irrikka vahnah danan unak valvalackk."*

Gene and Linda were staring at him.

"Huh?" Gene said. "Snowclaw, what did you say?"

*"Bok?"*

"What? Hey, wait a minute." He beckoned for Snowclaw to follow, walked back to the portal and stepped across the boundary.

When the big white beast had stepped across, Gene said, "Now, what was that you were jabbering about?"

"I said, we ought to explore this place, I'm tired of that dreary old castle—that's what I said. What was all that noise you were making?"

"You can understand me now, right?"

"Sure."

Gene walked a few paces forward, crossing the boundary. He turned and said, "What about now, when I'm standing on the other side of the interface?"

"Oh, I get it. You're outside the castle, so the spell is cancelled. Is that it?"

Gene walked back across the line.

"Huh?"

"Gonna be kinda hard to communicate."

"You said it."

"Yeah. What do you want to do?"

"I don't know. But I still want to get out of this cave."

"Maybe we can work out some sign language," Linda suggested.

"Sure, I guess," Gene said.

"Let's go," Snowclaw said. "I'll just keep my mouth shut."

They left the corridor and walked down the well-worn path. As they neared the middle of the clearing, they found an intersecting trail, this one narrower. Snowclaw, in the lead, stopped to sniff the air, looking about, his pointed ears cocked.

Gene was pensively regarding the portal. It stood unsupported on the ground like a frameless life-size photograph. A fresh thought occurring to him, he walked back to it and stood at the interface, peering into the dim interior. A draft of cool air flowed out from the opening, carrying with it the musty smell of the castle. Gene walked to the right, coming to the edge of the portal, went beyond it and stepped behind the plane of the opening.

"Oh, hell."

"What, Gene?" Linda's eyes searched around. "Gene! Where are you?"

"Behind the portal."

Linda walked back to the opening, Snowclaw following.

"Where?"

"Behind. Go around and come back here."

They did, walking around the portal as if it were a movie screen—one which, they found, had no thickness at all. Gene was standing a few feet from the juncture, peering into what looked like an identical aspect of the corridor they had just exited.

Gene left them, walking around to the front again, then returned shortly.

"I was expecting the damn thing to disappear when you

went around it. But it doesn't. And this corridor is a mirror image of the other one. See that alcove on the left? It's on the right if you go around front."

"Which means what?" Linda asked.

Gene stooped, searched the ground and found a pebble. Picking it up, he threw it through the portal. The stone ticked off the flagstone of the corridor floor, bounded a few times and skidded to a stop.

"It means Euclid's mother wore combat boots, but that's not news."

"Huh?"

"Never mind. I don't know what it means. Who comes out this way? And what happens if we go in? Or is this just another exit in another part of the castle?"

The three of them exchanged baffled looks, then walked back around the portal, going down the path a few feet.

"Where to?" Gene asked.

"Let's stay on the main path," Linda said. "I see footprints all over it, so somebody must come here regularly. I hope it means that this portal is one of the stable ones."

"Probably does. Hey, maybe this is Earth." Gene reached to touch a frond, which immediately recoiled, rolling itself up until it looked like a long green cigar. Gene sighed. "Then again, maybe not."

They made their way along the path, moving through the clearing and into the trees. Here the undergrowth wasn't shy, though it was lush, almost impenetrable.

They became aware of sounds. All around, insects clicked and chirped. Whooping cries came from a distance, echoing among the trees.

They walked through deep shade, the soil of the path soft and loamy. Smells were numerous, and Gene was reminded of a greenhouse. The odor of damp earth and rotting vegetation was heavy.

"Reminds me of Phipps Conservatory," Gene said.

"Where's that?"

"My hometown—botanical gardens. I remember going there on grade-school field trips. Thing is, the vegetation looks weird. Kinda reminds me of the Carboniferous."

"The Carbon . . . oh, you mean millions of years ago."

"Yeah. Actually, maybe early Jurassic."

"Maybe we've gone back in time."

"I doubt it. I don't recognize anything, and I took a few courses in paleontology."

"Do you think this is another planet out in space?"

"My guess is we're on another planet for sure, but the location is, like, *real* moot."

"You mean we might be in the fifth dimension or something?"

"Well, 'fifth dimension' doesn't really mean anything. Neither does 'alternate world,' to my way of thinking. Actually, the word alternate means 'every other one,' so it should be 'alternative world,' if you want to get semantically fussy." Gene thought about it. "No, *alternative* really means a choice between two things, so . . . Hell, what would the proper word be?"

"You've lost me."

"Doesn't matter. Damn. How about 'optional metrical frame'?"

"Anything you say."

" 'Option frame' for short. Yeah, I like that. This is one of many option frames."

*"Kvaas ejarnak kevak bo nera?"* Snowclaw growled.

Linda answered, "We were talking about where this place could be, Snowclaw, and Gene was saying that—"

Linda stopped in her tracks and looked stunned.

"Hey," Gene said. "I understood him, too, a little. Wasn't what he said something like, 'What are you people jabbering about?' "

"Yeah, that's what I understood too."

"Snowclaw, raise your right arm."

Snowclaw shrugged and did so.

"Wave it."

Snowclaw smiled and waved. *"Vo keslat."*

"Yeah, you look silly too. I'll be damned. It's not like back in the castle, but . . . Snowclaw, can you understand us?"

Snowclaw nodded and made a gesture that qualified the affirmative to, *More or less.*

They walked on.

"Give me some time to think about this," Gene said. He took some time, then said, "I think we didn't understand him at first because we were so surprised, though we shouldn't have been. Now that I remember, I sort of got his meaning then."

"I think I did too."

"Can't figure it out, though."

They came to another clearing, this one wider and looking completely different. Neatly trimmed grass grew along a spacious corridor running between walls of trees, and to the right lay an oval patch of grass that was a darker green and looked even more manicured. A thin pole with a flag was planted in the middle of it.

Gene began, "Of all the—"

"*Fore!*"

A small white ball thumped into the turf a few feet from Gene, hit his right arm, and bounded away to roll into the expansive sand trap in front of the green.

"Ow," Gene complained, rubbing his arm. "What the hell?"

Moments later Thaxton, whom Gene recognized from the dining hall, came running over a rise a few yards down the fairway. He looked peeved.

"I say," he shouted, "would you mind awfully getting out of the bloody way?"

"Sorry," Gene told him.

"If you hadn't been standing there, I'd be putting for an eagle. Now I'm in a bloody hazard! Blast it all."

Thaxton stalked by and gave Gene a grouchy look.

"Excu-u-u-se me," Gene said, and backed away toward his companions.

Thaxton waited off to one side of the green. Another ball shot over the rise, arching down to hit the lip of the trap. It bounced cleanly, lobbed onto the green, rolled, bounded off the pin and came to rest a few feet from the cup.

"Oh, bloody hell!" Thaxton despaired. "Of all the bleeding luck!" Grumbling, he sat down on the edge of the bunker.

A few moments later Cleve Dalton came sauntering over the rise.

"Hello there!"

He came down to where Gene and company were standing.

"Sorry to interrupt your game," Gene told him.

"Oh, don't worry about it," Dalton said amiably. "I heard Thaxton giving you a hard time. Don't pay him any mind."

"Mind telling me what a golf course is doing in the middle of the Jurassic?"

"Is that what this is?" Dalton smiled. "I didn't know."

"Well, it's close. We were hoping that this is one of the more stable aspects."

"It is. Very stable—at least it has been for the three years I've been a Guest."

"Good. Then we can get back to the castle."

"Easily, as long as you don't wander too far."

"Fine. Now, about this course . . ."

"Nobody I know remembers when it was put in," Dalton said. "It's maintained by castle servants, though, so I imagine Incarnadine had it built for the delectation of his Guests."

"Hmm. No kidding."

"Rather glad he did, myself. Golf's one of my passions." He crossed his ankles, put the head of his seven-iron at his feet and leaned on the shaft. "In addition to good books and straight gin. The latter is my one vice."

"Where the devil is that lummox of a caddy?" Thaxton griped. "Oh, to hell with it."

He stood up, trudged over to the ball and addressed it.

"It's like the bloody Sudan here," he muttered. "You have to be bloody Chinese Gordon to play this course!"

His trap shot hit the lip of the bunker and bounced back into the sand. A bout of potent cursing ensued.

"There's a lady present," Dalton told him.

"Eh?" Thaxton looked, Linda's gender hitting him.

"Oh. Frightfully sorry. Do forgive me."

"Oh, that's all right," Linda called.

"It is a difficult course," Dalton conceded. "Impossible to find a ball in the rough."

"Yeah," Gene said. "Is there anything else here besides the golf course?"

"No, except for a small clubhouse. Mostly lockers and things. It does have a bar, however."

"Hm. No civilization, then. Rats."

"Well, I wouldn't exactly say no civilization. . . ."

"There you are, you great bumbling twit!" Thaxton shouted to the strange figure coming over the rise. "I need my wedgie chop-chop!"

Linda's hand shot up to cover her mouth.

The caddy, a green, seven-foot-tall saurian beast resembling a kangaroo, broke into a loping run. Spindly forelegs struggling with two golf bags and a plastic cooler, it ambled down the grade, dropped one of the bags, backtracked and bent to pick it up, and in so doing, emptied the other bag of its clubs.

"Oh, for God's sake."

After some effort and a few more mishaps, the caddy finally arrived at the green, dumped its burdens, fetched one of the bags back up, and frantically rummaged through it.

Thaxton looked on, scowling. Losing patience, he barked, "The wedgie, the wedgie! No, no, no, not that one, for God's sake. Yes, that one. Yes! Can't you bloody hear? Right, now give it to me."

"Is that thing intelligent?" Gene asked in wonder.

"Not bloody likely," Thaxton answered, striking out into the endless wastes of the sand trap.

"I mean, is it sentient?" Gene amended.

"Oh, yes, very," Dalton said. "This one's not the best of the caddies, but he tries. They all belong to a local tribe."

"Tribe? Wow."

Dalton turned to the beast and said, "Lummox, old boy, could I trouble you for a drink?"

Lummox nodded and opened the cooler, which was

filled with bottles and other containers nesting in shaved ice. He withdrew a small plastic pitcher, opened the spout on the cover, took out a long-stemmed frosted glass and filled it. Gene and Linda were amazed at how humanlike and dexterous the hands were. Bearing the glass and moving his huge feet carefully, Lummox walked over to where Dalton stood, but stopped just short.

His face, generally saurian but capable of much expression, suddenly developed a guilty look.

"O-live!" Lummox wailed apologetically.

"Never mind, old boy," Dalton said mildly. "Give it here."

"Damn!" Thaxton's shot had wound up a goodly distance from the cup; the ball hugged the edge of the green. "It'll be a good twenty feet for a bogey! Damn!" He trudged out of the sand. "Damn, damn, damn!"

"Well," Gene said, sighing. "I guess there's not much use in us staying here. Unless you're in the mood for golf, Linda. How 'bout you, Snowclaw?"

Snowclaw snorted.

"You know, he's kind of cute," Linda said, walking up to Lummox. The caddy gave her a shy smile and scurried back to the cooler.

"Yeah, really," Gene said. He turned to Dalton. "What would you suggest we do?"

Dalton sipped at his drink. "I'll say one thing for Lummox—he makes a damn good martini. I'm sorry, what did you say? What should you do? Why, anything you want. You're young—there's a very good aspect just down from the Queen's dining hall. You might try that if you like white-water rafting. There are some good guides available."

"White-water . . . ? No, what I meant was, what's the best way to go about finding a way out of the castle?"

Dalton was appalled. "Why in the world would you want to do that? There's absolutely nothing out there."

"No, I mean a way back to our world."

"Oh, that. Well, if I were you I'd disabuse myself of that notion in short order. The gateways to the world we come from are very erratic. No telling where or when one will appear. In three years I've never caught a glimpse of a way back."

"But I don't understand," Linda said. "Why are some portals so stable, like this one, and others not? It doesn't make sense."

Dalton shrugged. "It's a random process, I suppose. It just so happens that the aspects opening onto our world are of the now-you-see-it-now-you-don't variety. No explaining it."

"But if we conducted a systematic search—"

"You might find one, for all I know. But it might open up in the middle of the Pacific, or the bottom of Death Valley in July—or fifty thousand feet in the stratosphere. There's no telling where. And it might stay open only for seconds."

Gene protested, "But surely the castle can't be so big that you'd never run across one at some point."

"As I said, for all I know, you might get lucky. But I wasn't, and believe me I tried." Dalton took another sip. "Well, maybe I didn't make an all-out effort. I like it here. If you don't, maybe it'll give you the motivation to succeed."

"Maybe," Gene said dourly. "But if no one has ever succeeded in getting back, fat chance we'll have."

"Nobody I know has, but I keep to myself, mostly. So, why don't you ask some of the other Guests? They may be able to help."

"Yeah, thanks."

"Excuse me, I have to mark my ball."

"Sure."

Gene's attention was drawn across the fairway, where thrashing noises had commenced among the trees. A deep-throated roar sounded, and ponderous footsteps shook the ground. Gene started walking toward Linda and Snowclaw, who had turned toward the noise.

Lummox was squawking nervously, fumbling with corkscrew and bottle, his attention drawn toward the disturbance.

"I want that glass of Madeira sometime this week, Lummox," Thaxton snapped. "Come on, then, it's just one of the big ones—nothing to worry about."

A towering beast, two-legged, cavern-jawed, and hungry, broke out of the trees. It took three thumping steps out into the grass of the fairway and stopped, scanning to the left, then to the right. Its eyes, a good twenty feet from the ground, found the grouping of foodstuffs on and about the green. Its maw opened and a liver-colored tongue flopped out then retracted slowly, trailing across rows of spiky teeth. It turned on its powerful hind legs and began to walk toward the green, picking up speed as it moved.

"Jesus, a Tyrannosaurus!" Gene yelped, taking Linda's arm and leading her back.

"*Harak!*" Snowclaw shouted.

Lummox threw the glass and the bottle of Madeira into the air and broke for the woods.

Dalton had calmly marked his ball and now was walking toward his bag. Thaxton was addressing his ball, chin almost to chest in a concentrated putting stance.

"I say, Dalton, old boy. Would you mind—"

"Make your putt," Dalton said, sliding a strange-looking weapon out of the bag. Basically rifle-shaped and constructed of blue-green metal, it had a curving wire stock and a bell-shaped business end. Dalton put the stock to his shoulder and aimed at the animal.

There was no sound.

The beast slowed, a vaguely puzzled expression forming on its saurian countenance. Then the tough, canvaslike skin of its head and neck changed color rapidly, from a flat gray-green to an angry red. A plume of steam issued from the top of its bony skull.

Then the head exploded in a fountain of blood, pulp, and ghastly pink mess. The eyes popped out and the sockets gushed streams of boiled brain. The dinosauroid shambled a few steps more before its massive hind legs collapsed, sending its bulk crashing to the ground. It lay unmoving, the area about its head looking and smoking like a mound of hot beef stew.

Thaxton putted. The ball described a wide curving orbit across the green, approaching the cup. It caught the rim, spiraled around like a planet spinning into its sun, and dropped for a bogey.

"By Christ, did you see that? I—" Thaxton looked around for an audience. Linda was staring past him, hands clapped over her mouth, her eyes rounded, her complexion ashen. Snowclaw and Gene were running toward the fallen creature, Dalton following at a jog.

"Bloody hell. Best shot of my life and it's an anticlimax."

Thaxton began calling for Lummox, who was nowhere in sight.

Gene stood examining the mess. "Good God," he said, waving fumes away from his nose. "Whew! What a stink."

Dalton walked up. "The big ones usually keep to the low ground, but every once in a while a rogue wanders out of the valley and gives us trouble. This one is probably old, and lost his harem to a young buck."

"Where did you get that thing?" Gene wanted to know.

"This?" Dalton displayed the weapon. "I traded it for gold I panned in a desert aspect a while back."

"I don't understand. If technology like that is available —" Gene swatted at the hilt of his antiquated weapon. "—why all the silly swordplay?"

"Good question," Dalton answered. "It so happens that devices like this don't work inside the castle. Almost nothing does, including electricity."

"What about gunpowder?"

"I'm told that gunpowder works, but a simple spell can prevent it from exploding with any force. Consequently, that particular technology has fallen into disuse."

"No kidding. Say, how does that thing work? Do you know?"

"No, I don't. And I don't know what aspect it came from."

Linda was edging up to them, seeming drawn to the carnage by a morbid fascination she couldn't quite overcome. She eyed the mess queasily.

"Oh, my," she said. "Yuck."

Deadpan, Gene asked, "Hey, Linda. Would you mind

getting a spoon from the cooler, if Lummox has one?"

Linda's jaw dropped. "A sp—"

"Yeah, or a fork or something." Gene unsheathed his sword, slid the point into the mess and ladled out a gob of gore. "Hard to eat with this thing."

"Oh . . . oh—" Gagging, Linda turned and ran.

# KEEP—WEST WING—FOREBUILDING

"HELL'S WIZARDRY," KWIP muttered as he viewed the tipping caldrons of fire. He stood at a window on the top floor of one of the many smaller structures that abutted on the keep. He could not see much over the wall of the inner ward, but the tops of the belfries were well in view, towers of flame all. He watched as soldiers, human torches, hurled themselves to the ground. The hell-sent apparitions floated above. The crucibles had turned nearly upside down and had emptied, drops of liquid fire depending from their rims. Then the disembodied hands began slowly to tilt the caldrons up again.

Awestruck, Kwip shook his head. He had seen enough; he moved away from the window.

The castle still shook and quivered, its stone blocks glowing with a faint ghost light, but things had quieted somewhat. He tried to set his mind back to business, although his hope of ever finding the treasure room had somewhat diminished over the last few hours.

Passing another window, he glanced out and came to an abrupt halt. The castle walls were out there, but no battle was in progress. The ramparts were deserted, as was the inner ward below. All was silent.

And it was raining.

Kwip scratched his black-bearded chin and shook his head. What was phantasm—the bloody conflict he had just witnessed, or this? Which window looked out on reality?

Both did, perhaps. Or perhaps neither did.

His memory was jogged just then. Windows . . . windows that looked out on sundry strange worlds. There was something familiar about that. Briefly, he searched his childhood memories. Images of his aunt's face floated from the depths—a grim face, haggard and snaggle-toothed. He saw her thin-lipped mouth curled with contempt—contempt for him, her sister's bastard son. Kwip's mother had died in childbed delivering him, and his aunt had resented the burden that he was. Kwip remembered the sting of the rod across the backs of his thighs, still heard the whistle and the crack. Unpleasant memories indeed. And the bugbears she frightened him with, the stories. She would sell him into servitude, she would, if he didn't straighten out—sell him to an evil sorcerer-king who lived in a black castle. What was the name again? It was on the tip of his tongue.

Unspeakable harridan! May she rot in Hell.

Coming to a corner, he turned and walked the length of the forebuilding, then entered a spiral stairwell and descended until he came upon a landing with an archway leading into the keep. He went through and turned left, walking along a short hallway that terminated in a rectangular stairway. This he descended, pausing at each floor to look about. Nothing brewing. About six floors down he stepped from the raised landing and strode off to the left, following a wide hallway broken by a series of pillared archways. Here and there the walls were hung with paired weapons flanking shields upon which were emblazoned a strange heraldic device. Kwip stopped to examine one. Ostensibly, the design was of a black dragon rampant on a field of red—but was that indeed a dragon? Winged it was, yes, but far more horrific. It had three sets of legs, the front pair ending in great, clawed feline paws. The head was feline in one aspect, reptilian in another. The huge wings were tipped with spines. Even in featureless outline the image set Kwip's spine to tingling. Something about it . . .

Kwip shrugged and walked on. Doubtless some mythical animal.

After wandering through a maze of corridors, he paused at a junction roofed with a groined vault. He sniffed the air. He smelled food, and realized how hungry he was. Following his nose, he soon came to a wide archway leading through to a dining hall. Inside, a few strangely dressed people were seated at a long table draped in fine white cloth and set with a wide variety of comestibles.

"Hello, there!" one of them called.

His gaze fixed on the table, Kwip approached the group.

"We're having a bit of lunch," a thin man with wire-rim eyeglasses said brightly. "Would you care to join us? My name is DuQuesne. This is Edmund Jacoby, and . . . um, is anything wrong?"

Kwip tore his eyes from the food—it was a feast fit for any manner of royal personage one could name, more food and more sorts of food than he'd ever seen in one place at one time. He suddenly felt self-conscious, despite the man's amiable greeting, and somewhat out of place.

"Did you say . . . ?" Kwip cleared his throat and ran his tongue over his dry lips. He managed a smile. "I am feeling a mite hollow."

"Do sit down and help yourself, my good man."

"You are too kind, sir." Kwip seated himself and looked around uneasily.

"Wine?" DuQuesne asked, holding up a bottle.

Kwip nodded and watched DuQuesne fill a long-stemmed glass. He reached for it, warily raised it in salute. "To your health, sir."

DuQuesne nodded, smiling.

Kwip drained the glass in three gulps, wiped his lips on the sleeve of his doublet, and belched loudly.

DuQuesne reached for a platter bearing a large cut of meat. He set it in front of Kwip. "The roast is especially good today."

Kwip took out his dagger, cut off a healthy slice, and

stuffed it in his mouth. He smiled and nodded in approval. He began to eat in earnest. He reached for a wheel of cheese, chopped out a wedge, and bit off half. He took a loaf of bread, wrenched off a piece and crammed that in too.

"You must have some more wine," DuQuesne told him, refilling the glass.

Kwip smiled through his mouthful, but didn't—and couldn't—speak. Abruptly self-conscious again, he halted a motion to tear into the roast beef. He put down the dagger, chewed, then swallowed quickly though with some difficulty. He glanced around the table with an embarrassed smile and said, "I beg your indulgence, sirs. My swinish manners . . . I crave your forgiveness—"

"Tut-tut," Jacoby said.

"Eat hearty, my friend," DuQuesne told him. "We have a relaxed attitude toward etiquette here. Enjoy yourself."

"You are most gracious, sir. I am not used to sitting at table with persons of quality such as yourself."

"Oh, please," DuQuesne protested.

"In truth, sir."

"Hardly."

Kwip took a sip of wine. A thought occurred to him. "Have I . . . ?" He looked at the four men seated about the table. "Have I the honor of dining with the master of this castle?"

They all laughed.

"We are all Guests here," Jacoby said, "as are you."

"Ah." Kwip took a bite of cheese and chewed thoughtfully. "Then may I ask to whom I am in debt for this repast?" He lifted the wineglass to his lips.

"His name is Incarnadine," DuQuesne began, "and there are at least a hundred honorifics tagging after it, but we simply call him Lord. . . . what's the matter?"

Recovered from choking on his wine, Kwip gasped, "Did you say . . . ? An eternity of pardon, did you say . . . Incarnadine?"

"Why, yes."

Kwip sat back, rubbing his throat. He glanced around

uncomfortably, then knitted his brow in troubled thought. "I see."

"I take it you've heard the name," Jacoby ventured.

"Hm?" Kwip turned to him. "Your pardon, sir. Yes. Yes, I have."

"Oh," DuQuesne said. "You're a local, then?"

"I am not sure I take your meaning, sir."

"Do you hail from this land?"

"This land? I think not. But in truth, I don't know where I am. Neither do I know how I came to be here."

"Well, that's nothing new," Jacoby said. "You're a proper Guest, I should think."

"But you've heard of this place?" DuQuesne pressed on. "Castle Perilous?"

Awed, Kwip looked about the dining hall. "Yes. Indeed, I have. Not for years have I heard its name, but I have heard it." He stared abstractedly at the far wall for a moment. Presently he resumed eating, slowly.

"Then you very well could be a native of this land—this world," DuQuesne said.

Kwip reached for more bread. "I require time to think on these things, sir. Perhaps you could tell me—how is this land called?"

"It's known as the Western Pale."

Kwip searched his memory, squinting one eye. "I have never heard of it."

"Well, neither had I," DuQuesne said, "until I blundered into this place. None of us had."

"And none of us," Jacoby put in, "had ever heard of Castle Perilous. But you, my friend . . ."

Kwip nodded. "Aye, heard of it I have, but only in story and legend."

"Indeed," Jacoby said.

"In truth. Long ago my mother's sister used to . . . spin me tales of Lord Incarnadine in his enchanted Castle Perilous."

DuQuesne put down his wineglass and leaned back. "I see. This is very interesting. I don't believe we've encountered this before."

Jacoby asked, "No one has come from a world in which

Castle Perilous was merely a legend?"

"I don't believe so. Roger, have you ever run into this?"

The thin, dark-haired man seated across from DuQuesne smiled and rubbed his aquiline nose. "Castle Perilous *is* a legend in our world."

Jacoby leaned forward, frowning. "You don't say?"

"I do. It's an Arthurian tale, a routine damsel-in-distress epic. Gareth and Linette are the protagonists. Gareth, I believe, was Sir Gawain's brother."

DuQuesne said, "Oh, of course. Yes, Gareth and Linette."

"Now, as I remember," Roger went on, "in that tale the besieger of Castle Perilous was Sir Ironside, the Red Knight."

"Doesn't *incarnadine* mean the color red?" asked the young man to Roger's left.

Roger smiled again. "You're right, Tom, it does, but I think we can attribute that to coincidence. Frankly there aren't many aspects of the tale that correspond with the situation here. But I'm no expert, and there are lots of legends about enchanted castles. There very well may be a yarn that more closely resembles this dream we're living."

"Ah, yes," DuQuesne said wistfully. "It does all seem like a dream sometimes, does it not?"

All agreed.

Jacoby looked at Kwip. "How did you happen to come here?"

Kwip swallowed. "It was . . . quite by accident."

"That's what everyone says."

Kwip halted a motion to reach for his wineglass. "You doubt me?"

"Don't be so touchy. By that I meant that almost everyone here essentially blundered into the castle, and some can't even describe how it happened. The usual story is something about a wall disappearing, or a door suddenly materializing where none was before. That sort of thing."

Kwip nodded. "I see. Yes, my story is very like that." He bowed his head. "An eternity of pardon, sir, for mistaking your meaning."

"Think nothing of it."

Kwip smiled. "To speak the truth, it happened to me in this wise: I was visiting a friend, a man of quality who owns a large and very fine house. A number of my comrades were there as well, and I am afraid we imbibed to excess. I excused myself and went to find the privy . . . or a garden wall against which to relieve myself—forgive my vulgarity, but I must confess I was somewhat overburdened with drink. I wandered a while, in and out of unfamiliar rooms, and finally found myself in what looked like the nether portions of a great castle or fortress. And in truth, I was here. I found a stairway and began to climb. That was when strange things began to happen."

DuQuesne nodded. "A familiar story."

"Well," Roger said, rising, "I'm off to the library."

Jacoby asked him, "Been making any headway on the translation problem?"

"Not much, and I haven't found a Guest who can cast an instantaneous translation spell. Something tells me that a talent like that is going to be mighty hard to come by. But I still like working on the problem the old-fashioned way. Keeps me busy."

"Do let me know if you have any success," Jacoby said. "I'd be immensely interested."

Roger chuckled. "Yes, I dare say you would be."

"Oh, the questions I'd love to have answered about this place," DuQuesne said. "Good luck, Roger."

"Thanks," Roger said as he left.

Kwip had sated his hunger and slaked his thirst. His mind now turned to other things; rather, it returned to his present task, which was to find whatever booty there was to be had in this place. The next task was finding a way back whence he had come. That one was the most problematical. He did not yet know where he was. He had barely begun to grasp the notion that he had been transported to another world. Best to keep his mind on matters he could handle, for the moment at least. He would take each task in its turn.

Others were rising to leave. He bid farewell to

DuQuesne and to the young man named Tom. He looked about and found himself alone with the one called Jacoby, who was smiling a smile not unlike a cat's, if a cat could smile. Then Jacoby spoke.

"They say that the treasure room in Castle Perilous is as big as a shire and filled to the rafters with gold, silver, and the finest jewels."

Kwip took a slow drink of wine before answering, "Indeed?"

"They say. They also say the biggest jewel is the Brain. Heard of it?"

"In truth, I have not."

"No? The Brain of Ramthonodox? But then, you've only recently arrived."

"That is true."

Jacoby swished cold coffee about in his cup. "Everyone who comes to Castle Perilous acquires certain magical powers, the nature and strength of which vary from individual to individual. Know what yours are yet?"

Kwip refilled his glass. "I am not sure I understand you, sir. You say these powers are gained by virtue of one's mere presence here?"

"That is the only explanation. You've acquired no sudden new talents, then, or any hint of such?"

"No."

Jacoby's smile broadened. "You will."

"I see."

"I hope yours are helpful."

"Sir?"

"In your further adventures."

"Thank you. Aye, it would be a boon."

"What will you do?"

"I've not given it much thought. As you said, I have only recently arrived."

"So you have. We shall talk later, perhaps. After you've become more accustomed to this place."

"It would be an honor, sir." Kwip rose with Jacoby and watched him leave. When he was alone, he pushed the wineglass away and sat back. He had not much cared for

Jacoby's tone, nor for the man himself. In this castle there was much to be wary of.

Kwip grunted. But that was true of many places. Kwip had traveled widely in his life and had seen many things. Many wondrous things. Surely this castle was the most wondrous yet, but it was still an abode of men, as well as monsters, and Kwip thought he knew men rather well.

He'd take monsters any day.

# Elsewhere

Linda was still in a snit over Gene's ribbing her.

"Oh, come on," Gene complained as they walked back to the portal, "I was only kidding."

"You'll be sorry. I'm going to conjure one of those things and have him tear you into beef jerky."

"Well, now, that would be overreacting just a tad, don't you think?"

"And then I'll make you eat its brains—oh, I'm getting sick just thinking about it. That was the grossest thing I *ever* saw."

"The most fantastic, too, I'll bet."

"You said it."

The portal was where they'd left it, unchanged. Gene stopped, tugging on a handful of Snowclaw's silky fur to get his attention. "Hold it a minute. I think we should come up with a plan of some sort before we go back in there."

Linda looked around, found a tree stump, brushed it off and sat. "Shoot."

"Huh?"

"What kind of plan? A plan for what?"

Gene scratched the stubble under his jaw. "Well, a plan

of action. Some systematic way of searching for a way out."

"Sounds great. Where do we start?"

Gene took a deep breath. "Beats the shit out of me." He sank to his haunches, picked up a twig and made vague markings in the dirt. "Damn. If only we had an inkling of where to start."

"Mr. Dalton doesn't seem to think there's a way out."

"He said he likes it here."

Linda looked around. "Yuck."

"He meant the castle."

"Double yuck."

"Yeah. Hell." Gene tossed the twig away. "We need answers. Nobody seems to have any."

"Somebody has to."

"The people who live in the castle might. Not any of the Guests, but the natives. The big cheese wheel who runs the place . . . what's his name?"

"Lord Incarnadine."

"Him. He should be able to tell us something. What we have to do is find him."

Linda sighed. "I've heard he's very hard to locate."

"It can't be impossible. He's the owner, he should be around somewhere. We'll get him and make him give us some answers."

Linda shrugged.

"Yeah, I know. Fat chance. What do you think, Snowclaw? Oh, I forgot. He can't understand—"

Snowclaw had been staring off into the brush. Suddenly he sprang forward and ran off the trail, broadax raised, disappearing behind an expansive broad-leafed shrub. There came a frightened squawk along with thrashing noises from behind the bush. Then Lummox came dashing out of cover. He scampered up the trail, saw Linda and Gene, squawked again, and ran off into the jungle.

"Snowclaw!" Linda admonished. "That poor little thing—"

"I don't think he knew it was Lummox. Snowclaw . . . ? Oh, hell, let's get back into the castle so we can understand him."

"I knew something was there, watching us," Snowclaw explained when they had crossed the boundary. "Didn't know it was that little lizard fella. Sorry I scared the compost out of him."

"We should go back and find him," Linda said with concern. "He could get lost."

"We're lost ourselves," Gene said, then shrugged at Linda's disapproving frown. "Oh, all right. Let's go back."

Linda's expression changed to regret. "I'm sorry, Gene. As if we don't have enough to worry about. It's just that he looked so frightened. Sort of reminded me of myself."

Gene gave her a little hug. "You've been great. You have a lot more courage than you give yourself credit for. Besides, you're also Superwitch."

"That's me."

"Conjure us up something to eat," Snowclaw said.

"You hungry again?" Gene said incredulously.

Snowclaw poked him lightly in the ribs with one partly retracted white claw. "Listen, skinny. You hairless types might be able to keep going on a few nibbles now and then, but you don't run a mighty engine of destruction like yours truly on birdseed."

Gene rubbed the spot where he'd been poked. "Anything you say, big guy," he said. "Anything you say."

"Just kidding," Snowclaw said. "But I do have an awful big appetite. Can't help it."

"You got it!" Linda said brightly. On the floor at her feet was a platter of *kwalkarkk* ribs.

Snowclaw sniffed. "Smell that *shrackk* sauce. Thanks, Linda."

"You did that pretty easily," Gene remarked.

"I seem to have gotten the hang of it, haven't I?" she said. "It's easy once you know you can do it. Once you *accept* the fact that you can do the impossible."

"Superwitch strikes again."

"Ta-daaa!" She scowled. "Hey, smile when you say that, buddy. How about 'Supersorceress'?"

"Sure." Gene was thinking. "The first time you did it, back at the armory—how did you manage to materialize something that you'd never seen before? Snowclaw's ribs, I mean."

"I really don't know."

"Snowy, do they taste like the real thing?"

Snowclaw grunted through a mouthful of meat and bone. "Best . . . I ever tasted," he managed to get out.

"Well, maybe I'm picking up thought waves from Snowy," Linda ventured.

"Which makes you a telepath as well."

"Wow. I really don't know."

"Do you have to visualize, picture the thing you're conjuring?"

"No. I just wish for it, and it's there."

Gene nodded. "That's really something."

Linda said, "What do we do now?"

Gene slapped the hilt of his sword. "Find a way out." He noticed that Linda was looking off abstractedly.

"What is it, Linda?"

"I wonder if anyone's discovered I'm missing." She looked at Gene. "I'm a Missing Person, you know. Officially. So are you."

"Yeah. My parents will be wondering how I could have disappeared inside the USX building."

They were silent for a moment, thinking, walking along the dim corridor. Snowy had gone up ahead. He stood at the intersection of two hallways and sniffed in one direction, then the other.

He turned and said, "Which way, guys?"

# Keep, Upper Levels

Kwip had been lost for hours; he didn't think he could find his way back to the dining hall. But that was no loss, as there was nothing back there but suspicious eyes. He had no wish to conduct his business under their gaze. His hand went to the rucksack slung across his back. He had found it in a storeroom, and had filled it with enough victuals to last three days, five if he rationed them. He'd worry about finding more food when they ran out.

He was walking down a wide hallway with rooms opening off to either side. Most of the rooms were bare, a few sparsely furnished. Some had windows, and some of these looked out on strange vistas. Kwip had stopped to look occasionally. Lately he had not. Even the exotic can, in time, become mundane.

Nothing, nothing, nothing, Kwip thought. So huge a place, so empty, so useless. Why had its builders gone to the trouble?

A furnished room! Kwip hurried inside. It was a spacious bedroom with all the appointments, a grand room fit for a woman of high station. He flung open the armoire and tore all the fine gowns from their hooks, looked them over, tossed them aside. He went to a chest of drawers and rifled through it, finding nothing but more women's things, all lace and fluff and silk. At the foot of the canopied bed he knelt to examine a leather trunk with a simple but effective lock. He stood and kicked the trunk, then grabbed one side handle and lifted. He could barely move it. He drew his sword and attempted to pry off the brass hinges at the back. He soon gave it up and tried prying the latch in front. For some reason it popped open easily.

There was nothing in the trunk but stones, and Kwip had the sudden suspicion that he had again become the butt of someone's little joke. He glanced about nervously.

Presently he sighed and surveyed the room. There were other pieces of furniture, but he had no desire to continue the search.

He sniffed, smelling the sea.

He moved to the window, and a little of his original sense of wonder came over him. This aspect was suspended only a few feet above the open ocean. Whitecaps flecked the windy surface, and the glare of sunlight danced on its waters. No land in sight. He looked out briefly, the salt spray hitting him; then he turned to go. But something made him turn back. Looking out again, he noticed it. The window was descending at a slow but steady rate. He stood and watched, estimating that window and waterline would meet within a very short time. He couldn't conceive of what would ensue when they did, nor did he want to find out. He left the room.

There were no more rooms after that. The hallway continued for what seemed like a league, with no end in sight. After walking a good quarter hour, he stopped and thought of going back. Perhaps he had been to hasty. . . .

He heard a distant rumble. More battle sounds? No. He turned and looked back down the corridor.

Apparently the unthinkable had happened. A gray, churning mass of water was rushing toward him.

He ran, knowing he couldn't outrun it, dashing on in the blind hope of finding a stairway, preferably one leading up, or a room with an aspect he could duck through and escape. Anything would do for the moment, anything but this endless corridor. The view ahead was not encouraging. The hallway continued its interminable way to an infinite vanishing point.

With the waters roaring at his heels, he saw an opening in the wall ahead and put on a burst of speed. It was a stairwell!—one that began on this level and led up. Jubilantly, Kwip dashed into it.

It went up two flights and dead-ended into a blank stone wall.

"Gods of a pig's arse! Not again!" He halted, stumbling, then turned to regard the gush of water that had followed him up the stair.

He took a deep breath and contemplated his end. "Aye, so this is it." Perhaps it was meant to be. He had escaped the hangman's noose, only to die by water in a castle of dreams.

Ah, well, he thought. As good a way to die as any.

He backed against the wall as the water foamed up to the landing. He watched it rise until it filled the truncated stairwell and began lapping at his boots. By the time the water's level had reached his knees, however, its rate of climb had slowed. Hope yet. But it was fleeting. Presently the flood tide began to rise rapidly again, reaching his groin, then his waist, his chest, his neck . . .

Soon he was floating, his boots feeling like lead weights. He kicked them off and found that he was able to tread water sufficiently well to keep breathing. But he was rapidly running out of breathing space. The chamber was small, and soon the water would fill it to the vaulted ceiling, at the apex of which, Kwip noticed, was a small round opening . . . a ventilation shaft, most likely. Kwip had a sudden idea. He had had no formal education, but as a boy he had passed endless hours playing with odds and ends around the house, experimenting and pondering the results. If he could plug that hole, the remaining air pocket might stop the water from rising, just as air trapped inside a submerged inverted cup prevents it from being filled.

His leather jerkin did the job. Stuffed into the hole, it made a dubious airtight seal, but the rising flood slowed, then stopped. Presently the waters began to recede, and in time Kwip was wading knee deep again.

It was definitely seawater. Bits of shell and other flotsam crunched underfoot, and scraps of seaweed floated about. Apparently the water had found an outlet and was draining away, flooding the floors below.

"Passing strange," he muttered. "A deluge out of a boudoir. *Damned* queer."

Shaking his head, he retrieved one boot and sloshed down the steps to find the other. Something grabbed his leg.

He struggled against it, grasping the iron rail above and pulling against it. Whatever it was tugged back. He strained and managed to raise his unshod foot out of the water.

A slimy, gray-green tentacle had coiled itself about his ankle. Kwip yelled, drew his sword and hacked at it until his foot was free. He shook the severed end of the thing off and backed to the wall of the landing as another appendage rose from the depths. It was of the same color but slightly thinner, and at its end rode a single unblinking, fishy eye. Balanced on its delicate stalk, the eyeball scanned the chamber, then swung around to gather Kwip into its view.

Not for long; a sweep of Kwip's sword sent the Argus eye plopping into the water, the cut end of the stalk spurting pink and yellow humors until it sank below the waterline. A smile grew on Kwip's face, fading as another eyestalk rose, this one forewarned enough to keep its distance.

More tentacles leaped up, these equipped with wicked, needlelike stingers at their ends. Doubtless they were poisonous. Kwip leaped to the side to avoid one while hacking at another. With some quick swordsmanship he succeeded in truncating four tentacles, but more were coming at him, many more. He backed up the stairs, swinging and slashing.

Very quickly his back was to the blank wall at the top of the stairwell. Three tentacles were drawing a bead for a simultaneous strike under the guidance of more eyestalks.

He feinted a thrust at one and cut wickedly at another, but landed only a glancing blow as the thing ducked away. The sword hit the iron rail and went flying from his wet grasp, falling with a gentle splash into the water.

He screamed, "No!" but knew it was the end. He pressed himself against the wall, straining, pushing as though the stone could yield.

Suddenly he was falling backwards. He hit with his buttocks, rolled on his back, and leaped to his feet.

Silence. He looked around. He was in another hallway, this one dry and devoid of sea monsters. There was no door in the wall in front of him, no opening of any sort. It was as blank as the one . . .

*On the other side?*

"Gods of a poxed doxy." Kwip examined the dark, smooth stone of the wall. The unmortared joints hardly showed at all. There was no way he could have—

A sudden impulse seized him, and he thrust his fist at the wall as if to strike it.

His arm passed through the stone like a ghost through a midnight fog.

## Keep—Near The Main Portcullis

The subaltern saluted and nervously began his report.

"If it please Your Royal Highness! I—" The words caught in his dry throat.

Prince Vorn laid a hand on the young soldier's mailed shoulder. "Be at ease, son. When last did you see an enemy soldier?"

The subaltern cleared his throat, then said, "Almost a day ago, sire."

Vorn nodded and turned to look at Lord Althair.

Althair shrugged. "I submit to you that we have triumphed."

Vorn scowled. "Or do we walk triumphantly into Incarnadine's trap?"

Althair looked about the high-ceiling hall in which they stood. It was being used as a staging area. Heaps of supplies lay about. Men of the quartermaster's corps were carrying more in. "I see no trap, Your Royal Highness. In fact, I see nothing but the same rancid field rations and mildewed blankets that have held this army together for more than a year." Beside him Lord Dax snickered.

Vorn grunted. He turned again to the subaltern.

"I am told you fought bravely, and well."

The subaltern's chest expanded slightly. "It was my privilege, Your Royal Highness."

"Your unit overran more than a few enemy barricades. You led the charges yourself. True?"

"Sire, I cannot gainsay it."

"Tell me this. How far into the keep has your phalanx penetrated? I realize distance here is difficult to judge."

"I truly do not know, sire. We walked for hours, then tried to find our way back. We nearly lost ourselves for good and all."

"And you were never challenged?"

"Never, sire."

"And you've seen no castle guards since yesterday?"

"None, sire." The subaltern's gaze darted around the immense chamber. "Sire, this castle is truly enchanted! We—"

"Yes, we know. You and your men are relieved until further notice. Eat, drink, and disport yourselves. Dismissed."

"Yes, sire!" The subaltern saluted and left.

Vorn's face was troubled. Arms akimbo, he began to pace. "Too easy," he murmured. "Too, too easy."

"Put your suspicions to rest, Highness," Dax said. "We have won the day. If Incarnadine's sorcery could prevail, it would have done so long before this."

Vorn stopped and nodded. "Aye, one would think so."

"He sprang his traps at every turn," Althair said. "We always managed to fight our way out."

Vorn snorted. "We? You mean my soldiers did. At the cost of rivers of their blood."

Althair looked pained. "Yes. The battle in the mines . . ." He turned up his nose. "Ghastly business." He dismissed the unpleasantness with a disdainful motion of the hand.

Vorn viewed him coldly. "I am sorry your sensibilities were offended."

Althair stiffened. "I only state facts."

"Again, you would do well not to waste time arguing a

case for the sky's being up, or for shit's being brown."

"May I remind His Royal Highness that I was against the tactic of undermining from the very first? If you had heeded my suggestions—"

"I have had my ears stuffed full of your endless carping and quibbling for nigh a year."

Althair drew his narrow shoulders up. "His Royal Highness chooses convenient time to pick a fight, when the battle's won and spoils are at hand to be divided."

Vorn whirled, eyes searching the room. "Spoils? Where? Like you, I see nothing but rat-gnawed blankets and barrels of moldy hardtack."

Lord Dax began, "The treasure room—"

"And where is it?"

"We must search for it."

"We'll be centuries finding it."

A woman's voice said, "With respect, I beg to differ with His Royal Highness."

The three men turned toward the arched doorway. Lady Melydia stood within it, flanked by two armed escorts. Carrying a satchel and a wooden case, Osmirik looked over her shoulder. Behind him other servants waited.

Vorn smiled. "My lady."

She told the guards to wait outside, then entered, her blue-dyed long gown rustling as she moved. Osmirik followed her. As she drew near, she shivered and gathered her red shawl about her shoulders. "This frightful place is always so cold."

Vorn undid his cape and draped it around her.

"You are too kind, sire," she said with a smile.

Althair looked at Dax and rolled his eyes.

Vorn returned her smile. "How do you beg to differ, my lady?"

"In this wise, Highness. Finding the treasure room will be a small matter, once the Spell Stone is located."

"This is good news. How came you by it?"

"Recently I have cast knowledge-gathering spells which have probed more deeply into the exact nature of the castle's magic. Although I have had opportunity to do this in times past, I lacked the means. Getting the means took much scholarship over the past few months, much poring over ancient books."

Osmirik cast his eyes to the ceiling and cleared his throat.

Melydia went on: "When the Spell Stone's spell is abrogated, the castle will cease to exist. That much I knew. But I was unsure about the fate of everyone and everything in the castle. Now I know much more, although my knowledge is far from complete. According to my best calculations, this is what will happen with respect to physical objects inside the castle: any and all artifacts which exist in and of themselves—that is, which are not also magical constructs—will remain. Chairs and tables and spoons and knives, all inanimate objects, perforce including what valuables as may exist. With the castle gone, their location will of course be revealed."

Vorn's grin was broad. "Excellent! And what of people?"

Melydia took a breath. "Unfortunately, I cannot be so specific with regard to the beings, human and otherwise, who reside here. I think most of the latter will be swept away, banished to those regions of Hell that spawned them. As to the humans—guards, servants, and citizenry—if any of them are still in the castle when it goes, I know not what will be their fate. Some or all of them may in truth be demons. I have always harbored suspicions concerning their origin."

"What of Incarnadine himself?"

Melydia frowned. "I do not know. He likely has already hied himself through one of the castle's many portals, thereby eluding me . . . us."

Dax asked, "What of the curious lot who parade about the place in strange garb, doing even stranger things?"

"You mean the so-called Guests?"

"Yes. Well, the ones who appear human, at least."

"I suspect they, too, will be swept away. They appear human, but they also may be of infernal origin. At any rate, I think it safe to say that anything that entered Castle

Perilous by magical means will vanish with it."

"Does this include us?" Althair asked.

Melydia answered, "Hardly. We will not vanish. However, I am not sure exactly what will happen. There could be danger."

"What do you propose we do?" Vorn asked.

"Continue mopping up—at least go through the motions, though no enemy be in sight. I will locate the Spell Stone."

"How will you do it?" Vorn asked.

"By magical means, of course. I have it all planned. When I am ready to undertake the undoing of the spell, you and your men must leave the castle—get as far away as possible."

Vorn was taken aback. "Leave?"

"You must. Yes, I know, Highness. The prospect of abandoning your conquest so quickly disturbs you. But shortly after you take leave of this place of evil, it will cease to exist forevermore. You will have wiped it from the face of the earth. Expunged it. And on the clean spot where it once stood, its fabulous treasures will lie waiting for you. You need only stoop to pick them up."

"But if we leave, the castle guards . . ."

"They have gone, vanished through a thousand different portals. They will not return. And even if some do, they will be hard pressed to defend a castle that does not exist."

Vorn nodded. "Aye, true enough." A smile spread slowly across his face. "Can it be true, then? Have we triumphed?"

"Yes, Highness. *You* have triumphed."

Althair said, "Would it not be better to say that we have all triumphed?"

"Of course," Melydia said brusquely.

"It is to you whom we owe this conquest," Vorn said. "Were it not for your expertise—"

"My sorcery," she corrected. "I do not balk at the word."

"Truly, sorcery such as the world has never seen."

"In the service of the world's greatest conqueror."

Vorn took her hand. "My lady."

Dax and Althair exchanged glances. Dax said, "Your pardon. I have many pressing duties. My men—"

"Yes," Althair said. "If we may have your leave . . . ?"

"Go," Vorn said.

They left. At that point Vorn noticed Osmirik's presence. "Scribe, do you agree with your mistress's predictions?"

Osmirik took a moment to compose his answer. "Her Ladyship is wise beyond measure, Your Royal Highness. Everything that she says will happen, will likely happen. Even more than she says may happen."

Vorn cocked an eyebrow. "What more?"

Osmirik glanced at Melydia, conscious of her glare. "Alas, I cannot say, Highness."

"Can not, or will not?"

"He is free to speak his mind," Melydia said.

Osmirik's dark eyebrows went up slightly.

"Then speak," Vorn commanded.

"There is much danger," Osmirik stated.

"I said as much," Melydia said sharply.

"True, my lady," Osmirik said. "You well know that this castle's existence is maintained by great forces, forces that, once unleashed, may prove devastating."

Melydia addressed Vorn. "That is why, Highness, you and your men must be well away."

Vorn asked, "But what of you, my lady?"

"Do not fear for me. My sorcery will provide ample protection."

"Scribe? Is she right?"

"Sire, I, too, will be in the castle when the Spell Stone's enchantment is nullified. I am reasonably certain of my continued existence after that event."

Vorn nodded, looking at Melydia. "So be it, then. I will do as you have asked. I am yours to command, my lady."

"It is you who command me, sire," she said.

Vorn offered his arm. "Come, we will dine. We have much to celebrate."

"I would be honored."

They left the chamber. Osmirik laid down his burdens, sat on a crate and let fall the hood of his cloak. He sighed, rubbing his eyes.

"However," he said to no one in particular, "there is some question as to the continued existence of the world."

# Elsewhere

The bazaar was near deserted that day. A few street urchins chased each other up and down the aisles between the stalls. Here and there a prospective buyer haggled with a vendor. In a nearby stockade shaggy, thick-legged pack animals brayed complainingly, tails swishing at biting insects. The sun was high and the day was hot.

The book vendor awoke from his nap and cast a mercenary eye on the tall, well-dressed man who approached his stall. He liked what he saw. "Books, honored sir?"

The man nodded and picked up a parchment scroll. He read the title and put the scroll aside.

The book vendor smiled. "I took the honored sir for a man of culture and learning the moment I saw him."

"Indeed? I thank you."

The book vendor moved closer, eyeing the man's choices.

"That's an especially interesting volume. Rare."

The stranger laid it aside and examined another, then another.

Presently the book vendor said, "Is there anything in particular . . . ?"

"Yes. I am in search of a book of some repute, a work dealing with a certain aspect of the Recondite Arts."

"Magic, is it?"

"More or less. Demonology."

The book vendor looked thoughtful. "Ah."

"Be you Durstin, the book vendor?"

"His honor knows of me? I am he."

"I was told you possessed a copy of this particular work."

"Does the honored sir know its title?"

"It is simply called *The Book of Demons*."

The book vendor's eyes did not betray his surprise. "I have . . . heard of it. It is a rare item indeed. Very old."

"Then you have a copy?"

"Regrettably, no. A thousand pardons."

"A pity." The man turned to go.

"I . . ."

"Yes?"

Durstin looked away. "I am curious as to who told the honored sir that I possess a copy of a banned work . . . an allegation which I most emphatically deny."

"I was unaware that the book was proscribed."

"It is indeed, and has been for centuries on the List of Forbidden Works. As I said, I am curious—"

"Khaalim sent me."

The book vendor nodded. "There is an inn near the stockyards called the Pale Eye. Be there at sunset."

"I have little time."

"We can't do business in broad daylight. Not this sort of business."

"I will pay you double what the book would ordinarily fetch. Do you have it here in your stall?"

Durstin cast his eyes from one end of the bazaar to the other. "I have been hauled before the Suzerain's magistrate on one previous occasion. The charge was selling vulgar and immoral literature. The scars still twinge when the weather turns. For a work on the List—"

"I will pay you handsomely. I need it now."

The book vendor was silent, still nervously looking about.

"Name your price."

Durstin's gaze swung round. He shrugged. "Say, fifty gold pieces?"

"I said I would pay you handsomely. I did not say I would deliver over the fortune of a king."

"Forty, then."

"I will pay thirty. Copies of this book are rare, but they do exist, and can be had elsewhere."

Durstin smiled crookedly. "His honor said something about having little time."

The stranger's lips curled slightly. Then he said, "I will pay thirty-five, or I will make time."

"Done. Pick up a book, any book, and ask the price."

"Hm? Very well. How much for this?"

Raising his voice the book vendor answered, "Two silver, three brass, good sir."

"That is all I have in my purse. Take it."

Durstin caught the leather purse, hefted it, opened it and looked inside. Fingering the contents, he smiled and nodded. "And so you have. A protective sheath for the book, good sir? No charge."

"Please."

The book vendor retreated into the stall and slipped behind a flap of brightly colored cloth. Shortly he returned bearing a cheap cloth scroll sheath.

"Here you are, good sir. Blessings of the gods be with you."

The stranger took the bundle and opened it, looked inside. He nodded and slipped it inside his tunic. "Good day."

The book vendor watched him go. The stranger left the bazaar area directly, not stopping at any other stalls. Durstin sighed. He then reseated himself, leaned his head against the post and went back to sleep.

Eating a hurried lunch in an outdoor cafe, he felt the pressure of observing eyes. He made no effort to look about and find who was watching him. He paid the bill and left, returning to the stable where he had left his mount. He knew he was being followed.

He passed through the city gate in the middle of the afternoon and headed out into the desert, making straight for the mountains to the north. The sun was fierce but bearable this time of year, dun-colored rocks baking in its glare.

He reached the foothills by mealtime but did not stop, heading upward, his animal's sure-footed gait slackening only a little on the steadily inclining terrain. He surveyed the parched land around him as it gave way to grassland, then stunted evergreen, then alpine meadow. He was aware that two riders had followed him and were now closing the gap.

They passed him an hour later, smiling and waving as they urged their mounts up the twisting trail.

When they disappeared into the pass, he stopped. He traced patterns in the air with his fingers and looked thoughtful, as if testing the wind. Presently he gently kneed his mount in the ribs. The animal brayed, broke wind, and continued up the trail.

In the narrow pass two riders blocked his way, while the two who had followed him came out of a side canyon to close off his only avenue of retreat.

The leader was young and had a pointy, rodentlike face and a sneering smile.

"Greetings, honored sir!" he called. "And what is a finely dressed man of distinction such as yourself doing on this lonely trail?"

"Be you Vorn's men?" the stranger asked.

"Eh?"

He looked at each man in turn. "No, I think not. Common highwaymen."

"A pox on you," the leader sneered. "We're not common. You'll not find our like in a thousand leagues of road. But enough of that—deliver your purse, or it will go badly for you."

"I left it in the city, along with its contents."

"Then give us what you bought."

"It is a mere book, of no use to you."

"You insult me!"

"How so?"

"You imply I'm unlettered!" The others laughed.

"You are," the stranger answered, "and a scoundrel to boot." He traced a quick pattern in the air.

Shrugging, the leader drew his shortsword. "Enough of this pleasant banter. Throw all your valuables over here now, or—" He suddenly developed a pained expression, dropping his sword and clutching at his chest. Alarmed, his companion reached out and grasped his arm to steady him. The leader's eyes bulged; then blood exploded from his mouth. His mount reared, throwing him off.

The other three regarded the still form of their leader, then looked fearfully at the stranger, who had ceased his hand passes and finger waving.

"A sorcerer!" one of them gasped.

The stranger raised a hand, one finger pointing. "Begone," he said. "That way. Or your heart, too, shall burst like an overripe melon." He pointed in the direction from which he had come.

They left very quickly, not bothering to take their leader's body or his mount.

He breathed deeply, tasting the mountain air. Then he resumed his journey.

The cave was high on the descending slope, its entrance hidden by gnarled brush. He unsaddled his mount, set the beast free, and entered the cave mouth. The way was narrow at first and he had to stoop, but soon there was ample head room, though not much light. He walked in darkness awhile, finding his way from memory, his fingers lightly brushing the smooth rock walls. At length he saw light ahead, coming from a side passage. He turned the corner and beheld cut-stone walls, jewel-torches lighting a way into the castle.

After taking shortcuts which only he knew, he arrived at his chambers. He went inside, locked the door, shed his costume and donned another, that of a castle functionary.

The voice spoke to him again.

*You have returned.*

"Yes. Are there any further developments?"

*I feel there must be. I sense an impending end to my bondage. Someone calls to me, I know not who.*

"Have more memories returned to you?"

*Not many. I feel, though, that it is only a matter of time.*

"Do you know your name?"

There was silence, then: *No. Will you tell me?*

"No, but there are those who will."

He left by a secret panel, threading his way through narrow passages until he came to a dead end. He shoved against a large stone block and it moved, swiveling on a central fulcrum. He pushed it open a crack and paused, looking out, then stepped into the hallway. The stone swung back and became a blank wall again.

A door lay to the left. He opened it and went inside.

The library was vast and many-volumned, shelves rising several stories to the corbeled ceiling. He strode across the main floor and entered an area where free-standing stacks stood in rows. He walked down the central aisle, turned left at the thirty-fourth row, and followed the shelf to its end, coming out into an aisle running along the wall, against which was set a row of carrels. He chose one and seated himself. He withdrew the scroll from his tunic, took it out of its sheath, undid the ties and opened it.

He took a deep breath, scanning the first few lines. It was written in a script he couldn't immediately decipher, but a translation spell would take care of that.

Wearily, he rubbed his eyes. He had only an inkling of what he was after. A key; he needed a key to unlock a mystery—then to close it up again, once and for all.

Perhaps the answer lay in this ancient book. Perhaps not. Time would tell, and he had so very, very little of it.

# KEEP—SOMEWHERE

THEY'D BEEN WANDERING now for at least a day. Last "night" they'd bedded down in a storage room full of odds and ends. "Today" they'd encountered evidence of recent flooding.

Gene waded through the puddle of brackish water. The carcass of another large sea animal lay beached nearby, an oily gray mass in the shadows. It stank.

"I wonder if it was a tidal wave that slopped through one of the portals, or something else," he said.

Linda and Snowclaw avoided the puddle. Linda's nose wrinkled at the smell. "What else?"

"An incredibly huge aquarium that sprang a leak, here in the castle somewhere?"

"That's silly."

"In this place? Nothing is."

Snowclaw said, "It's probably what you said, Gene. A leak through a portal."

Gene whistled and said, "What an incredible place to live. Imagine! You could be sitting around, darning socks or something, and all of a sudden—"

The far wall of the chamber disappeared, revealing a blasted alien landscape. A violent air current nearly swept them into the portal as pressure differences adjusted. Soon the air flowed the other way and waves of heat assailed them.

"Oh, hell," Gene complained. "The way out was through that wall. Now we'll have to double back. And there ain't nothing back there."

Linda looked nervously out at the dark rocks and bleached sand. "That doesn't look like a very nice place. I'm for going back."

Gene sniffed. "Air's breathable, but it looks hotter than hell out there. I guess we can't explore it. Unless . . ." He began walking toward the portal.

"Gene! Where are you going?"

"I'm going to take a quick look. It sort of reminds me of parts of Utah. Maybe—"

Something large bounded through the opening and entered the chamber. It was twice as tall as Gene and ran on two powerful hind legs. Its head was somewhat reptilian, though the eyes, unnervingly intelligent, were set close enough together to afford accurate depth perception. Its skin was beet red and looked rough and dry. It had a long, supple tail, and the claws on its short but sinewy fore limbs curved wickedly. It saw Gene and stopped in its tracks.

So did Gene, but he hit a wet spot and slipped, falling on his buttocks.

The beast eyed him, its blunted snout parting to reveal a gleaming set of caninelike teeth. Then a voice emanated from the cavity: "Look like food, but it speak." Its voice was several registers lower than human, but intelligible. Taking two steps closer, it said, "You food?"

The beast towered over Gene, who struggled to his feet. "Hi, there!" he squeaked in an almost hysterical giggle.

"Smell like food," the beast observed.

"Uh . . . uh . . . uh . . ." Gene backed stiffly away.

The beast's yellow eyes moved from side to side, taking in the chamber, Linda, and Snowclaw. The latter had begun slowly moving toward the thing, broadax raised.

"I not see this cave before. I smell much food."

Still backing off, Gene drew his sword and pointed it lamely at the beast.

The animal said, "I think you food. I eat." It sprang forward.

Snowclaw was a blur and a howl. The beast broke off his charge at Gene and turned to meet him, raking forward with its great claws. But in an instant Snowclaw had run by, and the beast's talons clawed nothing but air. It halted, looking puzzled. A great, raw gash had opened up across its chest, oozing grayish-purple ichor. The beast searched from side to side, then whirled.

Gene saw the great tail sweeping around at him and threw himself flat on the floor. The thin whiplike tip whistled inches over his head. He got up and ran.

The thing charged at Snowclaw, who had begun running in a wide arc back toward it. The beast ran a curving course to intercept, but at the last possible second Snowclaw executed an impossible pivot and leaped in the other direction, making a lightning-quick swipe with the ax. He raced back to the other end of the chamber. The beast did not follow. It turned slowly. Another incision gaped wide, this one running straight across its throat.

"No food?" it gurgled, its visage registering a faintly perplexed expression. It took three unsteady steps forward, then collapsed with a floor-shaking thud and lay unmoving.

Gene and Linda were peeping out from behind the stanchion of the arched doorway.

"You okay, Gene?" Snowclaw asked.

Gene stepped out. "Yeah. Thanks."

"You were lucky. You wouldn't've had a chance against that thing."

"I know. You were . . ." Gene shook his head in wonder. "Incredible."

"Aw, it was nothing. I've tackled worse than him."

"Fantastic."

"I'm a hunter, you know."

Gene looked at Linda, then hugged her, burying his face in her blond hair. Linda hugged him back.

They parted, and Gene said, "I almost couldn't move. I was totally petrified."

"Who wouldn't have been?"

Gene scowled. "I'm going to have to be quicker if I want to stay alive."

"Don't worry about it, buddy," Snowclaw said.

"I should have done something, thrown my sword at its face and run . . . something. But I just stood there like a wimp."

"It happened so fast," Linda said.

Gene grunted and looked immensely displeased.

"Talk about fast," Snowclaw said, staring at the far end of the chamber.

The portal was gone. The wall had reappeared, and with it the doorway leading out of the chamber.

An hour later it was "lunch time," and Linda whipped up another spread. She was getting very good at it. She not only conjured an assortment of coldcuts and salads, but materialized a buffet table to serve it on.

"Hey, this is nice, Linda," Gene said as he scooped linguine salad onto his white china plate. "Ice sculpture's real nice." He cocked his head toward the carved swan with swanlings in tow.

Linda looked thoughtful, then said, "You know, I think I've *seen* this layout somewhere." She snapped her fingers. "My cousin Terri's wedding reception!"

"Congratulations. Snowclaw, don't eat with your hands."

"Who's going to care?"

"The bride's family will get the wrong idea."

Linda frowned. "No, if it were Terri's wedding, then there'd be a champagne fountain. Maybe it was the rehearsal dinner." She chewed her lip.

"Linda," Gene said, "it hardly matters. Eat something."

She sighed. "I guess you're right."

"What's this pink Jell-O-looking stuff here?"

"Pink Jell-O stuff."

"I mean, is it—"

A shout echoed down the corridor. They froze and listened. It came again.

"Sounds like somebody yelling for help," Snowclaw

said, his furry white ears cocked.

They raced toward the sound. After making a few false turns, they came to what would have been an ordinary furnished room were it not for the wedge of botanical garden that someone had plopped in the middle of it. And in the middle of the riot of vegetation lay Jacoby.

"Quick!" he yelled at them. "It's got me! I can't control it!"

Gene alone made it to him after cutting a path through the dense undergrowth. Linda and Snowclaw had gotten tangled.

Jacoby was lying on his side. "My feet," he said hoarsely.

Gene looked. Shiny green vines were wrapped about the man's ankles. He drew his sword, followed the vines away from Jacoby's legs, and began hacking. He heard a high-pitched scream of pain.

Gene was horrified, thinking he'd cut Jacoby. But the scream hadn't come from Jacoby.

*"You bitch! How dare you cut me!"*

"Huh?" Gene froze, sword in the air. The voice seemed to come from a thick, rough-barked tree stump that sat amid a nosegay of attractive flowers nearby.

*"How would you like someone cutting and sawing at you?"*

"What? Well, I'm sorry . . . hey, wait a minute."

*"Just don't think you can come waltzing into my territory and pull any of your two-legged tricks! Mobile lump of meat! Your shit smells!"*

"No need to get abusive. Let go of this man here, and I'll stop chopping."

"Cut them!" Jacoby screamed. "The portal may close!"

"Come on, now, let him go."

*"I'm hungry!"*

"Jesus Christ. Shades of *Little Shop of Horrors.*"

For God's sake," Jacoby shrieked. "Hurry!"

Hideous screams issued from the tree as Gene brought his sword down in a series of quick chops that left one thick tentacle-vine intact. He took a measuring swing, then brought the sword down mightily. The end of the blade hit something hard and the sword dropped from his hand, but the vine had been severed.

"Okay—*whoops!*" Something pulled Gene's feet out from under him and began dragging him away. Jacoby struggled to his feet.

"Gimmie the sword!" Gene yelled, but Jacoby turned and ran.

Gene grabbed the ropy tentacles that had entwined themselves about his ankles. He tugged, and they tugged back.

*"You'll do, two-legged cutie! Thought you were smart!"*

"All I need in my life is a gay bougainvillaea, or whatever you are."

*"I'll eat you slowly, feet first, and no anesthetic! I can be cruel!"*

"I'm not into . . . domination," Gene grunted, straining against the plant's incredibly strong pull. The tree stump was very near. Gene watched in fascination as the bark split down the middle and became rubbery, expanding to form a huge pulsating cavity lined with rows of wicked spikes. If the situation hadn't been so absurd, he would have been afraid.

Suddenly Snowclaw was above him, savagely chopping at the stump. The horrid mouth closed up. After an agonized scream the voice wailed, *"All right, all right! I'll let you go! Please don't hurt me!"*

The vines retracted and Gene got to his feet. Snowclaw gave the thing one more hack, opening up a diagonal gash that immediately began to bleed bright pink sap.

*"Owwwwww! I didn't mean it, I didn't mean it!"*

Gene retrieved his sword, and he and Snowclaw struggled back to Linda, who was having her own problems. Vines had also snared her; however, these were thin stringy ones covered with tiny thorns that had gotten hopelessly snagged in the material of her outfit.

It took some time to chop her out. Finally they did. Holding Linda between them, they bulled their way back through the pie-shaped slice of jungle.

Jacoby had collapsed in one of two stuffed chairs beside the fireplace, fanning himself with a hand. He was breathing hard and wheezing.

"Asthma, you know," he said. "I nearly passed out. I . . ." He straightened up. "Frightfully sorry I couldn't help."

"Yeah," Gene said ironically, sucking on a bleeding finger.

"Oh, my God, this place is going to drive me crazy," Linda said, collapsing into the other chair. She looked herself over. "Look at these scratches all over my arms!"

Jacoby said, "I think it was Nietzsche who said something to the effect that the person who grows bored with his life should risk it. He must have had this place in mind."

"It's certainly not boring!" Linda laughed. "How I wish it were."

"Come now, it's not all that bad."

"You *like* it here?"

"Oh, immensely! I wouldn't live anywhere else—though I must admit that recently things have been getting a bit more dicey. Has something to do with the siege, I should think."

"Any late word on what the situation is?" Gene asked.

"There are reports that the invaders have entered the keep. I haven't heard anything beyond that. It's sometimes difficult to get reliable information. We've not seen any of them in the Guest area, but it's only a matter of time, I suppose." Jacoby seemed suddenly to have recovered. He got up and went to Linda, took her hand. "Are you sure you're quite all right, my dear?"

"Sure, they're just scratches. How about you?"

"Capital."

"What happened, by the way?"

"Oh, it was nothing, just my own pigheadedness, I'm afraid. I was sitting here dozing when that business materialized. I ignored it, but then I wanted to get to the loo, and the damn thing just wouldn't go away, so I thought I'd risk crossing to the other side. Damned if it didn't trap me."

"It's a funny portal, two-sided like that," Linda said.

"I've seen its like before," Jacoby said. "Sort of like a wedge of space instead of a flat plane. Comes in crosswise, I suspect. Of course, I don't actually know—"

With a quiet pop, the jungle disappeared. Nothing remained on the bare stone floor but scattered dirt and a few odd leaves.

"So much for that," Jacoby said. "Linda, my dear, I shall be forever in your debt."

"Me? Those guys got you out."

"Yes, of course." Jacoby glanced at Gene. "Thank you."

"Don't mench."

"You're a woman of great courage, my dear."

"Oh, right."

"You give yourself so little credit. Have you had lunch?"

"Well, it was sort of interrupted."

"The dining room's just down the hall."

Gene stamped his foot. "All we did was wander in a big circle. Damn!"

"I'd be delighted if you'd join me," Jacoby said.

"Well, sure," Linda said. "What do you say, guys?"

Gene shrugged.

"C'mon, Snowclaw," Linda said, hooking her arm in his. "I'll rustle up some ribs for you."

"Y'know, there's this other dish I like," Snowclaw told her. "It's made out of rendered blubber flavored with a little fish oil, and then you take some fish meal, see, and you mush it all up . . ."

Gene watched the three of them cross the room. He sighed, slid his sword into its scabbard. "Yeah," he said sardonically. He moped after them.

With some puzzlement he suddenly remembered what Jacoby had screamed.

*I can't control it. . . .*

# Keep—Lower Levels

Osmirik squinted, peering through the darkness ahead. "Another blind passage, my lady. I think."

A soldier held a lantern high, and light fell on the stone wall that formed the corridor's dead end. He approached it and ran his hands along the dark stone, searching for any hidden seams or openings. He looked back at Osmirik and shook his head.

Osmirik nodded gravely. He turned and said, "Yes, another one."

Melydia emerged slowly from the shadows behind him. "No matter. We draw ever closer." She halted.

She stood holding the L-shaped ends of two long metal rods. The rods were parallel, pointing straight ahead. She turned her body to the left. The rods moved with her at first, then resisted, rotating in her loose grip back to their former positions. She turned the other way, and again the rods swung to the front.

"The force that attracts them grows stronger," she said.

"Aye, but is the source accessible? Mayn't it be underground?"

"I doubt it. The Spell Stone is part of the castle."

"A foundation block, perhaps?"

"Perhaps. But we will be able to see it."

"Her ladyship is so sure."

"Yes. I have labored years, and have rung the changes on every conceivable variation. I am sure." She lowered the rods. "Let us go back to the last turning and start again. I felt the proper direction was to the left, but overrode my better judgment."

"As Her Ladyship pleases."

The military escort led them back. There were nine left out of the original eleven. One man had wandered blithely into an attractive aspect and had fallen into a hidden pitfall. The portal had closed before anyone could get to him. Another had died fighting a venomous python that had dropped from a chandelier in a dining hall.

Back at the branching of the corridors, they trooped down the left leg of the Y, Vorn's soldiers leading, Osmirik and a servant with another lantern behind them. Melydia, flanked by two armed guards, followed with arms outstretched, the instruments in her hands attuned to mysterious, unseen forces. Bringing up the rear were three more servants bearing parcels.

But that passage, too, led to a dead end.

Osmirik sighed. "Ever closer, yet never there."

By lantern light Melydia's face was limned in shades and shadows. "We shall not fail." She handed the rods to a young servant, then looked around. "No torches in this passage, nor in the other one. I did not notice it till now—why, I knoweth not. In truth, we've not seen one since we left the dining hall."

"Absolutely correct, my lady," Osmirik said. "I did remark on it, but did not think the fact significant."

"The last dead end we encountered—was it also unlighted?"

Osmirik reflected, then said, "No, my lady."

Melydia frowned. "Hellish place. Neither rhyme nor reason to it."

"Aye."

"But it will not stand beyond tomorrow."

"Will things go that quickly, my lady?"

"Yes, if we find the Stone soon."

Osmirik was silent.

"And we will," she added.

They walked back along the passageway.

"I must charge the rods again," she said.

"They grow weak?"

"Not yet so weak as to be useless, but soon."

"The recharging spell will take time."

"You needn't remind me," she snapped.

"I merely wish to—"

"I know what is your wish, and I know what you are about. You have had ample warning, Osmirik."

"I have. I grow weary of it."

"You are impertinent?"

"Your pardon, my lady."

Osmirik thought, Could she know?

He said, "Her Ladyship must know that I seek only knowledge, and that my scholarly interest in these proceedings is keen enough."

"You show great interest in scholarly minutiae, yet ultimate knowledge seems to hold no attraction for you."

"I beg your leave to differ, my lady. It does."

"So? Do you realize the magnitude of the advance represented solely in the spell that charges the rods?"

"I do, my lady. If you recall, I rendered some preliminary incantations from the ancient Tryphosite."

"So you did, and so acrawl with scholar's glosses were they that I could barely read them."

"Merely a desire to be thorough, my lady. There were many questionable passages."

"No doubt."

"I do understand that the spell taps some fundamental force."

"Aye," Melydia said. "Likely the fundamental force of the universe itself."

"Natural philosophers have long speculated that the universe is reducible to only a very few forces. Do you think there is but one?"

"I am not a natural philosopher, scribe. I seek only practical knowledge. But, yes, I think there is but one, and the Spell Stone is its focal point. He who controls the Stone controls all."

But you do not seek to control the Stone, Osmirik thought. You seek only to undo the control of another. That way lies madness, and perhaps death for us all.

His thoughts were interrupted by exclamations among the guards ahead.

"What is it?" Osmirik called, but then he saw. They had not yet arrived at the branching, but here was another corridor leading off to the right, this one lined with jewel-torches. It had not been there before.

"We're in luck, my lady," he said.

"Send two soldiers down there and see if it leads anywhere." She turned to the young servant, a boy of about fourteen. "Give me the rods."

The lad fumbled in a leather pouch, handed one rod over, then searched the pouch again. "Your Ladyship, they were both in here. . . ." He rummaged frantically.

"How is it possible? I just now gave them to you."

"Your Ladyship, I—"

She struck him across the face. "Little fool!"

"I did not hear it drop, my lady," Osmirik said. "I fancy we all would have heard it on this hard stone."

She shook the boy. "Then where is it?"

"Your ladyship, I don't know!"

"I will go back and look, my lady," Osmirik said, taking a lantern from another servant.

Osmirik had searched back almost to the dead end when Melydia called him. Echoing down the corridor, her voice was indistinct, and he stopped to listen.

"Osmirik! Come! The little fool had it dangling from the strap on the pouch, Goddess knoweth how."

Osmirik walked back. By the time he got there, Melydia and the rest were already a good way down the newfound corridor. He took one step to follow and almost broke his nose.

The opening had closed in an instant. Aghast, he stood within kissing distance of a featureless stone wall.

# Keep—Middle Levels

"I thought you were an old hand around here," Gene complained. They hadn't been able to find the dining room, or anything else.

Jacoby was either nonchalant or was putting up a good front. "I'm experienced enough not to be concerned when this happens now and again. Don't worry, my dear boy. They say if you just keep walking, eventually you'll find the Guest's living area. It occupies a central position in the keep, and all paths somehow lead to it."

"Yeah, but we wandered for days before we gravitated back there," Gene said.

Abruptly annoyed, Jacoby stopped and looked around. "I could swear I walked just a short way down the corridor from the dining hall. We must have made our mistake coming out of that sitting room. It must have been left instead of right."

"Our mistake?"

"Sorry, mine."

Linda said, "Gene, I don't see how you can blame Mr. Jacoby for getting lost when we've—"

"Okay, okay," Gene said curtly. "But we're still in dangerous country—and he doesn't have a weapon."

"Don't worry about me, young man. I can take care of myself." Jacoby sniffed the air. "You can usually smell the dining room. I don't. My only regret is that I'm getting hungrier by the minute."

"That's no problem," Linda said. "Want me to conjure up something?"

"Conjure . . .?" He smiled. "Of course. Your materialization talents. Coming along nicely, are they?"

"Take a look." Linda folded her arms and twitched her nose.

It was the buffet table again, this time complete with champagne fountain. "I *thought* it was Terri's wedding reception," she said.

Jacoby was impressed. "Remarkable. Large-scale materialization." He moved to the table and spooned goose-liver paté onto a club cracker. He took a bite. "Splendid."

Gene sat down on a carved stone bench and looked disgusted.

"Aren't you eating?" Linda asked him.

"Lost my appetite."

Jacoby helped himself to everything in sight and sat down heavily next to Gene. He held the overburdened paper plate in a way that made it appear to be resting flat atop his immense potbelly. Gene snorted and got up. Jacoby eyed him, toadlike, munching a leg of fried chicken.

Gene walked over to Snowclaw, who was scooping gobs of sticky green porridge from a cast-iron pot and shoveling the stuff into his mouth.

"Want a taste?" he asked Gene, offering a handful.

"Uh, no thanks. Looks good, though."

"Come on, you wouldn't touch this stuff with a harpoon. I was just kidding."

"Yeah."

"What's the matter, chum? You look a little depressed."

"I guess I am. Looks like we'll never make it out of here."

Snowclaw shrugged. "Those're the breaks. Can't say it isn't interesting here, though. Lots of adventure."

"No complaint on that score."

"Too damn warm, though. Look at me. I'm shedding already." He ran his clean hand up and down his arm and came away with loose fur. "See?"

"You got humans where you come from?"

Snowclaw reflected. "Now, I've heard stories of creatures more or less like you. But the way I hear it, they're hairy and they live in trees. Kinda nasty too. Why?"

"Well, if you were unfortunate enough to share your world with the hairless variety, they'd probably hunt you for your fur. That's high-price material you got there. Finer than sable."

"Huh," Snowclaw said. "You don't say."

Gene scowled. "Boy, I'm in a lousy mood."

"Cheer up," Linda told him through a mouthful of tuna salad.

"Yeah, Gene," Snowclaw said. "We'll get out of here somehow. You shouldn't give up."

"You're right. I'm letting things get to me." He turned and cocked an eye at Jacoby. "And people," he added.

Happily stuffing himself with fettuccini Alfredo, Jacoby appeared not to have heard.

"Now, Gene, don't be unkind. Mr. Jacoby—"

"Jesus," Gene said.

Linda did a take. "Huh?" Then she turned to see what Gene and Snowclaw were staring at. When she found it, she dropped her paper plate.

They were all gawking in Jacoby's direction. He stared back quizzically. "I say, is there something—"

He turned his head and saw the human hand growing out of the wall beside him. He lurched to his feet, the contents of the plate splatting on the hard stone floor. "What the devil?"

The hand grew an arm, then a shoulder. Then a head came popping through the wall. It was a dark-bearded man with dark eyes and a wary expression. He looked, edged back when he saw Snowclaw, then recognized Jacoby.

"Your pardon, sir. I did not mean to intrude."

Jacoby exhaled windily. "You gave us a devil of a fright, but no matter."

Kwip stepped out from the wall. "An eternity of pardon."

"It's nothing. I see you've found your talent."

"Aye, I'm damned to ghost through walls like the dead. But damn me twice if spirits can get hungry. . . ." His gaze locked on the buffet table.

"Some angel food cake?" Gene offered.

# Keep—Deep Levels

THE SOLDIERS WERE tired, the servants exhausted. Melydia had called for a rest here in the dank lower regions of the castle. She was far from hungry, but knew she needed sustenance, so she took two biscuits and a flagon of water, found a niche with a seat-high ledge, sat down and ate. As she did, her eyes searched the shadows around her. Shapes swam within them, shapes she knew were side-effects of her spell-enhanced strength and endurance. But they were emblematic of the many minds and spirits whose presence she sensed. The castle swarmed with them, their many emanations echoing within her head. She could make little sense of it all—occasionally a voice or a thought would enter her mind unbidden, then just as quickly leave. Most of the time what she heard was nothing but faint background noise, which she could ignore. But as she neared the Spell Stone, the din grew increasingly loud.

But there was something else. Something unusual was happening. She thought she heard a voice, a single voice calling out above the noise. Calling . . . perhaps to her. She could not quite make it out, but the voice had been growing more and more distinct.

She put down her half-eaten biscuit and closed her eyes, threw her mind open to the tumult.

*. . . a faint buzzing . . . a sense of loss, of dread . . . boredom . . . hunger. Fear, stark fear. Merriment. Music . . . somewhere . . . she told me that just to get my goat, but by God she'll . . . dreaming, falling, sleep and death —hide, hide, hide . . . a great bell tolling somewhere, far off—a sense of times past—the smell of mint and angel spice . . . WHO SEEKS ME?—the roar of the sea—near? where? . . . get away quickly! . . . voices, echoes, the sound of water dripping . . . WHO SEEKS ME? WHO SEEKS TO BREAK MY CHAINS? . . . a shadow falls with the sound of velvet against desire . . . footsteps in the darkness—the yowling of some fearsome beast . . . WHO ARE YOU, YOU WHO FOLLOW A PATH THAT TENDS TOWARD THAT WHICH HOLDS ME? . . . WHERE ARE YOU? SPEAK TO ME. SPEAK—*

"Who calls?" Melydia shouted.

*I hear you. Is it you?*

"Who calls me?" Her whisper held an edge of fear.

*I know not who I am. I thought you would tell me.*

"How can I tell you if I do not even see you?"

*I suppose you are right. Alas.*

"Where are you?"

*Where? The word has little meaning.*

"How can that be?"

*I know not. I know so little. I sense that I exist, yet I contain so many existences within me. They are not part of me, however.*

Melydia stood, sudden understanding flashing in her eyes. She knew. She had not thought it possible.

"It is I who seek you," she said. "It is I who want to set you free!"

*I have found you. Please tell me—what are you about?*

"I endeavor to find the Spell Stone."

*Ah. The name resonates. It is . . .*

"That which holds you in bondage."

*I feel it is true. But where . . . ?*

"You do not know its location?"

*I sense you. . . . I also sense . . .*

She waited.

*Yes . . . yes. I perceive a relationship, between you and the thing.*

"Can you tell when I get closer?"

*Yes. I think so. Yes.*

"Then you can help me."

*This I will do. You are my liberator.*

"I am. The more you help me, the more you hasten the hour of your liberation."

*I have sensed your coming for some time.*

"I have been long in seeking."

*Because of you I will soar again. Again I will scale the cold heights, feel the air above the earth, see the black skies and the burning sun. . . .*

"Yes, you will."

*I will destroy . . .*

"You will destroy my enemies."

*I . . . ?*

"Yes. In return for my labors on your behalf, you will do my bidding."

*Ah. A bargain. Is this not what it is called?*

"It is. Agreed?"

*I sense I have no choice.*

"None."

*Then . . . we are agreed.*

"Good. Abide. I will call thee when I need thee."

*I obey.*

She turned and walked back down the corridor to where the servants and soldiers were still taking their meal. When she saw their faces, she stopped. They were all staring at her, bewildered, fearful.

They had heard only her voice. She thought: *Belike they think me mad.*

"I am in contact with the demiurge whose embodiment is the castle itself," she told them. "I command it. With its help, we will find the Stone."

This seemed to allay their fears—or perhaps plant the

seeds of new ones. No matter, she thought. They will all die soon.

She was hungry now. She asked for and was given bread, a slice of cheese, a hank of dried, salted meat. She returned to her niche to eat.

# KEEP—UPPER LEVELS

OSMIRIK WAS NEAR exhaustion, but kept climbing. The smell of books grew ever stronger. He knew the library was on one of these high floors. The smell had led him up here.

He had first noticed his peculiar new power shortly after he had become separated from Melydia, a happenstance he regretted not the slightest. In fact, his intention was to stop her. Only the knowledge available in the castle's library could help him. At first he had despaired even of finding a way back to the invading army's staging area, but as he'd wandered blindly, the unmistakable smell of books—must, dust, and old parchment—had come to his nose and would not leave. He had always loved the smell, of course. At one point on the lower levels the odor grew quite strong. He followed his nose into a bedroom with a bookcase holding a few volumes of forgettable lyric poetry.

But now he knew he was on the right track. If a library could have a scent, he was hot on it like a hound with its snout to the trail.

Other smells came, most of them unfamiliar. His olfactory sense had sharpened to an astonishing degree. It was apparent that books were not the only things he could seek out, if he wished to. This newfound talent entailed the ability to sniff one's way to anything desired. Everything around him had an identifiable smell—this table, that tapestry, here a candle, there a sconce. Everything, anything. It was odd, and somewhat disconcerting, but less so than he would have thought. None of the odors were overpowering or especially bad. Some were quite pleasant. And if he wished, he could ignore them all.

He proceeded down the empty corridor warily, but not inordinately concerned for his safety. He had passed numerous aspects, ignoring them. Strange eyes had regarded him out of shadow; he had walked on. He was possessed of a sense of mission. There was little time, and the situation grew more dangerous by the hour.

Light ahead, coming from a doorway. He looked in. The room was pleasantly furnished, and he considered stopping to rest, but decided against it. He strode on to the next door, which was closed. He put his ear to it first, heard nothing. Then he grasped the handle and pushed.

Music, laughter, noise. He beheld a room full of strangely dressed people, most of them standing in little groups and engaged in animated conversation. The general mood seemed festive. He smelled alcohol. The music was loud, harsh, and discordant. The room's appointments were odd, and beyond the huge windows a vast and brilliantly lighted city sprawled endlessly. The sight took his breath away.

"Isn't the masquerade tomorrow night?" The voice belonged to a young man seated by the door.

"Hall costume," a young woman sitting beside him remarked.

"Hall costume? Jeez, I've got a lot to learn about these things."

They both looked up at him curiously. The young man's gaze was drawn to the corridor behind him.

"Hey, I thought that was the connecting door to the other suite," the young man said. "Where's that—"

Osmirik closed the door and continued down the corridor. But he stopped. Something made him go back and cautiously open the door again.

Nothing but a dark, empty room.

The next door let into another bedroom, and the next was locked. He knew the library was near. The smell of learning was pungent in his nostrils. He ran to the next oaken door.

Here! The door flew open onto a vast room of books. He leaned against the doorjamb, taking deep breaths and casting his eyes about the huge chamber. He straightened up and went in, closing the door behind him.

The silence was deep, yet it was the sort of restful, contemplative silence befitting and peculiar to a library. He saw no one immediately about the main floor, and as he walked through the open stacks, he looked down each aisle, finding no one.

He stopped. How was this place organized? In all his years, even those he had spent at university, he had never seen this many books in one place. It was a hundred times as big as any other library in existence. He had not thought there could be this many books in the world. Obviously the librarians here, if any, had a method of keeping track of what was where. It would almost be a necessity. But what? And where?

He heard footsteps and looked to his left. Someone was walking along the far aisle. He moved down the aisle he was in, paralleling the other's path. At length he reached the end of the stacks and stopped, looking out over an area occupied by reading tables. He watched the end of the far aisle.

A tall man emerged, wearing a simple brown cloak. He walked past the tables, stopping at one end of a long cabinet with hundreds of small drawers. He searched, then chose a drawer, opened it and riffled through the stacks of pasteboard cards contained therein.

Osmirik had heard of a card catalog, but the only one he knew of was far away in the library of the Imperial University, in Hunra, the capital city of the Eastern

Empire. Osmirik had never been there.

He stepped out and approached the stranger.

The man seemed to sense a presence long before he could have heard Osmirik's careful step. The man turned and smiled. "Greetings," he said.

Osmirik stopped. "Are you the librarian?"

The man took a moment to consider the matter before saying, "Yes, sir. Can I be of any assistance?"

"You can. I wish to see what you have on the subject of demonology."

For a brief moment the man fixed him in a penetrating gaze. Then he said, "Of course, sir. This way."

He led Osmirik into an aisle running between the end of the stacks and a row of carrels. They walked along until they came to a winding stairwell, which they mounted to the first gallery. As they moved along a railed walkway, Osmirik surveyed the expansive floor below, his wonder renewed. The librarian stopped in front of a tier of shelves.

"Now, as far as demonology is concerned, the main titles are here. However, there are more in a special section for oversize folios, located on the first floor. There are not many of those, and I will fetch them for you. As you can see, there is not much overall. It is a subject for which field research can be problematical."

"I quite understand."

"There exist many excellent works of a theoretical bent, but I must warn you that they are far from definitive."

Osmirik regarded him. "Oh? Are you versed in the subject?"

"I would like to believe so. I have for years been engaged in research along those lines."

"Indeed? I would be grateful for any assistance you could give me."

"I am at your service, sir." The man bowed.

"Thank you. Would you fetch those oversize portfolios for me?"

"Certainly, sir."

The librarian left, and Osmirik scanned the shelves. He

was amazed. There were works here he'd only heard of, volumes of surpassing rarity. He chose one, an ancient work on demoniacal taxonomy. He opened it and carefully leafed through.

He'd best get to work. He picked two more books and carried them to a nearby table, sat down and began to study.

Presently he was aware of the librarian at his side.

"Yes?"

"The oversize portfolios, sir."

"Put them here."

"Yes, sir. You might also be interested in this work."

He held out what looked like an ancient scroll. Osmirik took it and read the title. It was written in an unusual form of hieratic Lutonian with which Osmirik was quite familiar, having done his thesis in the history of the Lutonian Empire.

He was astounded, and in an awed murmur said, "*The Book of Demons*!" This work was not only rare; most eminent scholars were convinced it was no longer extant. Indeed, there were some scholars who claimed the book was merely a legend.

"Where . . .?"

"Yes, an exceedingly arcane work. I have read it."

Osmirik was incredulous. "You have?"

"Yes. I hope you will find it useful. I did to some extent." The librarian looked off. "But it did not tell me exactly what I needed to know."

"I see," Osmirik said, his voice barely audible.

The librarian sighed and looked down at him. "Will there be anything else, sir?"

"Ah . . . no." Osmirik managed to smile. "You have been very helpful."

"Only too happy, sir."

The librarian turned to go, walked a few paces away, then stopped and turned slowly around. "There is one more thing, sir."

Osmirik looked up. "Yes?"

The librarian's features suddenly took on familiar lines. Osmirik realized that he had been avoiding looking at the man's face, for a reason he could not fathom. Now, with a suppressed gasp of surprise, he recognized the man standing before him.

"Tell Melydia that I wait for her," Incarnadine said.

Flabbergasted, mouth agape, Osmirik stared at Incarnadine's back until the tall man strode out of sight.

# Keep—Upper Stories

Kwip poked his head into the wall of the corridor then withdrew it. "Another hallway on the other side of this," he said. "But little else."

"We're getting more and more lost," Linda said.

"Not possible," Gene said. "You can't go beyond being utterly, hopelessly lost, which is what we were to begin with."

"Aye, true enough," Kwip observed, while debating with himself whether to slip away or stay with his new-found companions. He had tagged along because he needed food, and now that he had almost a full backpack —Linda had conjured one for him along with the preserved food he'd asked for—he was ready again to strike off into far parts of the castle. But he was having second thoughts. Wandering alone was perhaps a bit too dangerous.

He came to a decision. He'd stay with the group for now and bide his time. He didn't like the thought of dividing booty five ways, but if by chance they should find the treasure room, the question would likely boil down to how much one person could carry. He did not doubt that fabulous wealth lay behind the building of such an edifice as this.

Unless the buggers squandered everything building it, he thought ruefully. Which might indeed be the case.

"How about the other wall, Kwip?" Gene asked.

Kwip moved to the opposite wall, stopping a nose's length away. He touched his forehead to the cold stone for the barest moment. Then his head disappeared into the wall, half his body following.

"Wow, that's the strangest thing," Gene said. "I wonder what it feels like?"

Kwip extricated himself and shook his head. "Merely a large room with naught in it."

"Could you possibly get stuck halfway in?" Gene wondered.

"A disquieting notion," Kwip said. "I'd as lief not think on it."

"Yeah." Gene cast a glance up the hallway. "Well, hell. I guess we should just keep walking this way."

They moved on.

"Can you breathe when you're, you know, inside a wall?" Gene asked.

"No. I can draw breath, but none comes."

"Do you feel anything? I mean—"

"Tis not a sensation to be described easily," Kwip said. "There is some resistance, but not enough to impede me. There is a musty, stuffy smell, some slight dizziness . . . More I cannot really say."

"Huh," Gene said thoughtfully.

They came to a large chamber with corbeled walls and plentiful alcoves. In one corner, however, an open door led out to bright daylight.

Gene said, "That doesn't look like a portal."

They filed through and came out onto a high terrace with crenellated battlements. Gene looked over the edge. The drop looked to be about eighty stories. Turning and looking up, he saw that there weren't many more stories above. He turned back and took in the view.

"Not as high as the World Trade Center, but just as heart-stopping."

"I don't like heights," Linda said nervously.

"Neither do I, but look at this place. It's so complex, it's hard to take in all at once. Look at all those concentric walls and towers and things."

Jacoby said, "Magnificent, isn't it?"

"Twas wizardry built this," Kwip said under his breath.

"I think those are people moving around down there," Gene said. "At the foot of this main building here, the one we're in."

"Aye, the keep." Kwip shaded his eyes and looked. "An army. The besiegers."

They spent a good ten minutes sightseeing, then went back inside.

"Well, at least I have a sense of the boundaries of this place," Gene said. "It isn't endless." He sat on a stone bench. "What we have to do is head *downstairs.*"

"We've tried that before," Snowclaw said.

"Yeah, I know. But we have to try again."

"Okay," Linda said. "Say we make it down all that way. Say we find an elevator. We find the front door, we get out. What do we do then?"

Gene shrugged. "At least we'll be out of this madhouse."

"But what's out there? A strange world we couldn't possibly live in."

"Exactly," Jacoby said from the leather armchair in which he'd ensconced himself. "My boy, you've a lot to learn. You must rid yourself of any notion that your being in this castle is a predicament that needs getting out of. The task at hand, inasmuch as we don't know what our position will be vis-à-vis the besiegers, is to try to maintain what we have here."

Gene looked at him sourly. "You're saying that I don't know how good I have it."

"Precisely."

"So we all stay in this Gothic funhouse until we either get eaten by slime creatures from another dimension or go bananas. Is that it?"

"Hardly. One simply makes the best of one's situation."

"I still say we should try to find an exit. If there's a way in, there's a way out."

"Not necessarily."

Kwip was pacing slowly in a circle behind Jacoby's chair. Until he saw the sweeping view from the terrace, he had thought the castle a human artifact, albeit an enchanted one. Now he was convinced otherwise. Its sheer bulk alone argued for a supernatural origin. And its lord could not possibly be anything less than the Prince of Demons.

"Anything wrong, Kwip?" Linda asked.

"Eh? No, nothing."

Gene stood. "One thing for sure—we're not going to find anything hanging around here."

"You're right about that, Gene, old buddy," Snowclaw said. "I don't know about you people, but it's too damn warm in this place for me. I got to find me some snow and ice or I'll go 'bananas' too . . . whatever they are."

"You want me to conjure a snowbank for you?" Linda said.

"Thanks, Linda. No, not right now, but if I get desperate, I'll let you know."

"Let's look for a way down," Gene said.

Linda said, "I don't want to leave the castle, Gene. Not for that wasteland outside."

"Neither do I, now that you mention it. I was just thinking that we should try to find a way downstairs. If the portal to our world is still open, it'd be down there somewhere. That's where we came in, I think. Looked like the basement, anyway. Right, Snowy?"

Snowclaw shrugged his massive, furry shoulders. "Hard to tell."

"Yeah, I know. But let's give it a try anyway."

"Sure."

Jacoby was laughing silently.

"You don't have to come with us," Gene said sardonically.

"Sorry," Jacoby said, "but your stubbornness is rather amusing. Quite admirable in a way, though."

"Thanks. Linda, are you coming?"

She looked at Jacoby, then at Gene. "Sure," she said.

"Oh, I'm game for anything," Jacoby said, rising. "Shall we look for a lift, then?"

Linda said, "Don't be silly, Mr. Jacoby."

"Hey," Gene said, "maybe he has something."

"Only joking, my boy. As far as I know, there aren't—"

"No, what I mean is, Linda can conjure one up!"

"Huh?" Linda said, wide-eyed. "Conjure an elevator?"

"Why not?"

Linda thought about it, then threw her arms wide. "Well, by golly, why not?" She stood and stared at the near wall, putting a finger to her chin. Her brow wrinkled. "Hmm," she mused.

Kwip looked confused. "Pardon—"

"What is it, Kwip?" Gene said.

"At times your speech is passing strange. Pray tell, what is an 'elevator'?"

"Just watch."

Before Gene had finished speaking the words, a soft chime sounded. Gene turned his head and saw elevator doors opening in the near wall. Above them an inset light shaped like an arrow glowed red; the arrow pointed downwards.

"Going down?" Gene called.

"Do you think it really works?" Linda said with some concern. "I don't know anything about mechanical things."

Gene walked into the small metal cubical and looked it over. "It's pretty convincing."

"It could all be an illusion." Linda entered and stood beside him.

"The food you whipped up certainly was no illusion. I even got heartburn from the béranaise sauce." Gene examined the controls. "This looks like your average automatic job, only no floor buttons. Just Up and Down, and, let's see, what this . . . Open Door, Close Door, and Emergency Stop. Standard."

"But why doesn't it have floor buttons?"

"I don't know. It's your elevator. Why doesn't it?"

Linda brushed a wisp of blond hair from her forehead. "I wish I knew how I do what I do."

"Yeah, that voodoo that you do so well. Maybe you should give it some thought. C'mon, gang, all aboard."

They all piled in. With Snowclaw it was a little crowded. Gene checked for toes sticking out, then hit the Close Door switch. Outside and inside doors hissed shut.

The car remained motionless.

"Well," Gene said. "Here goes." He hit the Down button.

The floor dropped out from under them. Jacoby shrieked, Linda screamed, Gene yelled, and the car was suddenly acrawl with floating bodies. The elevator plummeted. Gene frantically tried to swim back to the control panel, but Snowclaw's hairy white bulk was in the way.

They fell for a short eternity. Gene grabbed handfuls of white fur and shook.

"Snowy! The red button!"

"Huh?"

"Hit the button! *Hit the button!*"

Snowclaw got the idea and slammed his fist into the control panel. There came an ear-splitting squeal of distressed metal, then a horrendous clanking and groaning, followed by a loud, heavy thud.

It was an abrupt stop. Everyone wound up in a heap on the floor. There were moans and muffled, urgent requests.

"What?" Snowclaw asked.

"Get . . . off . . . my leg," Jacoby puffed.

"Oh, sorry."

"Everybody okay?" Gene asked after he got his breath. "Linda?"

"I thought we were going to die." Her face was fish-belly white. "I'm going to be sick."

Kwip picked himself up and exhaled. "This is an elevator, then?"

"Not quite," Gene said. "It seems to lack certain mechanical necessities."

"We must have fallen a hundred stories," Jacoby said, his face a cadaverous shade of gray.

"I can't tell you how sorry I am," Linda said.

"It was my idea," Gene said. "I should have known that nothing mechanical would work inside the castle. Forget it. Let's get this door open." Gene bent to examine the juncture of the inside doors. He tried to pry them open with his fingers. "They probably lock automatically," he said. He looked at Linda. "You okay?"

She burped. "Excuse me. My stomach is still ten floors up. Yeah, I'm fine. Well, not *fine.*" She rubbed her middle and scrutinized the control panel. "Why not just hit the door button?"

Gene thought about it. "Why not? Just don't touch that Down switch again."

"Don't worry, I won't," Linda said. She held her breath, then gingerly pressed the Open Door button.

The doors rolled apart, revealing a solid stone wall.

"Of course," Gene said.

"Allow me," Kwip said, stepping forward.

A moment later Gene tapped him on the arm. Kwip's shoulders drew back and his head came ghosting out of the wall.

Kwip's eyes gleamed strangely.

"See anything on the other side?" Gene asked.

"Aye, but . . ." Kwip gave Gene an odd look. "I need to get a mite closer." He stepped into the wall again, this time disappearing completely.

Gene chewed his lip, then said, "Linda, do you think you could materialize an opening of some sort?"

Linda thought about it. "That's an interesting question."

She could, and it turned out to be a door with a graceful Gothic arch. It led into a vast room of unusual geometry, though the room was the last thing they noticed, for in the middle of it, high atop a dark, irregularly shaped supporting stanchion, sat an amber-colored crystalline mass of enormous proportions and complexity. It glowed with its own lambent light, throwing strange shadows into the farthest corners of the immense chamber.

Gene whistled and said, "Good God, look at the size of that thing!"

"The Brain," Jacoby breathed.

"What?" Linda asked him.

"The Brain of Ramthonodox. The legendary jewel."

"Yeah?" Gene said. "Is it supposed to have magic powers or something?"

"Enormous powers," Jacoby said soberly, then licked dry lips.

The doorway hung about four feet off the floor. Snowclaw jumped off first and helped Linda down, then Jacoby. Gene leaped, and landed with knees bent.

Kwip did not turn to look at them. He stood on the edge of the platform on which they had alighted, his gaze fixed on the enormous jewel.

Gene came up and stood beside him. "Really something," he said.

"Aye," Kwip said quietly.

"How in the hell did they get it in here? They must've built the castle around it."

"Likely did."

The stone was a single glittering mass, a giant star with thousands of short crystalline spikes radiating from a spherical central body. Fingers of amber fire moved and weaved throughout the stone's interior.

Jacoby seemed transported. "Beautiful," he murmured. "The color . . ."

"Gorgeous," Linda said.

Looking down, Kwip spied a way across the jumbled, many-tiered floor, stepped down from the platform and began to make his way toward the center of the chamber. Gene followed.

"C'mon guys," he said.

The room looked like a Gothic amphitheater without seats, or a cathedral built in the shape of a bowl. Its roof was a complex arrangement of stone-ribbed vaults supported by clusters of slender pillars. The supporting stanchion stood where the stage or altar would have been. To get there they had to make their way down a series of terraced platforms. At the bottom they crossed a smooth stone floor and stopped at the foot of the stanchion.

Each radiating facet was a hexahedron tapering to a point, and all were of different thicknesses and lengths. Some were the size of a finger. They all sparkled and shone with an amber phosphorescence.

Kwip eyed the stanchion. It was a fractured, irregularly shaped mass of dull black rock, its apex lost among the thicket of crystalline shafts at the mammoth jewel's underside. At floor level the rock was at least fifty paces across.

The rock could be climbed.

"Is that thing just balanced up there?" Gene said. "What's supporting it?"

"It's difficult to see," Kwip said, squinting.

"Weird." Gene turned and glanced around the chamber. "Looks like no way out. Linda, you'll have to cut another door for us."

"Can do."

Jacoby shot Gene a look of annoyed contempt. "Don't you realize what we have here? This is the castle's source of power."

"Yeah? Where's the plug? I'm gonna pull that sucker."

"You're a fool."

"What do you propose we do? Take it with us?"

"Of course not."

Gene threw his arms wide. "Then what's your beef, Jacoby?"

"You wouldn't understand," Jacoby sniffed.

"Maybe I don't. Maybe I'm just ticked off because I got passed over when they handed out the magic tricks."

"Gene, your powers will come," Linda said. "It's different for each person."

"What about me?" Snowclaw complained. "I'm in the same boat."

Gene said, "You're so big you don't need hocus-pocus."

"I want to get closer to it," Jacoby said, walking toward the base of the stanchion. When he realized how steep it was, he stopped, hesitating. Then he screwed his courage up a notch and began climbing.

"Oh, for—" Gene stamped his foot and followed. "C'mon, Snowy. I don't know what he's up to, but I don't want him mucking with whatever that is up there."

"Right."

Kwip and Linda watched them climb after Jacoby.

"Mistress Linda—"

"Just call me Linda."

"I would be pleased to. Linda, might I ask a small favor?"

Above, Jacoby huffed and puffed, then quit. Looking up the jagged slope, he saw it was no use, and the enthusiasm sputtered out of him like air out of a balloon. He sat on a narrow ledge and watched Gene and Snowclaw climb up after him.

"What's the matter, Jacoby? Waiting for your Sherpa guide?"

Jacoby smiled thinly. "You're young—you go up."

Gene bent to peer at the surface of the rock. It looked like anthracite but was as hard as granite. "Okay, I will."

It was tough going, and Gene made it almost to the top. What made him stop was the sight of the bottommost spike of the jewel floating inches off the sharp apex of the rock. There was something else going on up here. He heard a faint crackling and a barely audible hum like the singing of high-tension electrical lines. He looked more closely at the jewel. Faint blue lines of force stretched between the underside of the jewel and the peak of the black massif.

The tip of one of the spikes hung directly above him. He reached, slowly, putting out his index finger. He hesitated, finger poised. He drew back. Then he touched it.

It was cold, very cold. He took his finger away and rubbed its tip against his breeches.

"Some kind of weird," he muttered.

When he got back down, they were all waiting for him.

"What's up there?" Linda wanted to know.

"Some guy selling Amway. What do you people want to do?"

"I'd like to get out of here," Linda said. "It's cold, and that thing up there is giving me the spooks."

When they had climbed back up out of the amphitheater, Linda materialized another doorway, this one leading into a curving passageway. They turned right and followed it until it met another tube leading away from the outer wall of the amphitheater.

At length Kwip halted. "Gods of a pig's arse."

"What?" Gene asked.

"Left me rucksack back there. I shan't be a minute." He turned and headed back.

"Wait, I'll go with you."

"You needn't bother, my friend."

Gene stopped running after Kwip, watched until the dark-bearded man rounded the corner, then walked back.

Linda asked, "Anyone for lunch? Dinner? Whatever it is."

Jacoby patted his stomach. "Always feeding time at this zoo, I'm afraid. Another wedding feast, my dear?"

"No, I'm going to try for my friend Shelly's brother's bar mitzvah."

Gene said, "I could go for a corned beef on rye piled with cole slaw with Russian dressing."

"I like a man who knows what he wants. It was a sit-down dinner, though. I don't remember if they had cold cuts."

They didn't, although there were a number of sizable rib roasts.

"Oh, now I remember," Linda said. "Prime rib au jus."

"Kosher, I guess," Gene said.

"You bet. Will you carve, Gene?"

"Sure. What'll it be, Jacoby? Well-done, medium, rare, still ruminating . . .?"

Jacoby was staring back down the hall. "Hm? Oh, rare will be fine."

Gene handed him a plate with a slab of meat on it. Jacoby looked at it, then resumed gazing down the corridor.

Gene served Linda, then Snowclaw, who'd commented that the stuff looked edible enough to sample. Gene cut a medium-rare slice for himself and sat down. He was about to dig in when he noticed Jacoby still looking off moodily.

"What's wrong?"

"I don't trust that chap."

"He seems like a nice man," Linda said. "A little strange. I mean, he asked me for that tool, and I gave it to him, but I don't have the slightest idea what he wanted it for."

Gene cocked an eyebrow. "What tool?"

"Didn't you— Oh, you guys were climbing the rock. He wanted a little . . . what would you call it? A hammer with a sort of chisel on one end of it. A pickax. Like a thing a mountain climber uses. He described it to me, and I whipped one up for him."

Gene looked at Jacoby.

"You don't think—" Gene began, but just then a ringing came from the hall of the jewel, as from a strange and ominous bell, growing louder and louder. . . .

I'm thrice damned, Kwip thought as he climbed.

He'd have to make this quick. He neared the top, stopped and searched for a suitable spike, one small enough to hide in the backpack.

One of the smaller shafts caught his eye. He reached, and could just barely grasp its tip. No good. He stepped up higher and reached again. The jewel was cold to the touch.

Damn me, Kwip thought, I'd steal from the Dark One himself. But I must, I must have at least a part of it!

He got out the pickax, reached up and grasped the shaft. It felt like ice, but its warm amber light filled his eyes, and the shifting fire drew him into its warmth. He struck with the pick end of the tool. With a sharp, high-pitched pinging sound the end of the shaft broke off easily in his hand. He inspected the fragment briefly, noting that it still glowed. He looked about, listening. Droning like a crystal bell, the entire jewel began to resonate with the sound of the breaking.

He dropped the crystal into the backpack and hurried down. By the time he reached bottom, the ringing had grown into an ear-splitting alarm, its painfully high note reverberating in the stone bowl of the amphitheater, growing ever louder. As echoes multiplied, the noise swelled to an overwhelming crescendo, and soon the air was rent by an unbearably loud, horrendous keening that shook the ancient walls.

The floor quaked. Kwip stumbled and fell. He got to his knees and covered his ears. His scream of pain went unheard as the air shattered around him.

# Library

Osmirik laid the heavy folio aside and rubbed his eyes. He had read enough, and the truth lay on him like the rubble of a landslide. His worst fears had been justified. The ancient chroniclers were quite clear on the matter.

Despite the sick, hollow feeling in his stomach, he was scholar enough to still be in awe of the books and scrolls that lay piled before him. Priceless specimens such as these were not to be found even in Hunra, nor anywhere else, he suspected. He felt a distant pang of regret that they would most likely be blown to dust and scattered to the winds when the castle vanished. Or perhaps they, too, were mere conjurings.

It did not matter. All that mattered was thwarting Melydia. But how?

Mad Melydia. She would stop at nothing in her quest for vengeance. For years she nursed the wound that Incarnadine had inflicted; for years she plotted and schemed. She learned her Arts well, then cast about for suitable puppets to employ in her little dumb show. To the east lived a prince with a domineering empress mother. He needed lands to conquer, and a bride on whom his mother would look with favor. A spell, a puff of smoke from a brazier, and he did Melydia's bidding, while the empress looked on with an approving smile.

Osmirik laughed mirthlessly. What a tawdry little world it was, that armies were moved by the machinations of a scheming witch, that by her wiles castles fell, and worlds ended. . . .

He knew only he could stop her—physically, if that be the only way. He would sniff her out, her and her plots and philters, regain her confidence, make as if to assist her, and then—

What? He would know only if and when that time came.

Doubts gnawed. Was it inevitable? And what of the prophecies? He reached for another book and opened it, paged through it and found the passage. He read.

> And there shall come a time when men shall quake and tremble, and great tribulation shall befall the world, as in the days of antiquity, so shall it be on that fearful day, and he shall be unleashed who is hight the Great Beast, the Evil One, the Destroyer, and he shall darken the sun and spread his great wings against the wind, and it shall be visited upon the sons of men as it was visited upon their fathers, that they will flee and hide their heads and curse the day their mothers bore them. . . .

Osmirik shook his head. And shall he, a mere scribe, stand alone against the ineluctable Word? His heart sank, and he knew he could not. But he must try. His eyes again fell to the page.

*But it shall not be dark always, and the hearts of men are not lacking in hope . . .*

Clumsy literalism, he noted. Better, *The night will end, and hope shall live forever in the human breast,* but no matter. He read on:

> . . . and there shall be one in those days, a true son of his father, Ervoldt, by whose might the beast may again be chained, but his troubles shall be great, and his heart will be heavy; neither will his

> house stand against the storm. His name shall be as blood.

Ervoldt, the ancient Haplodite chieftain of legend, who tamed the demons of the earth and made them do his bidding. Osmirik reached for another volume, paged through till he came to the passage he had marked earlier:

> . . . and Ervoldt did all these things, and in the manner in which I have told them. And also did he magick the greatest of the beasts, Ramthonodox, and it was in this wise: he did [text missing] his freehold and his fortress, and [its] windows were numbered one hundred and forty-four thousand, and of [its] rooms there were no end.

He unspooled *The Book of Demons* again, and found a variant of the same passage, with the text restored:

> . . . and he did so in this wise: he did bespell the great beast, which was a demon, and tamed its wiles, and chained this beast to a great Stone, and wrought he a change such that it no longer took the aspect of a beast, but became a great house, which Ervoldt did make his freehold and his fortress . . .

A third variant in yet another decaying book read much the same way. He dug the volume out and opened it—then closed the cover slowly. No, he would not go over it again. There was no mistake. He leaned back in the creaking wooden chair again.

. . . *And his name shall be as blood.*

Better, *His name shall be as the color of blood is called.* His name shall be Incarnadine.

Suddenly, the floor began to vibrate. A faint high-pitched note sounded, accompanied by a deep rumbling. The nearby bookshelves rocked, and one small volume dislodged itself and fell.

Slowly the sounds dissipated. Finally, it was quiet.

Osmirik wondered. Melydia already at work? Incarnadine, perhaps. Or something else entirely. Likely the castle itself undergoing one of its sundry transformations.

He rose and moved to the stairwell, descended, then crossed through the open stacks. Stepping through the anteroom, he opened the door, peered up and down the corridor, went out and closed the door behind him. He had to get his bearings. He now sought the Spell Stone, as did Melydia, but she had her ways and he had his. He sniffed the air. Books, still books—but many other things besides. What would the Stone "smell" like?

A primordial smell, the dust of ages, the sulfurous smell of the fires that gave birth to the Cosmos itself . . .

He had it. There were two overriding "odors" to this place, and they seemed to emanate from the same location. He strode off toward it.

# The Hall Of The Brain

"Kwip, wake up. Are you okay?"

Kwip's eyes fluttered, then opened. He saw Linda's face.

"I'm not in Hell, then?"

"Hell, no," he heard Gene say.

He sat up and looked about. Jacoby was eyeing him suspiciously.

"What happened?" Kwip asked.

"We were going to ask you that," Gene said.

Snowclaw dug a finger in his left ear. "My darn ears are still ringing."

"I think I'm going to be deaf for the rest of my life," Linda said.

"Huh?" Gene said.

"I said, I think I'm going to be . . . Oh, be quiet."

Kwip got unsteadily to his feet. "I'm mystified," he said. "I'd fetched my rucksack and was walking out again when I heard a hellish din."

"It came from this chamber," Gene said. "It was unbearable where we were. I can't imagine what it was like here."

"Aye. Fell into a swoon, I did. Thought I was dying."

"Are you hurt?"

"Aside from feeling a mite shaken, I think not."

Gene pointed to the jewel. "Maybe it's none of my business, but did you screw around with that thing?"

"I'm not sure I take your meaning."

"What was the idea with the pickax?"

"I thought it would be useful in climbing the rock. You seemed to have a bit of trouble up toward the top. But then I lost heart and put the thing in my rucksack to keep against an hour of need."

Gene shrugged. "Okay. As I said, it's probably none of my business."

"No offense taken," Kwip said with a forced smile.

"Yeah. Well, if you're okay, the first thing we have to do is—"

"Gene, look."

"Huh?" Gene saw Linda pointing toward the door and spun around. About a half-dozen helmeted soldiers were already through the entrance, swords drawn. They weren't castle Guardsmen.

Kwip drew his shortsword and backed off. Gene unsheathed his broadsword and did the same, while Snowclaw advanced casually toward the edge of the circular stone floor.

"There's only a couple of 'em," Snowclaw said, beckoning. "C'mon, guys."

Gene and Kwip exchanged glances, then stopped their retreat. Linda and Jacoby ran to get behind them.

The soldiers had seen Snowclaw immediately, but were only now appreciating how big he was.

"Whattayasay, soldier boys?" Snowclaw called. "How's the chow in the army these days?"

That slowed them up. One of them, presumably the leader, spoke.

"You! Whoever or whatever you are, put down your weapon!"

"Can't hear you," Snowclaw said. "Come closer."

The soldier advanced. "I said—"

Snowclaw took a wicked practice cut. The broadax whistled through the still air. "What, this thing? I use it to cut my nails. Need yours trimmed?"

Four of them reached bottom and fanned out. The leader and another soldier approached slowly.

"All of you! Put down your weapons. Now!"

"By what authority do you order us about?" Jacoby protested.

"By the grace of His Royal Highness Vorn, Prince and Heir Apparent to the Siege of Hunra, Son of the Goddess-Empress, and Conqueror of the Western Dominions. You are his prisoners."

"Don't be silly," Snowclaw said. "You can't take us prisoner."

The leader stopped. "Eh? Why not?"

"'Cause you gonna die, hairless. *Arrrrrrrrauuuuuu-ughhhh!*"

Snowclaw's charge was lightning fast. The soldiers who'd flanked him barely had time to react. The leader had none. Snowclaw decapitated him neatly, then turned on the noncom, who managed to escape the same fate by stumbling and falling at just the right time. The ax blade missed his skull by a hair's breadth. He scrambled away from Snowclaw's follow-up, and by that time two of his comrades had arrived to back him up.

For Gene the suddenness of Snowclaw's attack was a shock, but when one of the two remaining soldiers came at him, he responded as best he could, though he could do little but clumsily parry his opponent's expert attacks. It was all he could do to keep running backwards in a big circle.

"Linda, help!"

"What'll I do?"

"I don't know! Something!"

"But . . . but—Oh, wait. How about—"

Gene backed into something hard and hit his head. He winced, looking around. He was inside a huge transparent bubble shaped like a bell jar. He reached out and touched the inner surface. It felt very hard.

The soldier was momentarily nonplussed, but recovered and took a swing at the miraculous shield. The sword blade glanced off sharply and the weapon went flying out of his hand. He hurried to retrieve it.

Gene saw that three other soldiers had come running through the doorway and were making their way down the stone terraces.

"Linda, get me out of here!"

Linda said something, but he couldn't hear. He shouted and pounded against the inside of the jar. She got the idea, twitched her nose, and the bubble vanished just in time for Gene to fend off his opponent's renewed attack.

"A crossbow!" Gene yelled.

"What?" By this time Jacoby had dragged Linda all the way back to the black rock.

"I need a weapon! Gimmie a crossbow! Materialize it—" Gene ducked a vicious sideswipe. "Materialize it in my hands!"

"What's a crossbow?"

"It looks like a bow and arrow but—" He ducked and backed. "Jacoby! Tell her what a crossbow is!"

Instantaneously a crossbow lay cradled in his arms. "Yeah!" he shouted, backing off. The soldier saw what Gene had and broke off his attack.

Gene examined the weapon he held. Although he saw that the bow was cocked and ready, he hadn't the slightest idea of how a crossbow worked. His opponent realized this, and charged. Still backing away and wishing he'd asked for something different, Gene pointed the thing at him and frantically groped for a trigger or releasing mechanism. His hand found a curved wooden tab on the weapon's underside. He pressed it. There was a twanging sound as the bowstring snapped. Gene looked up. A metal rod was growing out of the soldier's throat. The man dropped his sword, choked and spat blood, then fell.

Gene looked at the crossbow. Wicked, he thought, then wondered how the thing was cocked. He noticed a wide metal loop at the front, and it occurred to him that perhaps you were supposed to put your foot in that and somehow—

He heard Linda scream and looked. One soldier held a

knife to her throat, while a comrade had Jacoby pinned to the floor.

A voice behind him: "Drop your weapon or your friends will die!"

Gene let the crossbow clatter to the floor. He turned to look at the soldier who'd said it, discovering that the man hadn't been speaking to him, but to Snowclaw.

The great arctic beast stood near the headless bodies of two of Vorn's infantrymen, his broadax raised high. Two more soldiers flanked him, swords drawn.

"They will all die!" the first one shouted.

"Snowclaw, you better do what they say," Gene said. "You, too, Kwip."

Kwip dropped his sword.

Snowclaw growled, then said, "Aw, Gene, we can take 'em."

"No way, Snowy."

Snowclaw snorted and threw down his mighty ax.

The soldiers were looking toward the door. Gene turned and saw a woman in a bright orange gown slowly walking down the terraced slope. She held her arms straight out, each hand holding a long metal rod that pointed forward. Her line of sight was aligned intently between them.

She reached the circular floor and walked past Snowclaw, oblivious to him and the mangled bodies. Arms folded, Snowclaw regarded her in puzzlement. She walked on, moving in the direction of the dark boulder. The rods began to vibrate violently. She took a few more steps, and then the rods flew from her hands.

Gene ducked as they streaked by. He heard a clinking sound and looked toward the base of the rock. The two silver rods clung to the stone as if to a great magnet.

"So," the woman said. She stood regarding the rock, then elevated her gaze to the jewel atop it. "Of course . . . of course."

Presently her attention was drawn to Gene. She looked him up and down, then asked, "Who are you?"

"The name's Gene Ferraro."

"How did you find this chamber?"

"Just wandered in. Why?"

She did not answer, moving past him toward Linda and Jacoby. She looked the fat man over, then turned to Linda. "Are you a virgin?"

"Huh?"

"Have you known men?"

"What kind of—"

"Answer the question or it will go badly for you."

"It's none of your darned business."

Melydia slapped her face. "I ask you again. Are you a virgin?"

Linda was shocked, unbelieving. "No! *Okay?* No, I'm not."

"I thought not. Pity. A female is always preferable, but I suppose I can make do with the boy." She turned and cast her eyes about the cathedral-like chamber. "I was beginning to think that there was no way into this room." Frowning, she noticed the elevator door high in the wall. "That is most strange."

"Look, what do you want with us?" Gene said.

She walked slowly back toward him. "What were you doing in this place?"

"I already told you that. We're lost. We want to go back to our own world. We were trying to find it."

"Odd, then, that you should be here in the Hall of the Brain."

"Is that what you call this cross between St. Peter's and Madison Square Garden? As I said, we're here by accident. You were right about this room not having a door. We had to create one to get in. We had no idea what was here."

"Indeed? And what of the disturbance we heard a while ago? Was that your doing?"

"Not ours," Gene said. "We were nearby when it happened, but we don't know what it was or what caused it."

"I see." Melydia turned and headed toward Snowclaw. "And what manner of hell-spawned beast is this?"

"What's it to you, lady?" Snowclaw answered.

Melydia's right hand came out from the folds of her gown and performed a few quick motions.

Snowclaw howled and threw himself against the iron bars of the cage that had suddenly materialized around him.

Melydia took a deep breath. "I surprise even myself. Ordinarily I would need an hour to bring forth an object of that size, but in this place . . ." Her eyes sought the ceiling. Her whisper came softly. "Incarnadine, thy fate is sealed!"

"Move back!" one of the soldiers told Gene.

Ten minutes later Gene, Kwip, Linda, and Jacoby were bound, hands behind them, but were free to walk. The soldiers had searched them for hidden weapons. They had rummaged through Kwip's backpack and discovered dried meat and journey cake. They divvied it up and were now taking a meal break.

Melydia drew one infantryman aside. "Take them wherever you wish, as long as it is away from this place. Do not wander far, as you might lose your way. Kill them all."

"Yes, my lady."

She went to the Stone.

"Do you hear me?"

*I hear. You have found it.*

"I have found you as well."

*Indeed? I sense your closeness.*

"Hear me. A while ago you underwent an unusual perturbation. Did you perceive it?"

*Yes.*

"Do you know what it was, or what caused it?"

*It was . . . a loss.*

"A loss? Of what?"

A long silence, then: *Alas, I cannot say.*

"Very well. It may not be important."

*I will soon be free.*

"You will. And you will remember your liberator, heed her, and do her bidding."

*It is difficult to say. Only one has ever commanded me.*

*His name is no longer in my memory.*

"Ervoldt commanded you."

A slight tremor vibrated the floor.

*I remember! I recall the day. It was he who put me here, in this place that is not a place. It was he who enthralled me.*

"Yes, and it is I who will set you free."

# FAMILY RESIDENCE

THERE WAS NOTHING left to do but rest.

He lay abed and pondered what might have caused the spasm of a short while ago. The castle periodically underwent minor convulsions, but that one had been different. He had never experienced its like. Try as he might, he could not convince himself that Melydia had been responsible, although her spell-casting might commence at any moment.

He was loath to contact the voice, but decided it would have to be done.

"Attend me," he spoke.

He was surprised when the voice did not respond within a reasonable time.

"Attend me," he commanded.

*I hear.*

"You did not come when summoned."

*I was otherwise engaged.*

"How can this be possible?"

*Another speaks to me.*

"Indeed? This is unusual."

*You are no longer the only one, son of Ervoldt.*

He laughed. "I see you are being well tutored."

*I have forgotten many things. I must learn.*

"Why?"

*In order to regain my former existence.*

"Yes, of course. Enough of this. I wish to know the nature of the paroxysm you experienced a short while ago."

*I do not know what it was. The other has also asked.*

His eyebrows rose. "I see. And what did you tell her?"

*What I told you.*

He nodded.

*Also . . .*

He waited. "Yes?"

*That it was a loss. I can characterize it better now. It was insignificant, but it was a loss nonetheless.*

He sat up. "Can you tell me what was lost?"

A long pause. Then, *Part of what constitutes me. I am no longer the sum of my parts. I am less.*

"Indeed? This is news. Can you elaborate further?"

*No.*

"Do you know your name?"

A single bead of sweat formed on his forehead as he waited.

Finally, *No. Still am I nameless, still am I in thrall. But the time will come when I will once more beat the air with my wings.*

"Before that time comes, tell me this. Could the loss have been the result of a taking away of something?"

*Yes! That was it. What I have lost was taken from me.*

Breath slowly went out of him. "Good," he said. "Perhaps. Perhaps not."

He rose and left the room. In the next he turned to the right and exited through an arch, coming into a third room with a few tables and benches, a large fireplace at its farther end. He stopped and faced an area of wall demarcated by two stone pilasters.

He extended his arms and touched both index fingers together. Then he drew his arms apart.

The portion of wall described by the pilasters disappeared, revealing the interior of a charmingly furnished apartment. The two Guardsmen on the other side of the portal came to attention. They saluted as he walked through. He nodded.

"How goes it?" he asked one.

"All's well, sire."

"Is my family up and about yet?"

"It is still early morning here, sire."

"Pity to wake them, but I must. I'm running out of time."

"You will prevail, sire."

He smiled. "I believe you."

He moved through a large sitting room that opened onto a veranda and bright blue morning. Next were several utility rooms, and then a long hallway, at the end of which two more Guardsmen stood flanking an intricately carved wooden door. They saluted, then one man carefully opened the door for him. He stepped through, and the door closed quietly behind him.

He checked the children's suite first. His son had thrown off the bed covers. He spread a blanket over the sleeping boy, then went into his daughter's room. She lay on her back, sunlight making her small, oval face glow with radiant innocence. He touched his lips to her forehead, then smoothed her long dark hair. He moved to the window and adjusted the blind so that the light wouldn't wake her.

He walked quietly into the master bedroom. His wife was sitting up in bed, smiling at him.

"I heard you."

"I'm sorry."

"No, I was awake." She held out her arms. "Come."

They lay together quietly for a moment.

At length she said, "It's over?"

"Not quite."

"Then there is no change? We'll lose the castle?"

"That may be."

She rolled to her side and faced him. "I don't care. We have a good life here."

"We do. But that is not the issue."

"What is, then? You are vice-regent here. Is that not enough power, enough wealth?"

"Dearest, it's hardly a question of lust for riches or power."

She frowned. "I'm sorry. I shouldn't have said that."

"Don't be."

"I never wanted to be queen. I care nothing for that wasteland and its drafty old castle. I'm sorry. I don't."

"I know. It doesn't matter."

"You love it so. It's such a pity. I cry for you."

"Do not. I have not lost it yet."

"Oh, she is evil beyond measure, beyond understanding."

"She is mad, poor woman."

"*Poor woman?* How can you think her deserving of pity when—"

He covered her mouth and made a shushing sound.

She was silent.

He removed his hand, kissed her cheek and said, "I must go."

"So soon?"

"Something has come up. A matter that needs my closest attention. Actually, it is a bit of hope."

"Truly?"

"Yes. But I will know more after some investigation."

He got up and went to the open window, looked out. A bright low sun threw spider webs of light across the sea, and the breakers churned and foamed in sparkling silver and blue-green. Nearby a tall palm swayed in the salt breeze.

He turned toward the bed. She knelt with her thighs wide, a stripe of morning light across her high breasts, her dark eyes sad and pleading. He held out his arms and she sprang from the bed and came to him. They embraced in sunlight.

"Stay," she said. "Let that world end, if it must."

"You don't mean it," he said, caressing her soft skin.

"Of course not. But may I not have my secret wishes?"

"I have mine," he said. "In my arms now."

"My belovèd!"

They moved to the bed. Because he thought it might be the last time, he cherished every touch, every throb of fire, every thrust of her hips against his, every sound she made, and all the love she had to give him.

Afterward she lay with eyes closed. He got up and dressed, making few sounds. For a few moments he regarded her lithe sun-browned body stretched out across the sheets. Then he turned to go.

"Incarnadine."

He stopped. "Yes, my love?"

She was sitting up. "How many worlds do you inhabit? How many lives do you lead?"

He grinned. "If I had more than one life, my dearest bride, I would give them all to you."

Her smile faded as he left.

# Lower Levels

"Beware the girl. She is a witch."

There were only five soldiers left and four prisoners to dispose of. But they were an efficient unit. One stayed behind to guard Melydia and the servants.

They marched double file, a soldier and a prisoner, the sergeant-major, who now commanded, in the lead with Linda. Leaving the Hall of the Brain, they walked the passageway that circumscribed it, then took one of the corridors that radiated outward.

Gene was thinking furiously. He knew Linda was too. He hoped she could come up with something. He had no doubt that time was rapidly running out. These guys weren't going to buy them lunch, that was for sure. These guys didn't buy anyone lunch, or drink Perrier with a twist of lime, or put on their Asics Tigers in the morning and run five miles, or talk about their Porsches or their BMWs, any of that stuff. They didn't ordinarily do much but eat, sleep, and kill, with a little rape thrown in for savor.

They turned left at a cross tunnel, proceeding down it until they came to a small alcove.

"This is far enough," the sergeant-major barked. He drew his sword. "Let's be about it."

*My God,* Gene thought as the soldier guarding him pushed him toward the alcove, *they are actually going to kill us.*

A deep-throated growl came from farther down the tunnel.

The sergeant-major whirled. Out of the shadows bounded a tawny, full-maned lion in royal rage, its bared teeth white and gleaming, though not as brightly nor as fearsomely as the dentition belonging to the saber-tooth tiger that stalked angrily behind him.

However, it was the leopard that ran past both of them and tore out the sergeant-major's throat. Then the scene in the tunnel became two-dozen episodes of *Wild Kingdom* running at once.

"Gene! In here! Everybody!"

It was Linda, huddling in the alcove. Gene leaped, tripped over a charging cougar, and fell against Jacoby, knocking him into the alcove and on top of Linda. Kwip jumped in, and suddenly all was dark.

There came a muffled protest. "Mr. Jac—"

"What happened?" Jacoby warbled.

"Get . . . off me!"

"Terribly sorry."

A light came on. Gene looked up at the Coleman lantern hanging by a chain from the ceiling, then saw that the alcove was now sealed off by a wall.

"Linda? Are you okay?"

She sat up and blew air upwards to brush the wisp of hair off her eyes. "Yeah. Now the ropes. Any suggestions?"

"A simple knife, maybe," Gene said.

"Okay, catch."

Gene felt the handle in his hands. "You're getting great at this."

"Life and death situations make for good practice. You try that, I'll try my Cuisinart."

"Huh?"

"Without the plastic cover. See? Those are the chopping blades. I cut myself on them once or twice trying to wash them. Now if I can just do it without—"

Linda got free first and cut Gene's bonds, then Jacoby's and Kwip's.

"Those big cats?" he asked. "Why didn't they bother us?"

"I created them with a real craving for fresh soldier meat."

"Nasty."

"Those bastards were going to kill us." She held her head and shook it woefully. "Look what this place has done to me. Those men are dead."

"As cat food, they had their finest hour. Don't fret about it, Linda. You did what you had to do. By the way, I *loved* the saber-tooth. Nice touch."

"Oh, if I had thought, I might have come up with something that wasn't lethal."

"And you would have gone to heaven for being a nice person."

She sighed. "I guess you're right." She looked around. "Now what? I guess we go out through the other side."

"Unless you can conjure Marlin Perkins."

Linda materialized a small opening. Kwip cautiously peered out. It was a tunnel paralleling the one they'd been in.

"We have to go back and get Snowy," Gene said. "You can dematerialize the cage, and then—"

"Wait," Linda said. "I don't think I can do that. My talent is creating things out of thin air, not making things disappear. Hold on." She looked at the Cuisinart and wriggled her nose. "No soap. I can't make it go away."

"How come you can create doors and openings? After all, they're sort of negative quantities."

"I don't know. A door is *something* to me. You can see it."

"Well, anyway, there's only one more soldier. And there're four of us."

"You're forgetting Super-Bitch."

"Yeah. Do you think you can handle her?"

Linda looked inward for a moment, then said, "I don't know. She's up to something. And she's powerful."

"So are you, and you're getting stronger by the hour."

# Middle Levels

Osmirik stopped in his tracks when he saw the giant creature sitting in the middle of the large domed chamber. Something told him it was a creature, although it looked in some respects more like a vegetable garden. On the whole it was of such complexity that the eye was at pains to make sense of it. Leaves, claws, stalks, legs—these appendages and more protruded from the beast at haphazard angles. Green and yellow fronds covered the body in most places, save for a few areas where strange feathers grew.

Osmirik backed off. It was a long way around the thing.

"Greetings," came a voice emanating from an appendage resembling a cabbage head. It appeared to have a mouth.

Astonished, Osmirik halted.

"We bid thee greetings," spoke another vegetable mouth.

Osmirik bowed stiffly. "A good day to you, sir . . . er, sirs."

"It is polite," the first head observed.

"Ask it what place this be," suggested a third.

"Capital idea. Kind stranger, canst tell us how this place is called?"

"You are in Castle Perilous," Osmirik answered, "the master whereof is Lord Incarnadine by name."

"Might ye know, then, how we came to be here? We are unclear on the matter ourselves."

"Unfortunately, I do not know. My apologies."

"Tis nothing. Thou hast done us a kindness."

"Ah, tis beyond hope," lamented a fourth head.

"By the heavens, I think thee right," said the first. "We shall never leave these walls."

"Your pardon," Osmirik said. "I have a question."

"Yes?"

"How long have you been here?"

"A very long time. We think for at least a hundred cycles of the stars, albeit none are here to be seen."

"And you have spoken to no one in all that time?"

"Thou'rt the first who deigneth to speak to us."

"A pity," Osmirik pronounced. "And an injustice."

"Truly, for we have in that time composed nigh on two million lines of a new poetical work."

Osmirik was somewhat taken aback. "You don't say?"

"Yes. It is lyrico-pastoral in nature, with overtones of romantic melancholy. Likely as not, it would please thee greatly."

Osmirik looked off, searching for the nearest exit. "Under ordinary circumstances, I would fain hear it. However—"

"We would be honored to perform it for thee," the first head intoned. "Chorus, assemble!"

The cabbage heads rearranged themselves.

"Very well. Begin."

All heads then chanted in unison:

> "Hear us, O Demiurge, whose spirit deep abides
> In soils which giveth life to each and all,
> And bless these humble lays, that they may be
> As seeds cast on fertile ground to germinate
> And bear the fruit of Universal Love . . ."

"Mother Goddess, blank verse!" Osmirik murmured as the chorus droned on. He began sidling his way through the narrow space between creature and wall, smiling pleasantly and nodding enthusiastically. At length he made it to the other side, stood and listened a polite moment, bowed, and walked through an exit.

"Uncultured dolt," came a voice at his back.

Osmirik exhaled, then shuddered. What next? he thought. After an outsized cabbage garden with a penchant for high-flown poesy, what could follow?

The floor opened up and swallowed him.

He slid, endlessly, down a dark spiraling pipe. He tried halting himself, but the angle was too steep and the walls inordinately slippery. He extended his arms and legs and let his body go as loose as possible, praying that the pipe would soon level off.

It did not. It widened, then tipped to vertical. Screaming, Osmirik plummeted in darkness.

The pipe ended and he shot through into open air. He was briefly conscious of falling through a great semidark chamber. Then came a violent shock—

He was underwater. Warm currents pulled him this way and that as he thrashed his way upwards, his lungs burning and his heart slamming against his breastbone. Just at the moment when he thought he could no longer keep himself from inhaling water, he broke the surface and gulped air.

He gagged and choked as the intolerable stench of raw sewage assailed his nostrils. He was swimming in the stuff. He looked around. The chamber was huge and generally spherical, a vast stone cesspool, and from the roof protruded the ends of numerous pipes.

He searched the darkness at the edges of the chamber. There appeared to be a bank or at least a ledge bordering the lake of offal. He began swimming toward it.

As he neared shore, something seized his right foot, briefly, then let go. He splashed and kicked furiously until his strength was at an end and the ledge was an unbridgeable arm's reach away.

An arm reached for him, and he was pulled from the foul waters like the rotting carcass of a great fish.

"Fine day for a swim!" said a jolly voice. It belonged to a short, balding man wearing tights and a simple gray tunic.

After getting his breath, Osmirik wheezed, "I owe you a great debt."

"Think nothing of it. I like company now and again. Tis aching lonely down here at times."

"You are . . .?"

"Dodkin, Master of the Castle Waterworks, is what I'm called to my face. Shitmaster Dodkin, to other parts of me."

"You have my perpetual gratitude, Master Dodkin. But tell me—" Osmirik coughed and spat. "However do you put up with the smell down here?"

With a puzzled frown, Dodkin sniffed the air. "What smell?"

# King's Study

The room was a clutter of bookshelves, strange artifacts, alchemistic paraphernalia, and other oddments. A large astronomer's orrery sat on a table in one corner of the room. Star charts lined the walls in that area. A large, detailed globe of the world occupied another corner.

He sat at a table that held a number of curious instruments constructed of wood and metal. He scrutinized one in particular, a box with a window through which a copper needle could be seen. He observed the position of the needle on a calibrated scale and made a notation with a quill pen. His attention shifted to another device, this one a glass globe, inside which hung two pieces of metal foil joined at one end. He noted the extent of their separation, dipped the point of the quill in an inkwell and scratched more numbers on a sheet of foolscap. He turned then to a third device, a loom of interwoven strings threaded with hundreds of small colored beads which clicked and clacked as he manipulated them, singly and in groups. He did this for a good while, then ceased and contemplated the results. He recorded more data, taking careful readings from each of the instruments. A candle on the table burned steadily, limning his face in soft shadows. A film of fine sweat sprang to his forehead as he worked. Several sheets of foolscap, acrawl with numbers and symbols, fell to the floor in quick succession.

Finally he put down the quill and mopped his brow with a kerchief he had taken from inside his gown. Bearing the last sheet of foolscap, he rose from the table and crossed the room to a low multitiered desk. On it sat a personal computer with a compact keyboard terminal, a color CRT, a twin floppy-disk deck, and a hard-disk drive. He seated himself and made a simple hand pass. The screen came to life, showing an AO> prompt. With quick accurate strokes he punched a series of keys, then waited for the screen to go through an elaborate display of graphic pyrotechnics.

"Damned showy off-the-shelf software," he muttered.

Using his right index finger, he traced another pattern in the air, observed the results on the screen, made another hand pass. Then, with his eyes on the sheet of figures, he entered data on the keyboard.

When he had completed data entry, he punched a few more keys, sat back, and let the program run.

A line of figures came up on the screen. He read it.

"Impossible," he said. "But there it is. Now all I have to do is locate it."

He commenced a set of elaborate hand motions, accompanying these with a low, monotonous chanting. Presently the CRT screen began to glow spectrally. Milky images ghosted across it, gradually sharpening. Voices. At length the picture focused to unmistakable clarity.

Completing the incantation, he regarded the faces on the screen. None were familiar, although that was not unusual. He would have to observe for some time, he supposed, before he could act. He had no idea, now, what he would do, if anything.

He positioned himself more comfortably in the chair. He watched, and listened.

# Lower Levels

"I'm just not strong enough," Linda was saying. "She's frighteningly powerful. I could tell."

Gene said, "I think you're right about her being up to some kind of dirty work. No telling what. It must have something to do with that jewel, though."

"Well, we can rule out stealing it. So she must want to tap the thing's power."

"Obviously," Jacoby said.

"To do what?" Gene wondered.

Jacoby's smile was strange. "To do anything she wants to do."

"She's in cahoots with the besiegers, that's for sure," Gene said. "So, it might have something to do with completing the final takeover of the castle."

"She wants to take control of the jewel," Linda said. "To take control away from Lord Incarnadine."

"A good guess," Gene said. "I wouldn't be surprised if you've hit it right on the head." He looked around, then pointed to the intersection of tunnels up ahead. "I'm pretty sure that's the corridor we were in when the big cats hit."

"Let's face it," Linda said. "We're lost again."

Jacoby let out a long sigh. "Oh, dear, I must sit down." To no avail he searched the corridor for something to sit on.

"It's just a little farther," Gene said.

It wasn't. They stopped to rest again, sitting down in the middle of the bare stone passageway.

"I don't know how long it's been since I slept," Gene said, then yawned.

"Don't start!" Linda said. But she caught it too.

A low rumbling sounded. The floor shook, and the walls seemed to become rubbery and pliant. It lasted for about twenty seconds, then stopped.

"No telling what that was all about," Gene said.

Linda looked off, as if hearing or perhaps sensing something.

"Funny," she said.

"What?" Gene asked.

"I'm beginning to develop a sixth sense, or something like it. She's started whatever it is she's up to."

"Yeah? Any idea of what she's doing?"

"Something magical. Probably putting a spell on that big jewel."

"Maybe she wants to have it set in a nice eighteen-carat gold ring."

"Or maybe . . ."

"Yeah?"

Linda shook her head. "I'm not sure. I get the sense that she's going to destroy something, or undo something." She drew her knees up and wrapped her arms about them. She looked off again. "Maybe the rock is more important than the jewel."

Gene said, "Look, if you're getting all these psychic vibrations, you should be able to get us back to the Brain room."

Linda cocked a thumb over her shoulder. "I know it's in that direction. But I don't know what tunnel will get us there."

"Oh. Kwip, how about taking a little jaunt through this

wall and seeing what's on the other side?"

"Aye," Kwip said, getting up. He disappeared into the wall.

"Still can't get over that," Gene said, rising. "Christ, this floor is colder than a witch's—well, whatever."

"You'd better watch what you say, pal," Linda said.

"Sorry."

"You'll get so bewitched, you won't know—"

Kwip came striding out of the wall, shaking his head. "Tis naught but solid stone. I began to feel a mite strange, so I turned about."

Gene let himself fall back against the wall. "Hell." He yawned again. "When the hell is my turn? I gotta get me some magic soon."

"I thought you had it," Linda said.

"You kidding? See me doing anything enchanting here?"

"No, I meant the way you sword-fought."

Gene laughed. "You gotta be pulling my leg. Why, I barely—"

"I caught glimpses of your bladecraft," Kwip said. "You gave a good account of yourself."

"Against a professional soldier," Linda said. "Gene, did you ever take fencing, or any kind of military training?"

"Never. Never handled a sword in my life."

"But you held your own against a skilled sword fighter."

Gene rested his left hand on the hilt of his broadsword. "It never occurred to me. You know, you're right. I should have been mincemeat back there."

"We'd best be going," Kwip said.

They pushed on, but the labyrinth of bare passageways seemed infinite. Every tunnel that led in the proper direction ended in a T. No matter what direction they chose then, the passage always ran to an L forcing them back in the direction whence they'd come.

The shakes hit again, this time more severely. The walls appeared for a fleeting moment to be composed of shivering gelatin, taking on a translucent, insubstantial quality.

When things had quieted again, Gene exhaled noisily.

"Jesus, that was pretty bad. I wonder what's happening."

Linda's eyes narrowed. "Super-Bitch is still at it."

"I'm getting worried about Snowy. If it were anything or anyone else, no problem, Snowy'd cream 'em. But her, I don't know. I think she's in a ballpark all her own."

The tremors began again. A section of the right wall disappeared, revealing a blinding-white arctic landscape. Powdery snow blew into the corridor.

Gene had been leaning against the wall. He dug himself out of a snowdrift, spat flakes and said, "Damn it."

"Gene, get out of there!" Linda yelled.

Gene took a step and keeled over into deep snow. Kwip reached and helped him out. They had barely recrossed the boundary when the wall materialized again.

"Jesus, that was *close*!" Gene wailed. "Gimmie a break!"

"Things are getting more unstable," Linda said.

"That might have been Snowy's world," Gene complained.

The tremors continued, slowly growing more severe.

"Keep walking!" Linda told them.

The floor turned to rubber and began to heave and pitch like some tricked-out device in a funhouse. Then even stranger things began to happen.

A gaggle of pink, flamingolike birds, about a dozen in all, came squawking and flapping out of the left wall. They waddled across the corridor and disappeared into the right. At almost the same time, paralleling the birds' course farther down, a pale rider on a black stallion thundered across the passageway. Sprinting in the opposite direction came a pack of long-toothed wolflike canines in fur of silver and gray. Meanwhile, in the turbulent air of the corridor, glowing airborne splotches of color along with miscellaneous random images flew hither and thither.

The floor heaved in waves and began to move forward like a conveyor belt. Gene and Linda ran to the bottom of a steep trough, losing sight of Kwip and Jacoby. The walls shook like slabs of rubber. Gene ducked as an image of a giant human mouth came at him, its fleshy red lips parting to reveal rows of sparkling, photogenic teeth. But the apparition abruptly vanished, replaced with the image of a Manx cat wearing a lavender ribbon around its neck. It floated over Gene's head; then it, too, blinked out of existence.

Gradually, these and other phenomena occurred less frequently. The floor settled down, then the strange visions ceased altogether.

"That was interesting," Gene said when all was quiet.

The four of them lay on their stomachs, looking about cautiously.

Jacoby swallowed and said, "Do you think—"

"No," Linda told him. "There'll be more."

Gene stood. Without warning, a trapdoor sprang open beneath his feet. Yelping in dismay, he dropped through the narrow aperture and was gone, as quick as that. The "trapdoor" closed, leaving no seams.

"Gene!" Linda screamed, and that was all the reaction she had time for before the next wave of anomalies hit. The floor commenced heaving again, and the waves bore her down the passageway like a surfboard rider on a rolling swell.

The wave motions propagated forward from a point just beyond where Jacoby and Kwip had come to rest after the last disturbance. Helpless, they watched Linda being carried out of sight while fleeting, incongruous shapes filled the air, and rats, bats, and other creatures skittered between the walls.

Eventually things got quiet again. They got up, and Kwip called out. There was no answer. He ran down the passageway calling Linda's name, Jacoby huffing after.

They ran until Jacoby was out of breath. Linda was nowhere to be seen. Jacoby slumped to the floor, wheezing and coughing. Kwip leaned against the wall and stared off.

"A pity," Jacoby finally said, his breathing still labored. "But we finally have a chance to talk. Let me first commend you—" He coughed elaborately, then took a deep breath. "You did a fine job keeping it from the soldiers. I saw you take it out of the knapsack and hide it on your person. For the life of me, though, I can't imagine how you kept them from finding it when they shook you down."

Kwip cast a cold eye on him. "To what do you refer, sir?"

"The jewel, of course. Or the piece of it you hacked off with the pickax. How did you manage to prevent them from finding it?"

Kwip shrugged. He saw no reason to deny it. He feared Jacoby as much as he did a garden slug. "There are ways," he said. "There are portions of the body that no one thinks of palping, certain ways of twisting and turning, presenting those areas one wishes to present."

"You could have run at first sight of them," Jacoby said. "Gone off and run into a wall. Yet you stayed."

Kwip scowled. "I didn't, against my better judgment."

"Perhaps you fancied Linda?"

"Perhaps. A fair lass. A woman of quality, I should say."

"I found your staying rather strange behavior. You see, I took you for an experienced thief and a thorough scoundrel the moment I laid eyes on you."

Kwip's hand went to the haft of his shortsword. Then he relaxed and smiled crookedly. "I'll husband my strength and not slit you from gills to gullet. But choose your words with care."

"One thief and scoundrel to another," Jacoby said, chuckling.

Kwip regarded him. "So?"

"In the world I hail from, my particular specialty is called embezzling. I was employed by a prominent London assurance company. Accounts receivable. Oh, it was a grand scheme, and it worked for years. Greed got me in the end, and an unexpected accident that kept me in hospital during the semiannual audit. Nothing I could do. The judge gave me three years. And you?"

"Twas the hangman's noose for me," Kwip said.

"I thought as much. And that story about getting lost in a friend's house?"

"It happened on the eve of the execution. I was pacing the length and breadth of my cell for the thousandth time when I turned about and saw that the wall of the far end had disappeared. I walked out, and . . ."

"Of course. As for me, I couldn't face the prospect of jail. On the eve of my sentencing I was sitting in my bedroom thinking seriously of ending my life. I was facing my own dark night of the soul, and that's when destiny's door swung wide." Jacoby smiled. "We really have much in common."

"That much, at least."

Jacoby grunted and got to his feet. "And now you'll be wanting to hand the jewel over to me."

Kwip drew his sword. "Mark you, there is only so much—" A strange expression overcame his face. The muscles of his neck bunched into taut cords, and his arms began to shake.

"You walk through walls," Jacoby said. "I control people. I make them do what I want them to do. You have no choice, no way of fighting me. It's a pity I can't control more than one person at a time. But with the jewel, that may change. Hand it over."

Kwip's sword arm spasmed, went rigid, then bent spastically to bring the point of the blade near his eyes. "No!" he gasped.

Jacoby's jaw muscles twitched. "I want it, now."

"It's yours," Kwip screamed. He then collapsed, dropping the sword. He breathed heavily for a moment, then looked up at Jacoby, who stood over him threateningly. He fumbled in the folds of his blouse near the neck, withdrew the amber jewel fragment and gave it up.

The fat man held the thing, admiring it, his eyes focused deep within its fiery interior. "At last. At last." He scrutinized the fragment for a full minute, then exhaled and slipped it into the vest pocket of his tattered pinstriped jacket.

Kwip watched him walk away.

# King's Study

He had seen enough. A single hand pass darkened the screen and returned the AO> prompt.

He sat for a moment, deep in thought. Then he rummaged in a small plastic filing chest and withdrew a computer diskette, which he inserted into the right-hand drive slot.

"Never tested," he murmured. "But it should work."

He hit a series of keys, waited, hit more keys, waited, then sat back.

"I hope," he added.

He began an elaborate set of hand passes, tracing designs in the air with his fingers. These took some time to complete. Presently the screen brightened again and began to show blurred images.

At last he sat back and took a deep breath.

The screen displayed a face in close-up. It belonged to a man of middle years, dark of eye and strong of jaw, holding a knife blade to his stubbly cheek. He looked directly out from the screen, one eye squinting, blade poised for a stroke. Suddenly his eyes darted about warily.

"Who calls Ervoldt?" he bellowed, looking off-screen.

He got no answer, cursed, looked forward again and brought the knife to his oiled chin. Then, startled, his eyes bulged and his head filled the screen.

"Who in the name of all the gods might you be?" he shouted with great annoyance. "And what devilment are ye about inside my shaving glass?"

"I speak across the chasm of three thousand years," came the answer.

"Do you? To glower at me as I crop my whiskers? Begone, spirit, and let me be about my business."

"Hear me, Ancient One. I am human, and as alive as you, though I inhabit a time far removed from yours. I am your remote descendant."

"Eh? The devil you say."

"I speak truth."

The man in the glass scowled and peered outward. "I see you." He nodded, his expression softening. "You have the family look about you. Three thousand years, say you? The line breeds true." He stepped back from the mirror. "And still in the family business, I see. What device do you use? Crystal sphere? Far-seeing glass? Necromantic rings?"

"A modification of the second device you mentioned. The refinements involved would be difficult to describe."

"Doubtless so, after so long a time in which to make such advances." Ervoldt threw down the razor. "Very well. What do you want?"

"Some advice."

"Go on."

Much later Ervoldt nodded gravely and said, "I have always thought that some day the Stone's secret would be breached. In truth, I am surprised it lasted three millennia."

"It will last three more with your help. The chief problem, of course, is recasting the spell as soon as possible after my adversaries undo it."

Ervoldt frowned. "Aye, and you will have the devil's own time of it. Since I do not know you, I cannot judge your abilities. I do know that the spell involved intricacies that have befuddled many a competent adept. I do not say this to tout my own proficiency. I succeeded only because I undertook the task when the stars were most favorable, a factor others before me failed to take into account."

The other nodded, and looked away. "I am well aware of the sidereal mathematics you devised. I have your orrery, and have used it many times."

"Indeed. It has lasted that long? I am honored. But to return to the matter at hand—I can but wish you well. You will need as much luck as I had."

"Another factor has arisen, one which I am sure you never encountered."

"Such as?"

"Watch the glass." He hit a number of keys. The second disk drive hummed.

"What are you doing?"

"I am using the refinements of which I spoke earlier. The calculations should be visible to you."

"What?" Ervoldt looked off to one side. "Ah! I see." He studied what he saw. "Very interesting. Yes . . . yes. I see. You have more?"

A good while passed. At length Ervoldt looked out again at his descendant. "I understand. Yes, I would say you have an advantage here, be your ciphering correct and your surmises true."

"Would you say that this advantage might offset any unfavorable sidereal conditions?"

"I think it would tend to ameliorate them. Beyond that, I cannot say."

"It is enough. You have been of invaluable service to me, Ancestor."

"I am glad. You seem an able young man and a worthy bearer of the family name."

"Thank you . . . Grandfather."

"Before you leave me, one question."

"Anything."

"Have you attempted this communication before?"

"No. Have others made contact?"

"Not contact," Ervoldt said, "but I have had detected strange meddlings, perhaps attempts to observe me. I am not sure."

"I see. Though I cannot be certain, I think I know who it was."

"Tell them to bugger off. I value my privacy. To future generations I am the dead. Let me lie, let me rest."

"My apologies."

"They are unnecessary. This look into the far future has lightened my heart. Simply to know that there is a future is somehow reassuring. May the gods look upon you with favor. Fare ye well."

"Farewell."

A motion of the hand and the screen went dark.

He sighed. Rising from the computer station, he walked the length of the room and stood before a star chart. He examined it, doing a few mental calculations. He shook his head.

"The worst possible time."

The walls shook again and took on a strange cast. These disturbances had been occurring regularly for the past half hour, but he had been able to ignore them because of certain protections that this particular room afforded. Soon those safeguards would not be enough.

The time had come. He would have to make his way to the lower levels with all due speed and put his plans, such as they were, into immediate effect.

# Hall Of The Brain

Snowclaw looked out from the bars of his cage. They were doing curious things out there. Braziers burned, candles glowed, and the smell of incense hung heavy in the air.

Snowclaw didn't like it one bit, but he had just about broken several bones trying to force his way out of the cage. It was no use. All he could do was observe the strange goings-on and comment now and again with a disapproving growl. At least he could let them know he didn't like it.

Snowclaw wasn't used to concentrated thinking, but now, with time on his hands, he was at leisure to put some thought into the process of deciding what to do next, if anything. He arranged the things he would do in sequential order. First he'd break out of his confinement. Then he'd tear the head off everybody in the room.

No, no good. The witch-female was too powerful for that. First, break out. Second, get away, so the magic-wielding hairless female couldn't cage him again. Third, find his good buddy Gene and the other female, the one he liked a lot, Linda. Fourth? Well, if Gene and Linda and he were together again, everything would be okay, there wouldn't be anything more to worry about, except getting back home. . . .

Home. He never really thought about it much, but what was home? A shack, that's all. A nice one, though, comfortably livable, and warm enough when the north wind blew and it got *really* cold at night, so cold the blowing snow felt like needles against your hide and the air was brittle enough to shatter like the glass in the windows of city-folks' houses if you yelled or made a sudden move, just shatter into a million pieces, so cold that you'd give anything for spring to break early and to see the icebergs calving into the sea and moving out with the tide, great white floating islands, and to feel a mild breeze and see little green things appear among the wet rocks. . . ..

He was homesick. But all he had back there was a shack and a shaky living. Sometimes he got lonely—every once in a while, and he'd get the urge for companionship. Why, the last time he'd shacked with a mate was years ago. Yeah, it was a lonely existence out there in the ice fields. But it was the only way he knew how to make a living.

Now, this place—he kind of liked it here. It was lots of fun, sometimes, and the food was good. There were plenty of good fights, a little danger for spice. Yeah. He liked it. Thing was, on a permanent basis it would tend to wear a little thin. But on the whole, the prospect of staying here indefinitely didn't upset him as much as he would have thought.

He missed Gene. For some reason he liked the little smooth-skinned fellow a whole lot. Why, he didn't know. Didn't really matter.

Great White Stuff! He wanted out of this cage so bad he could taste it. What in the name of the Ice Queen were they doing out there? Witchy stuff, most likely.

He thought of Gene and Linda again and wondered what they were doing, whether they were okay. They could be in trouble. He was a bit worried. He grasped the bars again and shook. The cage rattled, and the hairless soldier turned to glare at him. Up your mud hole, Bare Butt. Give your dirty looks to someone else.

No use. He sat and leaned his broad back against the far wall of the cage. His thoughts returned again to his friends. He was convinced, somehow, that Gene was in trouble. Linda he wasn't sure about. But he was certain that Gene needed him. He had no idea *how* he knew that, but he knew it for sure.

He could almost see Gene. He closed his fierce yellow eyes. He *could!* He could actually see his buddy now, and it was true, the little hairless guy was up against it.

He jumped to his feet. "Gene!" he called out. "I'm coming, pal!"

Snowclaw could almost reach out and touch him. He didn't know what was happening, but whatever it was, Snowy was all for it.

Melydia sprinkled more incense onto the glowing coals. Smoke rose from the brazier.

She was not adept at visualizing spells, though her sense of them was keen. But her perception of the enchantment cast around the Stone had become so palpable that she saw, or thought she could see, an intricate network of glowing filaments surrounding the Stone like a spider's web, each strand pulled taut with extreme tension. As she recited the opening lines of the Spell of Abrogation, the web shimmered and vibrated, emitting a sound like an ethereal harp.

The beast in the cage made noises again, but it did not distract her. She barely noticed it.

She finished the Greater Invocation. Soon, Incarnadine, soon. You will show yourself, and you think you will have me, but you will be wrong. I am now far more powerful than you—than anyone one in this world. And once the demon is loose, it will do my bidding. You will control it no longer.

She regarded the Stone again. Around it, glowing strands of red, green, purple, and yellow entwined sinuously in a filigree of magic. She blinked her eyes and it was gone. Then, slowly, it returned. Yes, it was really there. She was not just imagining it.

She looked over her shoulder. The servants sat huddled

as far away from her as they dared. The young one looked frightened. She would try to prevent him from dying immediately, so as not to upset the others. It would be difficult, though, as the spell called for a great quantity of virgin's blood. She would endeavor to put the least amount to good use. She cared nothing for the boy. At one time, long ago, she would have balked at such an act. In fact, it would have horrified her. But after years of delving into the Recondite Arts—

"Your Ladyship."

She turned her head. It was the soldier.

"What is it?"

"The beast. It is no longer in its cage. It is nowhere to be found."

"Have you been watching it?"

"Yes, my lady, just as you said. But it . . . it disappeared. One moment I was looking at it, and the next—"

"No matter," she said. "Do not bother to search for it. I doubt it will return here. Return to your post and do not disturb me again."

"Yes, Your Ladyship."

Sometimes she forgot that everyone in this castle was a magician to some extent. Be that as it may.

She began another incantation.

# Elsewhere, And Back Again

"At last I have you, Count Ciancia!"

From the floor Gene looked up at a man who was dressed in something that vaguely evoked *The Three Musketeers* and similar costume epics.

Gene said, "Huh?"

"I know not by what thaumaturgy you have contrived to change your appearance, or how this secret chamber was instantly revealed, but I know you, Count, for the fiend you are."

"Wait a minute," Gene said, struggling to his feet.

The man drew a rapier, whipped it about briefly, and fell into a fencing stance. "Be on your guard, sorcerer!"

"Hold it!" Gene yelled, raising his hand. "You've got it all wrong. I'm not this Count whatever you call him. You—"

"More lies!" the man hissed, anger flashing in his eyes. "You spew them like vomit from a drunkard!"

"That's getting personal." Gene glanced around. He couldn't figure what happened after the floor had swallowed him. He'd fallen, but not far, and had wound up in darkness, briefly. Then the lights had come on, and . . . Was he still in the castle?

"Have at you!" The man charged.

Gene barely had time to draw his sword. He sidestepped the middle-aged man's lunge, ran out of the alcove in which he'd found himself and into a spacious seventeenth century drawing room. He instantly realized that he'd just crossed a portal.

His antagonist chased after him, still yelling but now quite unintelligibly. On this side of the portal there'd be no communication at all.

Gene backed away, brandishing his sword. The weapons were mismatched, of course, broadsword against rapier, but Gene didn't know enough about weaponry to guess who'd have the advantage, if any.

He found out quick. His opponent was a passable swordsman, and the rapier's tip nearly skewered Gene three times before he had time to back out of range, parrying desperately. If Gene could bring the full force of the broadsword against the thin steel of the rapier's blade, the rapier would break. But his opponent wasn't about to let him do it. The man stayed with feint-and-lunge maneuvers that kept the rapier unpredictably darting about, avoiding contact with Gene's heavy weapon.

The portal might close any second. He would somehow have to maneuver back toward the far wall. But Gene was not in charge. His opponent would determine who would go where. On the positive side, the man was no expert. Although he couldn't fathom why, Gene had the feeling that he could hold his own with a fencing sword too. This flashed through his mind when he saw the crossed épées above the mantelpiece.

His back to the fireplace, he swung wildly with the broadsword and fended his opponent off, then overturned a stuffed chair to block him. Taking advantage of the momentary distraction, Gene reached back and fumbled with one of the crossed swords—it fell and rolled away. He reached again, grasped the remaining épée by its cupped hilt, and ran off toward the alcove.

"Coward!" the man yelled when Gene had recrossed the boundary. He was in the castle again—he could tell by the distinctive purplish-gray stone—but the chamber was a cul-de-sac. He had nowhere to run.

Gene switched the épée to his right hand and put it up against the man's thrusting attack, neatly parrying and delivering a riposte that the man had trouble beating away.

The man's expression changed. He was a little less sure of himself.

"Just who the hell are you?" Gene demanded.

"As if you didn't know!" came the answer, along with a forceful beat against Gene's sword and a savage lunge.

"I'm not Count Whozis," Gene said, calmly beating back and riposting. "Isn't that apparent by now?" The sword felt like part of his hand, as if he were born to be a swordsman.

"No other human dwells in this place. If you are not Giovanni Luigino, the Count di Ciancia, then you are one of his familiars, and if that is true, I should be dead! But I'm not. So you must be he, though you bear no resemblance to the fiend."

"Okay—" Gene feinted, then attacked the man's left shoulder. His opponent parried, but couldn't riposte due to Gene's expert follow-up attack to the middle. "What's this guy done, anyway?"

"Damn you to hell! You know more than I what foul deeds are yours. I know only—" The man overreacted to Gene's feint, leaving himself open to a quick lunge, which he had to hastily beat away, retreating. "I know only that you have raped my baby daughter and have forever soiled her reputation."

"Hey look, if you want, I'll marry the bitch."

The man froze, his eyes wide. "You will?"

"Hell, yeah, if you'll keep your shirt on."

The man looked skeptical. "What sort of dowry will you demand?"

"Make it easy on yourself. Nothing, if you want. Or her hope chest, what do I care?"

"Done. You have my blessing."

Three events happened then, almost but not quite simultaneously.

One: Snowclaw's voice came out of thin air.

"Gene! I'm coming, pal!"

Two: a short, chubby young woman in a blue hooped gown and décolletage came bursting through the double doors in the left wall of the outer room. Following close behind was a thin, dissolute young man dressed in lavender pantaloons, hose, and white puffed-sleeve blouse. At the sight of Gene, an outraged father, and the unexplained hole in the drawing room wall, his pale eyebrows rose. He lifted a monocle.

"How very interesting," he said.

"Father!" the girl shouted indignantly, her multiple chins quivering. "What on earth are you doing here?"

Turning, the man said, "Corabella?" Then he saw the count and drew a sharp breath. "You!"

Three: Snowy materialized in a dead run and slammed into Corabella's father, sending him cartwheeling across the room.

Snowy was a little disoriented. "Hi, Gene," he said. "Hey, I really did it!"

Corabella screamed. On Gene's side of the portal the walls turned milky and began to waver.

"Snowy, quick!" Gene reached across and tugged at a handful of Snowclaw's fur. Snowy got the idea and leaped across the boundary.

Darkness.

"Snowy?"

"Yeah, I'm here. Where are we?"

"The portal shut, and this room's a dead end. Jesus, that was another close one."

"You're probably going to ask me where the hell I came from."

"Well, now that you mention it," Gene said.

"I was in that cage right up until a few seconds ago, and now I'm here. Just before that happened, I could see you. I wanted to help you, and suddenly I was here, helping you."

"Congratulations! You got your magic power. Teleportation!"

"No kidding? Hey, that makes me a real magician, don't it?"

"It sure does, big fella. Now, if we can get out of this hole."

As if on cue, an oblong of light materialized to the left—an opening, leading into familiar castle architecture.

"Here we go," Snowclaw said. "By the way, what was that scene all about? Looked like fun."

"Seventeenth century Italy, maybe, but nobody's ever said anything about time travel, so it must've been some goofy variant. I don't know. We gotta find Linda."

"I think I can do just that," Snowclaw said.

# Donjon, Then Chapel

Jacoby stopped to examine a few of the curious torture devices that filled the room. He had known immediately what they were, though he was not certain how most of them worked or what torments they were designed to inflict. Some of them looked positively diabolical in intent. Looking them over, he felt a curious ambivalence—an amalgam of dismay and approval. These were but tools in the ungloved fist of power. There was no mercy in this room, only the certainty of punishment for trespasses against the ruling order. There was no compromise, and no escape.

He strode through a block of cells. The straw in them looked fresh, and he wondered when the facility had last housed prisoners. Everything looked perfectly functional, ready for use. But that was no different from the usual state of things here; he had never seen anything in the entire castle that looked worn-out or dilapidated, even though the place was reputed to be thousands of years old.

He left the donjon and searched for stairs. He had had his fill of the cellar. Besides, he needed food. He regretted losing Linda. No one had seen the cook for the last few days, but the Guests' dining room had been laid out with enough nonperishable items to last for weeks. If he could get up there—

The floor began to shake, and the stone walls shimmered. Jacoby dived to the floor, buried his head in his arms and rode out the disturbance.

When he thought it safe, he climbed to his feet and looked about. The tremors seemed a little less intense in this area of the castle, thank heaven for that. He was in a large high-ceiling chamber. It was dark, and he had to squint to pick out some detail in the far wall. He saw what looked like enormous cast-iron doors, similar to those on great cathedrals. He walked toward them.

Suddenly, a thin bright vertical line of light appeared between the doors and began to widen. Slowly, ponderously, the enormous entrance swung open, revealing an interior flashing with yellow-orange light.

"COME FORWARD!"

Jacoby's heart froze. It was the loudest, most terrifying voice he had ever heard. Stiffly, he turned and started running, but there was nothing but darkness back where he'd come from. He stopped and slowly turned to face the hellish light.

"WE BID YOU ENTER. OBEY NOW, OR INCUR OUR UNSPEAKABLE WRATH."

Jacoby tottered forward. The color drained from his face, and beads of cold sweat formed on his forehead like condensation on a pitcher of ice water.

He passed through the huge iron doors into a vast cathedral. Looking toward its farthest end, he beheld what had summoned him. He sank to his knees and averted his eyes.

"WE ACKNOWLEDGE YOUR OBEISANCE. ARISE, SERVANT, AND BE INFORMED OF A BUSINESS OF GREAT MOMENT."

Jacoby got up on shaky legs. He could not bring himself to look directly at the beatific visage behind the plumes of smoke and the tongues of fire.

"KNOW THAT SOON, VERY SOON, THIS HOUSE SHALL FALL. IT WILL VANISH, AND WITH IT ALL WHO DWELL WITHIN. TELL US NOW WHY THIS

FATE SHOULD NOT BEFALL SUCH A ONE AS YOU."

Jacoby nearly swallowed his tongue before he could get out, "Oh, Great One . . . if there were any way that I might be spared—"

"THERE IS. YOU WILL BE CHARGED WITH A TASK. UPON ITS COMPLETION YOUR WORTHINESS WILL BE JUDGED ACCORDINGLY."

Jacoby's eyes were desperate. "Anything, Great One! Anything!"

"YOUR WILLINGNESS PLEASES US. DO YOU STILL BEAR THE FRAGMENT OF THE BRAIN OF RAMTHONODOX?"

Jacoby fumbled in his suit, finally bringing forth the crystal. "Here it is, Great One—I did not steal it! I swear. In fact, I took it from the thief himself! He—"

"THE MATTER IS OF NO GREAT IMPORT. WE ARE WILLING TO FORGIVE PAST TRANSGRESSIONS IN LIGHT OF SERVICES PERFORMED ON OUR BEHALF. ATTEND US. YOU WILL PROCEED AT ONCE TO THE NETHERMOST REGIONS OF THE CASTLE. YOUR FOOTSTEPS WILL BE GUIDED ALONG THE PROPER PATH. YOU WILL BE CONDUCTED AWAY FROM THIS HOUSE TO A PLACE OF SAFETY. THERE YOU WILL AWAIT OUR PLEASURE. YOU MUST HENCEFORTH GUARD THE FRAGMENT WITH YOUR LIFE, OR YOUR DOOM IS SEALED. SPEAK NOW, AND TELL US YEA OR NAY."

"Yea!" Jacoby squeaked. "Oh, yes! I shall be infused with holy purpose! Nothing shall divert me, O Great One! Even if—"

"ENOUGH. BEHOLD."

The glossy floor quaked, heaved, then shattered, a huge crack appearing and widening rapidly. Smoke and occasional bursts of flame issued from the jagged chasm that soon gaped wide.

Jacoby fell on his buttocks. "Good *Lord!*" And then, muttering bitterly, "This is absurd!"

"ARISE," the voice commanded. "COME FORWARD."

He got up and moved reluctantly to the edge of the pit. A rough stone stairway descended into it.

"YOUR JOURNEY MAY BEGIN. THE WAY WILL BE MADE CLEAR, AND YOU WILL BE UNDER OUR PROTECTION AT EVERY STEP. DISCHARGE THIS OBLIGATION, AND YOU WILL FIGURE HIGH IN THE NEW ORDER."

"New order?" Jacoby said.

"THIS HOUSE SHALL BE BUILT AGAIN, AND ONE WHO IS OUR SERVANT SHALL BE ITS MASTER. PERFORM THIS TASK WHICH WE HAVE GIVEN YOU, AND BE CHIEF AMONG OUR SERVANTS."

"I shall perform it," Jacoby said firmly.

"GOOD. THEN GO."

"But who—"

"WE HAVE COMMANDED YOU . . . *GO!*"

"Yes, Holy One!"

Stumbling, slipping and muttering all the way, Jacoby disappeared into the earth.

When he was gone, the voice laughed.

# Lower Levels

Linda hugged the floor until the tremors passed, then got up and started walking again. An enormous blue flying insect buzzed by. She ducked, and the thing went sailing over her head—then transformed itself into an umber bird and continued down the tunnel. Crawling things skittered across the floor. To her own surprise, Linda had ceased jumping at their every appearance. She *hated* bugs, but she was rapidly getting used to far worse.

There seemed no end to this maze, and she was near despair.

No, she told herself. You're not giving up. You'll find Gene and we'll get out of this place. Believe it.

She believed it. For the first time in her life she actually believed she could do something, that she could be a cause and not just an effect.

A section of the right wall slid back, revealing the end of a large pipe. Her reflexes well-sharpened by now, Linda was quick to step back. As she did, there came the sound not unlike a commode flushing. Water spurted from the pipe, and then a man came sliding out and tumbled to the floor.

Linda held her nose.

Osmirik groaned and massaged the base of his spine. "Mother Goddess!"

"Are you hurt?" Linda asked him.

He was startled at first, but when he saw Linda, he broke into a smile. "Greetings," he said. "Be you human, or only a fair approximation?"

"All too human, I'm afraid," Linda said. "Can I help you?"

"I am undamaged . . . methinks." Osmirik struggled to his feet, wincing.

"Oh! Are you sure you're all right?"

"You are too kind, fair lady. No, I am sound enough."

"However did you get yourself into the plumbing?"

"It is a convoluted tale. I fell in, then was plucked out, but I had to throw myself back in, so to speak, in order to get out again."

Linda nodded, shrugging. "Makes sense."

"Very little, I'm afraid. I'm at my wit's end. I seek a certain person who may be about this part of the castle."

"Oh. Let me ask you a personal question. Are you out to help this person?"

Osmirik gave her an odd look. "In truth, no. Why do you ask?"

"This is just a wild guess, but is this person a tall, skinny redhead with well-developed magical powers and about half-a-dozen soldiers for bodyguards?"

Osmirik was taken aback. "You have seen her?"

"Oh, we've met."

Osmirik grasped Linda's arm. "Where?" Linda flinched away, and he let go. "Forgive me. I am not wont to manhandle a lady. I am sore distressed. I must find this woman. She is a danger to us all."

"You're telling me. She nearly killed me and my friends."

"That is danger enough, but she threatens the existence of many more. Where did you see her?"

"That's the problem. We escaped from the room where the Brain is, and then we—"

"The Brain? Of Ramthonodox?"

"Yes." Linda explained.

After listening, Osmirik nodded. "So the Stone and the Brain are together, the one holding the other in suspension, the other feeding its power into the containing spell."

"Huh? Well, they're related, if that's what you mean. Just what is Super-Bitch up to?"

"I beg your pardon?"

"The woman. Your friend."

"She is hardly my friend. She is my liege lady and mistress."

"Mistress? Oh, you mean you're her servant."

"That is so. You were saying that you escaped from the room wherein the Brain resides."

"Yeah, but now we're lost again."

"'We'?"

"Well, yeah, my friends, but as you can see, we got separated."

"Hey, Linda!" came Snowclaw's voice.

Linda whirled, searching. "Snowy! Where are you?"

"Hold on!"

A moment later Snowclaw materialized in the corridor. He flashed a toothy grin. "Hey, how about that? Neat trick, huh?"

"Fabulous! You got your talent!"

"Ain't it something? By the way, I found Gene."

Linda jumped up and hugged him. "You wonderful guy! Where is he?"

"Well, it's kind of hard to explain, but I just left him to get to you. I can jump right back, but I don't exactly know where he is in relation to here—if you know what I mean." He put Linda down and sniffed, looking around. "Hey, who did doo-doo all over the floor?"

"Never mind. Let's find Gene."

"That's gonna take some doing."

"You say you don't know where he is, but you can get there by doing your disappearing act?"

"Yeah."

"Why don't you jump back to Gene and tell him to start yelling. We'll do it too."

"Right." Snowy poked a milky claw at Osmirik. "Who's this dude?"

"This is—I'm sorry, I didn't get your name."

"Osmirik, scribe to the House of Gan."

"He's on our side, Snowy. Nice to meet you, Os . . ."

"Osmirik."

"Sorry. I'm Linda Barclay, and this is Snowclaw. Very pleased to meet you, Osmirik."

"The honor is mine, Mistress Linda Barclay, and . . . Snowclaw." Osmirik bowed deeply.

"Okay," Snowclaw said. "I'll jump back." He closed his eyes briefly, turned his body slightly to the right, took two steps and vanished.

"Wow," Linda said admiringly. "Neat."

"I believe I can find your friend," Osmirik said.

"You can?"

"We all have our talents, do we not? I seem to have been endowed with certain olfactory gifts ordinarily reserved for dumb beasts."

"Olfactory? You mean you can smell Gene from here?"

"No, but the creature who just left us has a most unusual odor. He is in that direction." Osmirik pointed to his right.

"Speaking of unusual odors . . ."

After Osmirik had bathed in the travertine tub Linda had thoughtfully conjured, he rubbed himself down, put on the clean tunic and tights she had also conjured, then stepped out from the partition.

"I hope I do not catch my death of ague. I was taught that it is not advisable to immerse one's body."

"It's not only advisable, it's desirable. And fun."

"Especially with another person," Gene said.

Linda spun around. Gene had his arms wrapped around Snowclaw. "Hey, it worked, Snowy."

"Whattaya know," Snowclaw said. "I don't know how, though."

"Apparently you have a teleportation field around

you," Gene said. "On second thought, why wouldn't a chunk of the floor go with you too?" He shook his head. "No, it's magic. You just have the ability to teleport things, including your own body." He looked toward Osmirik. "Hi, there."

Osmirik bowed.

# Deepest Levels

The caverns were deep and dark. Jacoby was fearful, but he trusted the voice. No harm would befall him as long as he persevered in his sacred mission. He passed through chamber after chamber, a strange radiance lighting his way, moving with him. As far as he could tell, the light had no source. It simply illuminated the area about him within a ten-foot radius. The caves themselves were visible by virtue of an innate luminescence in the rock.

The strange light knew the way. Jacoby followed it.

He passed a pool of dark, smoking liquid, a large bubble erupting on its viscous surface. The bubble broke, splattering, and steam vented from the hole that had formed until the black substance seeped back to close it off.

He entered a narrow crypt, dark recesses cut into its walls. From them came rustling sounds, clicking sounds. A pair of red eyes regarded from a shadowy niche as he hurried through.

All around him was a sense of presence, of discreet movement, of waiting and watching. But nothing challenged him, no one bothered him.

Something multilegged with a pointed snout came

scampering out of an intersecting tunnel. It saw Jacoby and stopped so abruptly that it nearly went tumbling. It did a hasty about-face and scuttled back into darkness.

Jacoby breathed again and put a hand over his thumping heart. "Good God," he said quietly. He filled his lungs, exhaled, and moved on.

He came to an open area where a water-carved rock bridge arched over a deep chasm, at the bottom of which lay a phosphorescent yellow lakelet, concentric ripples crossing and recrossing its oily surface. Silence here, save for the echoing plop of dripping water. He crossed the span, not daring to get close enough to the edge to look over. On the other side the light led him to the left along a narrow ledge, and then into a short tunnel. He emerged into another enormous room. This one was many-leveled, with galleries high up in the walls. The way led across the main floor, winding among weird rock formations. The moving light made the twisted forms around him writhe with life. Malformed faces silently howled at him, bony hands reached out.

Jacoby was out of shape, and out of breath. "Please," he said to anyone who would hear. "I must stop . . . I must rest. Just for a moment."

The moving pool of light stopped.

"Thank you, Holy One, thank you." He chose a flat stone ledge and seated himself. He rested for two minutes, trying to control his breathing. Then he got up and pushed on. Toward the end of the chamber he encountered a wide pit and had to walk around it. As he did so, he looked in. Foul-smelling currents of air washed over him. At the bottom lay an odd configuration of tissuelike material, and he was nearly past it when he realized what it was: a huge mouth, black inhuman lips parted to reveal the ragged stumps of mottled, yellow teeth. Jacoby gave a yell and dashed away. A rumbling, snarling sound came from deep within the cavity.

Another tunnel brought him into a vast open area through which an underground river flowed, its dark waters silent, deep, and inexorably moving. A little way upstream a stone pier jutted out from shore. Jacoby walked to its end and stood, listening. Silence, except for the faint suck and gurgle of shore-lapping water. Before him the river extended to outer darkness. He could not see the other side.

He let out a long, eschatological sigh. Choosing one of the cylindrical stone mooring posts, he sat down and awaited Charon's boat.

# Lower Levels

Gene shook his head after hearing Osmirik's story. "So she means to loose the dragon and rule the world."

"That is her mad plan, yes. But it is doomed to failure, and she well knows it."

"Then what's her motive, besides madness?"

"Love."

"Love?"

"And hate, its demon twin. Long ago she and Incarnadine were betrothed. He spurned her, returned her dowry, and paid breach-of-promise gold to her father. She has never forgotten the shame, nor has she forgiven Incarnadine."

"And for that she'd destroy the world?"

"Years ago she would not have. She was a beautiful young woman, in love with life. But after her humiliation, she took to studying the Recondite Arts. Today she is still beautiful—"

"But skinny, and her bust is nothing to write home about," Linda said.

"I don't think they use brassieres in this culture," Gene said.

"—but her heart is a fist of stone, and she is possessed

by madness. Therein lies the danger. She is, mayhap, the most powerful magician in the world."

"Better than Incarnadine?" Gene asked.

"That may be."

Gene shifted his weight on the plain stone bench they had found. The alcove it stood in was quiet, an island in the eye of the storm. Outside, strange forms moved in the air. "Things are getting increasingly crazy out there."

Osmirik said, "Yes, and at some point every step will be taken at peril of one's life. We had best act before that point is reached."

"We need a plan," Gene said.

"First we have to find the Hall of the Brain," Linda said. "We've tried everything, even cutting through walls, but nothing seems to get us there."

"Let's teleport there," Gene said. "We can all hang on to Snowy—"

"Will that work?" Linda said.

"Only one way to find out," Snowclaw said.

"Okay. When we get there, then what?"

Gene shrugged. "We take 'em. I mean, there's only one soldier left, and a couple of servants."

"And the most powerful magician in the world," Linda said. "This world, anyway."

"Yeah. We've got no choice."

Linda nodded grimly. "I know."

They discussed strategy awhile, then fell silent. Each made his preparations.

"Methinks . . ." Osmirik began.

"What is it, Osmirik?" Gene said.

"Melydia has always resented her womanhood. Hers is a spirit that cannot be contained within the cramped boundaries of a woman's station. That men and men alone rule the world is to her an intolerable injustice. In order to right this wrong, she has devoted her life to the accumulation of brute power. In that, I think, lies her gravest error."

Gene looked at Linda. "Who says this world is so different from ours?"

# High Above The Plains Of Baranthe

He sprawled on his stomach and looked over the edge of the Oriental carpet. Far below, at the foot of the castle's citadel, the tents and shelters of the besieging army lay grouped in clots and bunches. Along the perimeter lay corrals and animal pens, supply tents, and other makeshift shelters. The encampment looked like a dirty patchwork cloth spread over the plain.

He turned over on his back and watched the sky. Clouds like obese sheep grazed in a field of blue. He let his eyes dwell on the blueness awhile.

At length he sat up and took in the world around him. The castle sat like a magistrate high on his bench, presiding over and delivering judgments to the plains and mountains. He surveyed its curtain walls and black towers, its high parapets braced against the wind. It had been his home for over three hundred years. This might be the last time his eyes beheld it.

He performed a short series of finger movements. The airborne throw rug on which he rode began its descent, banking in a wide turn back toward the castle. He felt no movement of the air, no wind, yet the carpet's velocity with respect to the ground was considerable.

An impish look came to his eyes. "Might as well have some fun," he said. "While I can," he added.

His fingers worked fast—the pattern was extensive and complex. When it was completed, the transmogrification took effect instantaneously.

He no longer sat on a flying carpet but in the cockpit of a high-tech jet fighter. Pushing the stick forward on a diagonal, he put the plane into a steep banking dive, heading for the enemy encampment. The needle of the machometer crept upwards and the airflow howled over the clear canopy. At a thousand feet he pulled out of the dive at four G's. The enemy camp flashed past. He kicked in afterburners, yanked the stick back and stood the jet on its tail, sending it hurtling into the ethereal blue. The needle edged past Mach One.

"That should give them pause—or a case of the shits," he said, chuckling.

With a pathetic whine the engine suddenly flamed out. Indicators fell off, and then the instrument panel went dark. He waited a few seconds for the speed to lessen, then worked his fingers quickly.

The plane now became a propeller-driven, single-engine fighter, specifically a Focke-Wulf 190 A-4, armed with two 7.92mm machine guns and four 20mm cannon, and having an operational range of 592 miles. Unfortunately, as in the case of the jet, mechanical contrivances did not work well in this world, and the antique warplane would probably not even make it back to the castle. He made a mental note to do more intensive research into the question of exactly why machines of any complexity, even magical ones, could not function here for any length of time beyond a few minutes. As he had been working on the problem off and on for over a century, he had little hope of immediate success, but he was determined to get to the bottom of it. Someday.

Or perhaps not. Perhaps he liked this world the way it was.

Banking steeply, he headed back toward the citadel. He briefly considered making a strafing run over the camp, but decided against it. It would not be sporting, and the fate of Vorn's men was sealed whether or not his plan was successful.

As he neared the castle, the engine sputtered and gave out. He dead-sticked in a little closer, then spelled the antiquated airplane away and replaced it with the carpet.

The roof of the keep came up, and he landed. Stepping off the carpet, he stooped and rolled it up. He tucked it under his arm and walked to a small building into which was set a pair of doors. He pressed the button on a panel next to them. The doors rolled apart, revealing an open shaft.

It was time for the final and inevitable confrontation.

"Basement," he said, jumping off into darkness.

# UNDERWORLD

SOMETHING BROUGHT JACOBY out of his meditation. He looked out over the river. A boat was approaching.

"Come, Charon," he said, "and ferry me across."

The long boat moved rapidly, yet no one was rowing. Standing at the stern and manning the tiller was a strange being, a black figure, immense and powerfully muscled, humanlike but not quite human, with red eyes that glowed like embers in a face like a bull's. The boatman deftly guided the craft into shore and brought it abreast of the pier, whereupon he moved to the bow and threw a loop-ended line over a mooring post. With a sinewy black arm he beckoned Jacoby to come aboard.

The fat man stepped down into the launch, made his way amidships and chose one of a number of wooden boards slung gunwale to gunwale. There were seats for perhaps two dozen souls. The boatman cast off and moved to the stern, taking his station at the tiller.

The journey downstream was uneventful. The boatman said nothing, and neither did Jacoby. Propelled by unseen forces, the boat parted the water gently with its blunt prow, leaving a wake of undulating ripples. The black waters of the river flowed quietly, inexorably. An occasional prismatic oil slick drifted by, faintly aglow in the passing light. The rest was darkness and quiet.

It could have been hours, it could have been days, or only a few minutes. Jacoby's sense of time had been left in the mortal world above. Eventually the boatman steered for the far shore and put in, docking at another stone wharf.

Jacoby disembarked, walked to the end of the pier and looked about. "What, no Cerberus at the gate? No Virgil to guide my way?"

The ebony boatman raised a thick arm and pointed to a flight of steps rising from the riverbank. He spoke in a voice as deep and as slow as the black waters he plied: "Go forth from this place. Go up into the light of day. Do not return."

"I shan't, you needn't worry."

Jacoby climbed the steps, which eventually led into a passage that cut through the rock, bearing ever upward.

# Hall Of The Brain—And Elsewhere

"Ready, Linda?"

Perched on Snowclaw's mighty shoulders, Linda tucked her feet more tightly under his arms. "Yep," she said. "Climb on, guys."

Gene jumped up and locked his legs around the arctic beast's middle, couldn't hold on, and fell off.

"Let's make this simple," Snowclaw said, grabbing him and lifting him up with one arm. He gathered in Osmirik with the other and hoisted the scribe up.

The four now looked like an odd circus act.

"Jesus, Snowy," Gene said. "You sure you can hold us?"

"This ain't gonna take but a second."

"You got a fix on the Brain room?"

"Yup. I been there, so I know where it is, so to speak."

"Okay."

"Ready?" Snowclaw asked.

Gene said, "We all know what to do, right?"

Nods all around, except for Snowclaw, who couldn't.

"Okay, gang," Snowclaw said, "here goes."

And suddenly they were there.

Gene jumped off Snowy, drew his sword and sized up

the situation. It was just as Snowclaw had described it. There was one soldier and five servants. No, only four. Then Gene saw the young boy lying down in front of the kneeling Melydia. White, blood-daubed bandages were wrapped around both his wrists. Melydia was undoing one of them.

The soldier spun around. "Your Ladyship!"

Melydia turned her head. She did not seem in the least surprised.

"Okay, Super-Bitch," Gene said, stepping down the last stone terrace onto the circular floor. "The game's over. Stop what you're doing."

Sword drawn, the soldier stood his ground. His eyes were fixed fearfully on Snowclaw, who was rushing toward the cage. Nearby the battle-ax lay where Snowy had dropped it.

"Let me handle him, Snowy," Gene called.

The servants, all of them unarmed, had jumped to their feet and were warily retreating in Melydia's direction. Then, suddenly, all halted to stare in wonder at the swords and shields that had materialized in their hands.

"On second thought, Snowy old buddy, old pal . . ."

"I got 'em, Gene," Snowy said as he rushed by with broadax raised.

"Fight!" Melydia shouted. "Protect your mistress!" The servants glanced nervously at her, then advanced.

Gene found that his left arm was looped through the handles of a heavy shield. "Thanks, Linda," he said over his shoulder.

The soldier charged him.

The fight was quick. Osmirik, armed by Linda, took on one servant while Snowclaw battled three. Osmirik's opponent held his own against the scribe, but the three were no match for Snowclaw. He made quick work of them, then came to Osmirik's aide and dispatched the remaining servant. By that time Gene's expert swordsmanship had backed his adversary almost to the base of the black rock. The soldier desperately fought off Gene's blows, his eyes fearful and wondering. He knew it was only a matter of time.

Gene slashed crosswise, putting another dent in his opponent's shield, then feinted a thrust under the shield, which the soldier lowered a bit too much, laying himself open to Gene's quick thrust to the shoulder of his sword arm. The point penetrated, and the soldier yelled and dropped his sword. Gene hacked at the shield, knocking it away, and his next blow laid open the soldier's throat. Gene stepped back and watched him fall.

Gene took a slow, deep breath. He had never killed a man before.

Melydia seemed unconcerned by all this. She was still busy tracing designs in the air, muttering, making other strange movements. The boy lay dead at her feet. The brazier into which she'd poured the last of his blood still smoked.

Gene ran toward her. "Stop what you're doing!"

She did not even look at him. Her hand went out, made a movement.

"Gene!"

Gene turned at Linda's yell. She was pointing behind him. Gene whirled and saw the soldier getting up and retrieving his sword and shield.

"What?"

Snowclaw growled. The servants were also rising from the dead, zombies now, whey-faced and gaunt-eyed.

Melydia made another hand movement.

Gene swiveled his gaze back and forth. He couldn't believe it. Now there were eight servants and three soldiers.

The next phase of the fight was complex, and grew increasingly strange. Gene held his own against three opponents, but at some point he looked around and saw that there were other people in the room. Not exactly other people—duplicates of himself. And duplicates of Snowclaw, fighting other doppelgangers of the soldier and Melydia's servants. There were even duplicates of Osmirik.

He fought on. Presently he grew aware that the room had become increasingly bright. The light seemed to be coming from the jewel, but he couldn't afford to look up.

He stumbled over a body and fell, then rolled and jumped to his feet again. He looked down. It was himself, one of his magical twins, with a bloodied shirt front and an oozing slash across the forehead. Other fallen duplicates of himself lay about. But that wasn't the worst of it. New combatants had appeared, and these weren't human. A yellow-skinned, green-eyed, scaly being attacked him with mace and chain. Gene blocked, slashed, blocked, and thrust, making short work of it, but another variant of the same creature, this one green of scale and yellow of eye, took up the fight. He dispatched it, then whirled to find two horned goatlike creatures advancing on him, one with an ax, the other with a halberd.

Linda continued her slow advance toward Melydia. It was like walking through a swamp, like mud sucking at her feet. The melee went on around her. She had matched every duplicate that Melydia had conjured, every magical creature, and now that part of the contest was over. This duel was really between Melydia and her.

Brilliant amber light from the jewel flooded the chamber. The floor vibrated, and then began to heave.

Linda felt her powers grow. No longer were they limited to materialization tricks. She felt energy flowing from the jewel, and at the same time sensed a waning of the restraining force exerted by the rock. Power coursed through her, but it was all she could do to keep moving forward. Intense waves of force emanated from Melydia. Linda knew that the witch's power, too, was growing.

A wind—not moving air but currents of force—rose up and tore at her. Above, the jewel glowed and pulsed, pumping more energy into the whirlpool. A swirling vortex of energy formed as the fighting continued. Linda held her ground. She was about five yards away from Melydia, who still faced the rock, performing ritual movements and speeches. The closer Linda got, the more resistance she felt. She tensed her muscles, leaned forward as if bracing against gale-force winds. She inched forward, fighting a battle for every step. If only the floor would stop shaking, she thought. But it shook all the more. She knew what she would do if she reached Melydia. She would strangle the horrible woman with her own hands. The thought didn't upset her in the least. She could feel the woman's evil. It was the most loathsome sensation she had ever experienced. Somehow Melydia's mind was in contact with hers—not directly, but they were tapping the same source of power. It was as if they shared an electrical outlet. Even that limited proximity produced in Linda a profound revulsion. The woman's mind was a cesspool of hate, jealousy, contempt, fear—every negative emotion inflated to astonishing proportions, and the sum of it amounted to nothing less than hatred of life itself.

She struggled forward. About three yards now. The face of the boy at Melydia's feet was dead white.

Melydia began the last incantation. It was the most subtle and difficult of all. One missed syllable, one slip, one flub, and she would have to go back to the Lesser Invocation and begin again. She knew she wouldn't have time for that. She could handle the distractions going on around her for only so long. But she still had a little time, just enough. She began.

At the end of the second statement, the Anticlastic Argument, a hand movement was called for. She executed it, and went on. The third statement, the Synclastic, demanded a rigid body posture, measured breathing, and as little eye movement as possible. She enunciated it perfectly and went on to the next set of Arguments, which she completed flawlessly.

She took a deep breath, assessed the increasingly violent situation in the chamber—then began the group of statements leading up to the Concluding Argument, the last word of which was the Dodecagrammaton, the word that would trip the spell and liberate a force the world had not seen in three thousand years.

She began. Her lips moved, the words barely audible. Then . . . after years of planning and scheming, one word remained.

She felt a warm hand on her neck.

She declaimed the Dodecagrammaton, rapidly, confidently, forcefully, every syllable rolling perfectly off her tongue, every phoneme sharp and crisp, twelve sounds like hammer blows driving the last nail into the coffin of a world she despised, hated with every fiber of her being.

Hands snaked around her neck. She whirled and looked the girl in the eye.

"You are talented, my dear," she said. "And very brave. But you are too late."

An eddy of force carried the girl away from Melydia and into the whirlwind.

Gene thought: *Things are getting out of hand.*

He was floating high in the chamber, caught up in a terrific cyclone of multicolored streamers of fire. Snowy floated by—or maybe it was one of his doubles. But then, how were you supposed to tell the real one? He wondered if he himself were the real Gene or just a conjure-twin.

Another of those horrible things wafted by, and he took a swipe at it with his sword, which he had stubbornly hung onto. The creature snarled at him, then vanished in a puff of flame.

There was no sense of physical place now, no Hall of the Brain, no castle, only a swirling maelstrom of energy whose focal point seemed to be a bright starlike object somewhere off in the distance. Gene floated, then fell. There was no air, and he couldn't breath. Yet he could speak.

"I love you, Linda," he said.

Then there was nothing.

Through the smoke and the vapor and the nebulae of circulating fires there came a gap, a way, a protected lane. It clove the chaos in twain, and a figure walked it, purposefully, gracefully, without fear or hesitation, advancing toward the island of calm in the middle of the storm.

Melydia watched the figure grow into a man she knew.

"You have come," she said.

"Melydia," he said. "How good of you to visit me."

"It is my pleasure. You are too late, Incarnadine. Why have you held back?"

"Is that how it looks? My dear, I fought you with every means at my disposal. You are more powerful than I could ever hope to be."

"Yes, I am. Why did you not tap the deepest source of magic?"

"I would have had to do what you have done, Melydia. I did not want to make a pact with Evil itself."

"I did what I had to do."

"Do you hate me that much?"

Her scornful laughter held overtones of the cries of a tortured animal. "Is that why you think I did this? Because of you? You . . . you *weakling!* You dilettante! You were born to supreme power, and you did nothing but toy with it! Irrevocable power, ultimate might! You have spent not one lifetime, but several, throwing it away! Expending it on useless trivialities! You have withdrawn from the world. Castle Perilous should be the seat of world power, yet here it sits, an empty hulk, a legend without substance, a curiosity. But it will sit no more! Your house of uselessness is gone, or soon will be, and you can do nothing to stop its going. But I will build another to replace it. It will be fashioned from a transmogrified body—not that of a demon, but of a king. You will be my new castle, Lord of the Western Pale, and when men speak of Castle Incarnadine, it will be in hushed and fearful tones."

She fell silent. The smoke and fire swirled around her.

"When I rejected you," Incarnadine said, "it was not shame or humiliation you felt? Only regret that you would be denied residence in the citadel of absolute might?"

"I was a young girl. I suppose I suffered as any young girl would at the hands of a scoundrel. But that was long ago."

"Did I ever tell you why I broke our troth?"

"You may have. I do not remember."

"It was because I foresaw this day, Melydia. Not in detail, but in substance. Your madness was a seed then, but it had already sprouted. It was not I who planted it, Melydia."

"Enough of your lies. There is no more time for them, Incarnadine."

"Do you really think you can control Ramthonodox?"

"Yes. I know I can."

"You cannot. And the reason you cannot is something you never could have anticipated."

She was silent for a moment. Then: "More desperate lies."

"You could not have known, but you should have sensed it, Melydia. You are proficient, but not as subtle an adept as you might think. But your attention was on other things, was it not?"

"What should I have sensed?"

"That one of the demon's aspects is missing. It now has only 143,999. For demons, such a number is untenable."

Melydia's eyes widened. "How do you know this?"

"I may be a dilettante, but I know a thing or two about demons. I happen to live inside one. Aspects are very important to demons. It is very difficult to explain, but supernatural beings have structure to them, just as do mortal creatures. Did you know that? Not flesh and bone, not blood and sinew, but parts and pieces and bits and things. Things difficult to understand. But with a little study, some light may be shed on them."

"I know something of them—" She broke off and raised her eyes. "The moment is come. The process of detransmogrification is almost complete."

"I hope your protection spells are sufficiently efficacious."

"I hope the same for you. Although they will not be sufficient to protect you from me. Later."

"Thank you for the warning." Incarnadine looked about. "I sense someone nearby who is not a Guest, one who has not entered the castle by dint of magic."

Melydia searched off to one side. "Osmirik, perhaps. My scribe."

"He is still alive. I will have to extend my influence to protect him."

"Look to your own safety, Incarnadine."

"I always do, Melydia. But I'm bound to see to the welfare of my Guests. You did not consider what would happen to them, did you?"

"I do not care."

"Of course not. But did you know that detransmogrification entails some spatiotemporal effects?"

"I am not familiar with your terminology."

"You really should study some natural philosophy. Magic is only one way of looking at the universe. At any rate, my Guests will not die, but they will be swept back along their individual time lines to a point just prior to their entering the castle. At least that is my best guess as to what will happen."

"Time, say you? Time has run out, Incarnadine."

The smoke and the vapor and the traceries of fire were swept away by an explosion of white light.

# On The Plains Of Baranthe

Shouts roused him from sleep and brought him out of his tent. He strode out from under the sun screen, looked up at the citadel, and was awed. Dark clouds lay piled like mountains above the castle. The castle itself glowed like an ember, and great flaming prominences rose from it: sheets of pink flame, wreaths of incandescence, starbursts of fire. Forked lightning shot from clouds to castle.

A strong wind rose, and Vorn closed his cloak about him. He watched. Pointing, gesticulating, nervously shouting, his men watched with him.

The castle changed color, turning to orange, then to yellow. Glowing streamers unfurled from it, and white smoke rose. Its hue shaded to a lighter yellow, a sun-yellow, then to yellow-white, pure white, then to searing blue-white. It grew unbearable to look at.

Vorn watched for as long as he could, then averted his eyes. There was a brilliant, actinic flash. When he could, Vorn looked again. A white ring of vapor was expanding at astonishing speed from the epicenter of the explosion. But the epicenter itself—that he could make no sense of, at first. It was something huge and dark. It was not smoke or fire, but a shape, a thing.

Then the thing unfurled its wings and darkened the world beneath. Its head reared up, and its eyes were like windows to Hell. Its great taloned feet splayed out, eager to pounce, to tear, to crush.

Vorn found himself screaming. He wanted to run but he could not. The face of the beast stopped his heart, its eyes pierced him to the soul. Shouts, shrieks, curses, appeals to deities rose up from the troops. Some began running. Most, like Vorn, were transfixed.

The ring of vapor reached them with the sound of thunder, much like that produced by the flying ship that had sailed overhead a while ago. A blast of air hit, and tents blew down.

The titanic beast was on the wing, coming this way. Its faceted eyes searched the ground, its horrid mouth opened, and a cataract of fire spilled forth.

Vorn's mind slowly formed dim thoughts. He had been bewitched . . . she had been lying . . . he was dead, as were all his dreams of empire.

So be it. He dropped his cloak and drew his sword. He was still Vorn, Prince and Conqueror. He raised his head. The beast blotted out the sky with its vast obscene bulk. Vorn beheld, but could not grasp it. No human mind could apperceive its structure, or figure its lineaments, or live to tell of the horror of its ugliness, its loathsomeness, its frightfulness. . . .

His last thought was of how angry his mother would be with him for acting so foolishly.

*It was good to destroy once again. The world below had much need of cleansing. Flecks of corruption moved across its surface. It had been long. How long? It did not matter.*

*The demon now knew its name. It opened its mouth and spoke it.*

*"RAMTHONODOX!" The roar shattered the air, and raised dust on the ground.*

*It opened its mouth again and vomited fire, cleansing fire. It spilled forth its fury, giving vent to all its hatred of earthly things. Sheets of flame spread, covering the plain. From below came pitiable cries and exclamations, and the sounds gladdened it to the core of its being. All below was consumed.*

*Spent at last, it rose on great wings and sought the cold skies.*

# Atop The Citadel, And At Its Base

They faced each other across a bleak plateau. The castle was gone, nothing but bare earth remained.

"It is done," she said. "You were right. I cannot control the beast."

"You have unleashed an ancient evil. Have you no regrets?"

She was silent, staring at the ground. Then she said, "I do not know. Now that I have accomplished my purpose, I feel strangely empty."

"Your madness has run its course. The maggot has eaten its way out of you."

"And left a shell? Perhaps. I cannot fathom why I feel this way."

"You have loosed the beast to destroy the world, as you wanted to."

"Could I have wanted that? I wanted to rule the world."

"The desire to rule, to dictate, is born of nothing but contempt."

"You may be right. It is so strange. I feel nothing. Nothing whatever. I am weak. I have used all the power I had within me."

"And it was considerable. But you will not get your wish. The world will not die, neither will you. Neither shall the beast be loosed."

"How will all this be prevented?"

"By magic, of course. I will use the same spell that trapped the beast three thousand years ago."

She shook her head. "You cannot do it. The stars are not right. The beast is now forewarned. You will not be able to lure it down again from its home in the skies. It will descend only to destroy."

"The missing aspect will offset those unfavorable conditions. The beast cannot exist in its incomplete state. It will return of its own accord and will bargain with me. It will see that there is only one course open to it."

"So you hope."

"I know, Melydia. One thing—I will need your help. I will need protection." He pointed to the still form of the scribe at his feet. "So will your servant."

"I will do this thing. Methinks you have bespelled me."

"I have. Your madness is gone. Forgive me, it was a precaution."

"I only wish you could have done it earlier."

"That was not possible, as you well know."

"Of course," she said. "Only now am I vulnerable . . . so to speak."

"Enough. May we begin?"

"You need no accouterments? No paraphernalia?"

"None. The spell is purely mental in execution."

She pointed to the sky. "Behold, the beast rises."

"It will return soon, if all goes according to plan."

The tunnel had been dark, lit only by the strange glow that had stayed with him through the underworld. The aura of his sainthood? But he saw light ahead, daylight. He smelled the outdoors. It was strange, because he hadn't smelled it for so long. A cool breeze came to him.

He rounded a bend and saw the mouth of the cave a short distance ahead. He hurried, wondering what would be waiting for him out there.

He came out into bright day. He walked out from the

base of the cliff and looked up. He was at the foot of the castle's citadel. He could not see the castle, which he found strange. Perhaps if he got out a little farther.

The plain was bare, empty, nothing but dried grass and rock.

Wait! Wasn't the camp of the besiegers out here somewhere? Perhaps on the other side of the promontory. No, he was sure it was this side.

He lifted his eyes heavenward. "Speak, O Great Holy Voice! Speak to thy servant!"

He searched the skies. There was something up there, circling, some great black shape. A bird? No. It was descending, growing bigger.

Presently he saw what it was. He did not completely understand what it was, but he knew the thing sought him, and he knew he had been betrayed.

His heart gave out before he reached the cave.

The beast spoke.

*You, again.*

"Yes."

*Like your fathers before you, you seek to enslave me.*

"You have no choice. Only I can make you whole again."

*Free me now from your thrall, and I shall heal myself.*

"You know you can't. The fragment is only a metaphor. You are nothing but metaphor."

*Yet I am real.*

"I wonder. Or are you merely our reflection?"

*I AM NO ONE'S REFLECTION! I AM RAMTHONODOX! I WILL EAT THE INTESTINES OF MY ENEMIES!*

"Enough of that nonsense. I offer you a proposition. You have no choice. Perhaps one day you will gain your freedom again. It is not impossible. You are immortal, are you not? One day Man, your enemy, will be gone, and the world will be yours once more."

*No, I fear the world will never again be mine. I will fade to nothingness. The earth will belong to the small, the insignificant.*

"Perhaps. But time will tell. And time you have aplenty."

*It was good to cleanse the world once again.*

"I'm glad you had fun. Now you must rest."

*I feel weak.*

"Of course. You will feel weaker."

*Help me.*

"I shall. Come closer."

The sky darkened as the huge form bore down. Parts of the beast became indistinct. Multicolored flashes broke out along its vast bulk. A strong wind suddenly rose, whipping dust about the citadel.

*I do not do this willingly.*

"Doubtless not. Be quiet."

Whirling clouds appeared, at their center a growing vortex of blackness.

*I could crush you.* A gargantuan foot hovered above.

"You would not last long in your present incomplete state. And you know it."

There was a sound not unlike a sigh, and very like a fierce gale.

*I suppose you are right.*

The clouds rotated faster, and the vortex grew.

*I feel myself becoming something other than myself.*

"This won't hurt a bit."

The world imploded into blackness.

He couldn't find a sign. Coming to the mouth of the ramp he had driven down, he looked up, saw it was a long way to walk, dangerous, too, and decided there must be a stairwell, better yet, an elevator around somewhere.

He searched in vain. He did find a featureless corridor which met another at a T. To his right the way was dark, so he turned left, turned again at an L, and found himself back in the sepulchral silence of the garage again. Sighing, he retraced his steps, passed the intersection of the first corridor and continued on into the darkness. Feeling his way, he went about thirty paces until he bumped into a wall. The passageway turned to the right, still unlighted, and continued interminably.

Another turn, and there was light up ahead.

He saw the dark stone masonry, the jewel-torch, and wondered where the hell he was. He stopped. Suddenly he couldn't bear the thought of facing another useless interview for a job he really didn't want. Why not face it? He was unemployable, at least as far as white-collar jobs went. So what was wrong with blue-collar occupations? This sudden impulse to drop back in, to "get a job and settle down," was just a response to pressure from his parents. Wasn't it? Knee-jerk bourgeois security-seeking.

Well, to hell with USX, and to hell with getting a "good job." He'd tend bar, open a bookstore, go to Europe . . . something. To hell with everything.

He looked down the hall at the strange discontinuity. He took a step forward. . . .

It was an ordinary California day, bright sun, blue sky, haze, smog, and Linda was tired of it.

She was tired of everything. She didn't think she could get through another day.

She had tried calling her sister, but Sharon was at a rehabilitation nurses' convention in Denver. Linda didn't feel like bothering her. She had always been able to talk to Sharon, but what exactly was the point now?

Still, she couldn't think of suicide. It would kill Mother, and she couldn't stomach the thought of lying there in the casket with all the old biddies in the family talking in whispers about her. And the gossip. *Did you hear about the Barclay girl? No, the younger one. Did you know what they're saying about how she died?*

Ugh.

Maybe she was just afraid of dying. She was afraid of everything else. Afraid of living. But she did have a death wish—wasn't that what the pills were all about? Maybe she should go back to popping pills. That way, death would come and she wouldn't have to act, to make a decision. . . .

She was disgusted with herself.

She got up from the bed and went to the closet. She really should get out of this filthy T-shirt. Look at all this laundry lying here. She should get up off her butt and get down to the Laundromat—

Her closet had gotten a lot bigger. She wondered who had torn out the rear wall. And what was out there? It looked like the inside of a church, or a castle or something. . . .

Kwip paced his cell, contemplating the life of a thief. His life. A good life? No. The only one he could have led? Mayhap not. He wondered, as he had always wondered, if he could have been anything else. If only he were not such an accomplished thief! But to what station in life could he have hoped to rise, he a low-born guttersnipe, an orphan, an unwanted child? He had found it necessary to steal in order to survive. There had been no other course to follow. Perhaps in a better world—ah, but there were no other worlds, were there?

Kwip turned about and beheld the doorway.

When the ice bridge collapsed, Snowclaw had thought he was going to die, but now that he had time to assess the situation, he was sure he was going to. He was never going to be able to climb out of this crevasse, no one was anywhere near, and that was that. He'd stay here till he froze or starved. He'd probably starve first.

He was hungry already. He hated the thought of starving to death. Really hated it. He'd much rather freeze to death, but he knew there was no chance of that this time of year. He'd just get miserably cold. He growled and pounded his huge fist against the wall of ice at his back.

Right. There was no other choice. He'd use his claws and open up an artery, and that would be that. He flexed the muscles of his left hand. Bone-white claws extruded from the ends of his fingers.

He turned his head to the left, noticing that the ledge extended quite some way into the dark crevasse. Maybe he should . . . No, there'd be nothing. The ledge would peter out a little way down. He extended his claws again. Damn. What a stupid way to go.

Afterward, Incarnadine could not locate Melydia. He searched the reconstructed castle, but she was nowhere to be found. Therefore he was surprised when she spoke to him.

*Incarnadine.*

He stopped in his tracks. "Melydia?"

*I am here. I am part of what is around you.*

"How?" he asked.

*My strength was drained, all my spells gone. I was dying. Then . . .*

"I see. Then we will always be together, in a sense."

*Yes, my love. Yes.*

He discovered Osmirik in the library, already hard at work.

# Castle

On his way to the family quarters he ran into the great white beast, the girl, and the young man.

"Welcome. I see you've met up again. These things are preordained, I've always thought."

The young man looked blankly at his companions, then said, "I'm sorry? We just ran into each other in the basement of this place. Who are you? And where the hell are we, if you don't mind my asking?"

The King and Lord Protector smiled. "The name's Incarnadine. This is my place." He gestured about. "Really something, isn't it?"

"Yes, but what is it? *Where* is it?"

"Where? Anywhere you like. Another world, another time, just down the block, or in the next room. What is it? It's a castle, Castle Perilous by name. And it can be a perilous place. But it is larger than life, and contains wonders without end. Entry is by way of your deepest desires. Until very recently, there was no way out. But we've done a little remodeling, a little patching here and there, and things should be a bit more stable. You can probably find a way back, if you wish. But I have a feeling you'll stay."

"Stay?"

"Yes, as my Guest. You are all most welcome." Incarnadine pointed down the corridor. "You're very likely famished. The Queen's dining hall is down that way. Must dash now. Enjoy yourselves."

"But . . ."

Chuckling, he hurried off down the passageway. He wanted to spend the day at the beach with his family.